# Scorned Eternal

## Scorned in Blood Trilogy, Volume 3

Ana DiPinto

Published by Ana DiPinto, 2024.

SCORNED ETERNAL

**First edition. October 1, 2024.**

Copyright © 2024 Ana DiPinto.

ISBN: 978-1736141250

Written by Ana DiPinto.

# Table of Contents

To my Sisters

# Prologue

For days he had been frozen in time, captured by a man he once considered his ally, a friend even. In his head he could hear the words that came to mind, but he could not speak them out loud. Behind his frozen eyelids he could see the visions of a dream, but he could not open his eyes. Later, though how many days had past he could not say, he was rescued by the woman who not long ago tried to kill him. A woman who he had known centuries ago. A woman he had called his wife. They had once shared a life and dreams of building a family together until the night tragedy struck. A night that had changed the course of both their lives and would leave them separated throughout the ages until they would eventually be reunited through one man's acts of greed, revenge, and quest for power. A man Nikolai had learned was the son he once believed to had never been born. The son he conceived with his wife many years ago who he thought had been killed with the child still inside her womb.

The night that Una and Alex both showed up back into his life they were intent on destroying him and they had almost succeeded. Now Nikolai found himself standing next to Una in the warm summer night air taking his first breaths in days. The blood he drank from her veins had filled him enough to walk out of that mortuary, but he would need more if he was going to survive this night. Brand new dangers had come to light over the last few nights as Una had informed him. Alex was after the power which only one vampire possessed. Dac and Luca were on a new course of rivalry. Last but certainly not least there were vampire hunters, one of whom they had just left behind in that room in the mortuary.

"You should have killed him," Una had said about Jace. The wind blew her long black hair, and she brushed it from her face. Her voice carried with it the disgust she felt for the human they had left behind.

"I'm not worried about Jace right now, nor Luca or Dac fighting for that matter. They can work out their problems on their own. We need to get to Alex first. He will never be strong enough to defeat Luca and his plan as you've told it to me is ludicrous. Where is he? We need to go there now."

"And you need to feed. You won't be strong enough without more blood in you." Una insisted.

"Fine we'll head to the blood bank first, but then we go find Alex." Nikolai began walking in the direction that would take him to the blood bank that supplied the vampires with their blood, but Una grabbed his arm stopping him in his tracks.

"There's no time for that," she said.

"I will not drink blood from a human," Nikolai protested. He had not drunk the blood direct from a human in a long time and he was not about to start again tonight, no matter how much Una insisted. But he knew she was right. He could feel the weakness in his limbs. Una's blood had awakened him, but it was not enough to revive his full strength and as much as he hated to admit it, he was still recovering from when she stabbed him. "But you're right, we won't have time to make it to the blood bank and find Alex in time," he admitted before she had time to protest.

"There's a house on the edge of Aura Springs. That's where we'll find Alex. We'll figure something out on the way." Una led the way with Nikolai trailing behind her. What she meant by *they'd figure something out* was, whether it be human or animal, tonight Nikolai had to act like the vampire he was and use the tools he'd possessed to nourish himself. Otherwise, Alex will have his wish and Nikolai wouldn't make it out of this night alive.

They traversed at vampiric speed along the edge of the main highway covered over by the canopy of trees that stood tall and full. Nikolai knew why Una had taken him this way. It would provide him with plenty of opportunity to feed on humans who stalled their cars along the roadway or wildlife that roamed amongst the thickets. Either way, he would have to make a decision, and soon, as his body was giving him no other choice. The hunger forced its way through him, and he felt his energy steadily draining. His knees became unstable as he fell to the ground. He grasped at the dirt under his fingertips and tried to pull himself up. But he was weak from days of malnourishment and the poisons that had yet to fully leave his body.

Something slumped on the ground beside him. He looked over to see the half lifeless body of a man and standing above him was Una. Blood dripped down the corner of Una's lip and from the fresh wounds in the man's neck. Nikolai could smell the blood so fiercely he could already taste it. "Drink it," Una had yelled at him as she kicked the body closer. Nikolai snatched the body off the ground, bringing it close to his mouth. He could hear the man's faint heartbeat in tune with his own. Then instinct took over and he sunk his fangs into the already exposed artery and drank.

*What you do in the name of survival is not the same as what you do in the name of pleasure*, Dac had once said to him. It was these words that would ring true this night as he took a life for the first time in almost 70 years even if he had not been the one to have taken the first bite.

Nikolai's strength quickly returned with the fresh human blood that now flowed through his veins. Una led him to a car on the side of the road buried just far enough into the bushes that no human would have seen it in the dark cover of night. The keys still hung in the ignition. Una jumped into the driver seat. Nikolai hesitated but then climbed into the seat next to her. The man's smell still lingered in the car and the taste of his blood still lingered on Nikolai's tongue.

Moments later they pulled up to the place Alex was supposed to be. It was a wreck of a house long abandoned by its owners. The ceiling had long ago caved in from storm damage and years of neglect. The yard was littered with debris, dead leaves, and overgrown weeds.

The moment Nikolai and Una stepped inside they knew they were too late. The trails of blood and dirt across the floor told them so. The place was quiet except for the sound of a beating heart that echoed off the vacant walls. The cold touch of Una's skin sent a chill through Nikolai's spine as she grasped his hand intertwining her fingers with his. He squeezed her hand and together they followed the sound of the heartbeat. A door slightly ajar down the dark hallway showed the body of Alex. His throat split, his spine crushed, and all the blood drained from his body. He was dead the only way the undead could be. Nikolai and Una both choked back a gasp. Nikolai felt the tears from Una as they fell from her eyes and landed on the hand he was holding. Though he had not the chance to get to know his son, a pang of sorrow settled into his heart. He squeezed Una's hand just a little bit tighter than before.

Across from the carnage that had become of their son, in another room stood Dac. The knife in his hand dripping with blood from the still beating heart that rested on the tip of the blade. Luca's body lay on the floor. His chest open from where the demon's heart had been extracted. Dac cupped the heart in his hands letting the bloody knife fall to the floor. Nikolai and Una watched as he consumed the heart the same way his brother had once done, fulfilling his destiny. Fulfilling the curse of the demon. The curse of the seventh son.

# One

I t had been ten years since Jace had last stepped foot in Aura Springs. The day his house sold, and he packed his bags he swore he would never return to this place, and he mostly kept that promise. Of course, his cousin and his best friend lived here so he had to come back a few times, especially when the two got married and had their children. That was something Jace hadn't expected, but he guessed he shouldn't have been too surprised. He did see them together a few times and honestly, he was happy for the two of them. They made a sweet couple, and Alan was good for Janice and a good stepfather to her three other daughters. Which was the reason Jace was back in Aura Springs now. Janice's oldest daughter, Maeve, was turning sixteen in two days, and she had begged him to come to her birthday party. How could he refuse that?

The party was being held at the same hotel that his ex-fiancée Cloe had worked at before she died ten years ago. And three years before that he had lost one of his good friends, Harper. She had disappeared and was never found. Everyone knew that was the reason he left. It had been too hard for him to stay after all of that loss. If only they had known the whole truth.

"Will you be ok?" Janice had asked him over the phone when she first told him where the party was going to be. He'd be fine, he had told her. He had to be. It was a long time ago. He had moved past it all. Plus, he wasn't about to disappoint his favorite niece on her special day. "Better not let the other kids hear you say that." Janice laughed.

Jace was happy with how close the two of them had gotten over the years since she married his best friend, Alan. It was weird how it worked out. They hadn't been very close before, even when she first moved to Aura Springs. But now, even with him being so far away they had grown that close familiar bond that he had longed for. Even calling her kids his nieces and nephew and them calling him uncle, even though they were actually cousins. They felt like more than that now and having them in his life meant everything to Jace.

He, however, decided to stay someplace else during his time in Aura Springs. A small motel along the beach that he always stayed in when he came to town. He did his best to keep his eyes on the road ahead of him as he drove through town instead of taking in the scenery around him. A scenery of distant memories. Things he had rather forgotten. He stopped his car at the red light. The Aura Springs Café stood to the right of him. The smells of coffee and sugary baked goods filled the air around him or maybe it was just his mind remembering what it felt like to be inside that place. He swallowed hard pushing down the lump that grew in his throat. He rolled up his window, turned up the radio and waited impatiently for the traffic light to turn green so he could get to his motel.

It was late October. The leaves on the trees had all turned to pretty colors of yellow, orange, and red. He passed the train station that no matter what time of year it was it always looked like it belonged in another time. The wind began to pick up slightly and the smell of saltwater coming off the ocean filled the air. The number of other cars on the road beside him dwindled. With the weather cooling there were not many people staying at the motel or even on this side of town for that matter. After checking in at the front desk, Jace drove his car around the beige and blue building and parked as close to his room as he could. Once inside he placed his bags on the floor unzipping the smaller of the two. He pulled out a small tub of cream, a spray bottle and a plastic bag filled with bundles of hawthorn tied tightly together and placed them on the table. He opened the jar of cream rubbing it across his neck, temples, and wrists. Then he sprayed the room with his essential oil mixture and hung the hawthorn branches across the front doorway and the glass door leading to the balcony. He may not have seen any vampires in ten years, not since that night, but he still wasn't taking any chances.

Outside on the balcony the wind blew in brisk off the ocean. Jace stared out at the waves as they crashed against the shore. The sky was still blue with daylight. At least he still had that in his favor. A stranger ran along the shore with their dog running beside them splashing in the cold water. Jace breathed in the cool air and slowly exhaled as he tried to calm the jitters that crawled up his skin. Memories of a past life that he never truly forgotten threatened every corner of his subconscious.

He never knew what happened to the rest of the vampires after that night. He had kept to his word as best he could. He couldn't help the two vampires that got in his way. They had come after him. He had to kill them. That was an act of self-defense. But other than that, he killed only the vampire he set out to destroy. Then he walked away never looking back. Never coming across another vampire and never seeking one out. He put that life behind him. He wasn't a vampire hunter. Not truly. He was just an ordinary man once put in an extraordinary position. And over the last ten years he had lived an ordinary life. He still ran his business with Alan, although remotely from the other side of the country. He was here now for ordinary reasons, his niece's birthday party. But as the sun began to set his memories were anything but ordinary.

He stepped back inside his room, shut the door tight, locking the sliding door in place and closing the curtains making sure to cover every inch of the glass. He made sure all the hawthorn was still secured in its places. He switched on the desk lamp and turned on the tv, flipping through the limited channels that the motel offered looking for anything to distract his thoughts. Time to unwind and relax before going to see his family tomorrow. No one was expecting him until the next day. Any time he made this trip to Aura Springs he always done the same thing. Arrived a day early. Set up his room to protect it and himself from any vampires. And most importantly give himself time to decompress and sort out his thoughts before being dragged into whatever family chaos was about to ensue.

The problem was when he closed his eyes, he only saw her. The fiancée he lost ten years ago. Her golden skin and curly brown hair. Her smile that could light up the whole world. Then he saw the bloody water, the cuts in her wrist, and the puncture wounds at the back of her neck. He saw her lying in her casket looking like someone other than herself. Then he saw the pale skinned face of the vampire that had done that to her. The one who when she was human had once called herself Cloe's best friend. The one who begged for Jace's help and threw him into the world of vampires. He saw her eyes when he realized it was her that had killed Cloe. And then he saw her head roll to the floor when Sarah struck her with the axe after he had stabbed her in the heart with the dagger. The dagger she had given to him to protect himself. He often wondered in the days following if Harper had known he would find out the truth. Did she suspect he would end up killing her with that very dagger or did she think she would keep that secret forever? He wondered why Dac led him to her that day. Was it jealousy that she had turned to his brother for help, or had he truly been that evil once he felt betrayed? Luca had told him Dac had evil inside of him. Jace knew it to be true. He could feel it. How could he not? He was a vampire after all, but he also knew Dac truly cared for Harper. Whatever the reason, he would never know, and he was better off for it. He had not heard from Dac, Luca, or any of the other vampires since that night and he intended to keep it that way. His part in the vampire world ended the night he killed Harper.

He shuddered at the memory of it all. No matter how much he tried to escape it, it was always there. Lurking in the back of his mind. Following him wherever he went. Every dark shadow, or cold chill reminded him that monsters prowled beyond this world that humans knew. That every myth and every story had a little bit of truth to it. He had lost the love of his life, his best friend, and even a piece of himself to that world. Now he only wanted to hold on closely to those he had left. To protect them at all costs. So, he stayed away as much as he could. He cut ties to the vampire hunters and to this town as much as it would let him. Coming back only a few days at a time, only a few times throughout the years. And always keeping his deterrents with him and never letting his guard down.

He leaned back on the bed, resting his head against the headboard. The tv was still on though he did not pay much attention to it. Outside he could hear random cars passing by or kids playing across the street. He could tell the sun had fully set by now by the darkness beyond the curtain and how little the tiny desk lamp brightened up the room.

The stress of the long drive and the even longer day began to wear on him. He sipped from the water bottle on the nightstand next to him. He finally kicked off his shoes and pulled his legs up fully onto the bed. Maybe he could get a little rest before the morning. He pulled his cell phone from the pocket of his jeans and placed it on the table, not even bothering to put it on its charger. It would be ok until morning he thought as he sunk down into the bed, closing his eyes.

When he opened his eyes the next morning the room was bright despite the closed curtains. The sun was hitting directly in through this side of the motel. Jace didn't mind. He had slept a dreamless sleep and woke up refreshed before remembering where he was. He climbed out of bed and walked over to the bathroom to wash up and reapply his cream. He looked around the room. All the hawthorn was still in place untouched, unmoved. He breathed a sigh of relief, grabbed his room and car keys, and walked out to the front desk area where they offered a free breakfast of stale bagels and tiny boxes of cereal. He mostly just wanted a coffee since there was none in the room, but he grabbed a bagel anyway and ate it on the way to his car. Time to get over to Janice's. They would be expecting him to arrive any minute.

He was holding the coffee in one hand and the half of bagel he had left in his mouth so he could open his car door. When inside he placed the coffee down in the cup holder. Bit off another piece of bagel and then reached for his phone. It was still upstairs. "Damn," he muttered to himself. The morning air was cold compared to the day before. At least he hadn't parked too far away from his room, so he didn't have far to go to retrieve the phone.

He slipped the key in the lock and opened the door. His phone was buzzing on the table where he had left it the night before. When he reached for it, the screen had lit up with one missed call and one new text message. His heart sank into his stomach when he read the name on the screen. He swiped to read the text message.

*I heard you were back in town. We need to talk. It's important.*

# TWO

There was a familiarity about him, yet she couldn't place where she had seen him before. His face was like porcelain. His eyes were dark and hypnotic. He leaned in close to her. Chills ran down her spine. His mouth grazed her ear, she breathed in deep as he whispered, "come to me," before he disappeared.

Who was this man that haunted her while she slept? And why was she suddenly on her way to a place she hadn't been to in years? Why had both of her parents died? And most importantly, why couldn't she remember what happened the night they died? No, not just died, were murdered. Her parents were murdered, brutely murdered, right inside their very own home and yet she could remember nothing of that night.

Sophia was nine years old the night her parents died. She had hidden in the closet under the stairs in the foyer of her house the night it happened. But that's all she remembered about that night. Her mother shuffling her into the closet and closing the door. She sat there for what felt like hours in the dark with her hands over her ears and her eyes shut tight until the morning when her uncle found her. The next thing she remembered was waking up in her uncle's house, in a bedroom that wasn't hers knowing that her life was forever changed.

Now ten years later on the anniversary of her parents' death Sophia found herself ready to board a train to a place called Aura Springs. It was just before midnight when she packed a duffle bag full of clothes, pulled on a jacket, and snuck out of her uncle's house into the cold, dark night. The roads in Noxwood are steep in the mountains. Thick woods cover most of the grounds. Sophia stood at the edge of her uncle's property and waited for the rideshare service she ordered to come pick her up and bring her to the station. When she got there a light rain had begun to fall. She pulled up the hood of her jacket to cover her hair and sat on a bench under the wooden awning while she waited for the train. Noxwood had been her home for her entire life and now she was about to leave it without telling a single person and probably, she felt, for the last time.

She slept the entire ride from Noxwood to Aura Springs. The loud screech of the train's wheels against the metal tracks awoke her and the conductor yelled out, "last stop!" as he passed through the car. The abrupt awakening made her stomach queasy, but she hurriedly grabbed her bag, flinging it over her shoulder as she stepped off the train. The morning sun felt warm in contrast to the cool winds. She could almost smell the salt in the air coming from the nearby ocean.

Only two other people had exited the train along with Sophia. Not too many people are looking for a seaside vacation in the middle of fall, she guessed. Standing on the middle of the platform, Sophia looked around at her new surroundings. It had been years since Sophia had last been in Aura Springs. A few summers she had spent there with her parents when she was a kid. They had owned a house near the beach, and just recently Sophia learned they still owned it. She had thought her uncle had sold it off, at least that was what he had told her when she asked once if they could come here. As it turned out the property was part of the trust she received when she turned nineteen. She had no idea why her uncle had lied to her, but she knew even from a young age that her mother and father never truly trusted him. But when her parents died, he was the one that took her in and took care of her and for that she was grateful.

Despite all his shortcomings he made sure she had as good a life as he was able to provide for her. So maybe she did feel a slight ache in her heart when she left town without saying goodbye, but what she was doing she needed to do on her own and she knew he would never approve.

Sophia gave the address to the taxi driver as she hopped in the back seat. On the drive to her new house, she glared out the window watching the town pass by in a blur. When she arrived, she felt a pang in her heart with the vague memories she had of being here as a child. The key, she was told, would be in a lock box on the front door that only she had the code to open. The house was still fully furnished and when she opened the door and stepped inside a wave of unexpected emotions took over her.

She carried her bag up the stairs to her parents' old bedroom. After a nice warm bath and maybe some breakfast, next it would be time to find the woman that was supposed to help her get her memories back.

When Sophia had first told her best friend about the dreams she'd been having, at first, they both shrugged them off as stress dreams. The day of her nineteenth birthday a lawyer had reached out to her asking to meet with her privately without her uncle. That was how she learned about the trust her parents left for her, including this house, but as the days passed and the dreams continued, Sophia began to feel there was something more to it. It was like her mind was trying to tap into a memory she couldn't quite access. It was then her friend told her of this woman in Aura Springs that might be able to help her. She had offered to come along but Sophia wanted to come alone. So, she told her she changed her mind about making the trip out here and left another person in her life without so much as a goodbye.

Now in Aura Springs Sophia realized she couldn't get around much without a car, so she decided to rent one, but she only had cash because she did not want her uncle tracking her by her debit card usage. She found a local store within walking distance that sold those prepaid credit cards and bought one. Back at the house she used her phone to get online and reserved a car. Luckily, she found a place that would bring the car to her, so she didn't need to order another rideshare or a taxi. Once the car had been dropped off, she decided it was time to find this woman who could help her.

She pulled the rental car into the plaza parking lot. The shop she was looking for was fairly easy to find. The little bells over the door chimed when she stepped inside. A young girl stood behind the counter; Sophia was sure this wasn't the woman she was looking for but maybe she would know where to find her.

Sophia walked up to counter and asked the girl, "Do you know where I can find Sarah Higgins?"

"Oh, Sarah's not here today. Do you have an appointment?" The girl asked.

"Um. No, I don't. I was told she be able to help me with something. Do you know when she'll be in?"

"She doesn't spend much time here lately since taking care of her grandmother. Would you like to make an appointment?" The girl began clicking on her computer keyboard.

"Sure, that would be fine. How soon can she see me?" Sophia shifted from one foot to the other.

"She has an opening next week." She said glancing from the computer screen to Sophia.

"Nothing sooner? This is really important." Her voice cracked a little and the desperation in her tone surprised even herself.

"I'm sorry she doesn't. Like I said she doesn't have as much time these days as she used to, but how about I put you down for next week. I can pass your number and a message to Sarah and if something opens up sooner, she'll give you a call."

"That will be fine." Sophia gave the girl her information. She didn't expect to hear from her but what other choice did she have? So, she was surprised when Sarah called her a few hours later asking to meet.

The woman who had met her wore her copper-colored hair in a high bun on top of her head. She wore a long skirt with black boots on her feet. A black leather jacket covered her shoulders from the cold temperatures. It was after hours when Sophia met with Sarah outside of her shop. All the other shops had closed and hers and Sarah's cars were the only two in the parking lot. It was past dark, and the plaza was quiet. Sarah opened the door to the shop and led Sophia to the back room. She lit some candles and sprayed a mist of essential oils around the room before she began to speak.

"I have a feeling that what you are about to ask of me will require a bit of confidentiality." Sarah said.

"Yea, I suppose it does, but how did you know?" Sophia asked.

"Because your phone number is from Noxwood. I assume you made the long trip out here for a reason, otherwise you could have sought someone out a bit closer to home." Sarah flashed a comforting smile her way.

"A friend of mine gave me your name. She said maybe you could help me interpret this recurring dream I've been having."

"I'll do my best. Tell me about it. Try giving me as much detail as possible," Sarah said, and Sophia began describing the dream to her. She described every detail she could remember from the way she felt to the details of the man's face and the sound of his voice. Then Sophia saw the look on Sarah's face and a cold chill ran through her body.

"What's the matter? Do you know what this dream is?" Sophia asked her.

"This isn't a dream. It's more like a vision." Sarah stood up and walked over to a shelf pulling down a couple of glass vials of oils and a small plastic jar. "Take these," she said. "Keep the oils on you at all times and rub the cream in this jar on your wrist, neck and temples each day, after you wash up in the morning and before you go to sleep at night. This will keep the visions away for now." She then handed her a spray bottle like the one she just used when they first entered the room. "Go back to your hotel or wherever you're staying. Spray this around your entire space like I just did here. I will call you in the morning and we'll set up a time to meet again soon. I will need to get in touch with an old acquaintance. Until then stay safe."

Sophia nodded. She took the things from Sarah and put them inside her purse. As she walked back to her car suddenly, the night felt colder and darker than when she had arrived. An uneasiness settled in the pit of her stomach. Whatever this dream or vision was it had Sarah frightened and now Sophia was too.

Back at her beach house Sophia did as Sarah had instructed her to do and sprayed the contents of the spray bottle all over her house. She washed up and changed into a nightshirt and a pair of fleece pants then rubbed the cream onto her wrists, neck, and temples. She settled into her parents' old bed in the master bedroom. She wrapped the plush comforter all around her and for the first time in weeks slept a dreamless sleep.

She awoke in the late morning with an overwhelming feeling she needed to be somewhere. She glanced at her phone. She had seven missed calls. Four were from her uncle and three from her best friend. None of the calls came from Sarah as she had hoped.

Downstairs in the kitchen she poured herself a glass of water. Her stomach rumbled as she realized she had no food in the house. She needed to go shopping so she went back upstairs to get ready for the day. An hour later she was in her rental car, but instead of driving to the store she drove herself to the train station. The feeling in her gut was leading the way and that feeling was no longer hunger, but something else.

The late October weather was slightly milder than Sophia had expected. Aura City was a bit different than the mountain town of Noxwood that she was used to. The brisk wind that blew in between the tall buildings that littered every inch of the city barely made her shiver. Instead, she welcomed it as she kicked the leaves from under her feet. She kept her eyes to the ground as she walked the blocks that made up the city streets until she came upon a house that made her take notice.

The property stood back amongst the otherwise closely neighboring houses. High iron gates surrounded the place. The windows were boarded up and the front door hid behind locked iron bars. Sophia was drawn to the house as if it had meant something to her, though she had never seen this house in her life. Yet somehow, she could not turn her eyes away from it. Her feet stayed planted in place. Her hands stretched out and she wrapped her fingers around the cold bars of the gate. Out of the ground daisies grew along the edge of the yard. Did daisies grow in October, Sophia wondered? They must have because there they were. Their white petals and yellow middle stood out against the green grass and brown and red leaves that had fallen to the ground from the tree branches above. The late afternoon sun reflected off the white façade of the house in front of her.

"You shouldn't be here," a voice said to her. "If you knew what was good for you, you would stay as far away from this house as you can." The voice said. "Evil lives in that house."

Sophia dropped her hands to her side. She turned her head in the direction of the voice. A man stood to the right of her. He was older. His complexion was an ashen grey, much like the color of the grey sweatshirt and pants he wore. His eyes were void of life. His lips chapped and teeth yellow. "Sorry," Sophia had said.

"You will be if you don't leave from here right now," the man said as he walked away leaving Sophia standing there confused and frightened. Mindlessly Sophia reached down and plucked a daisy from behind the gate. She twirled the flower between her fingers as she walked away. Sirens blared as a fire truck raced down the street next to her. Cars moved over to the side of the road to get out of the way. She turned around watching the truck pass by. The odd man was at the opposite corner. He turned back to face her then continued walking away in the opposite direction. Sophia wrapped her sweater tighter around her shoulders and walked on. To where she did not know.

# Three

Jace looked at the text message on his phone from Sarah. *It's important*, the message said. He had not spoken to nor seen Sarah in the ten years since he moved away from Aura Springs. What could be so important that she was texting him now? The thought of it made his stomach turn. He had ignored the message all day while he spent time with this family, and even last night when he got back to his motel room. But now as the morning was fading into the afternoon another message came through, *please can you meet with me? Text me back*, the new message read, and he was finding it harder and harder to avoid the anxiety this message brought with it until finally he agreed to meet with her.

He parked his car at the edge of the driveway. Standing in front of Sarah's house brought back more memories of his past life. The last time he was here he and Sarah were getting into her car and driving off to Noxwood to confront vampires. When they returned from that trip, he didn't even say goodbye to her. He just got in his car and drove home. She had understood. He could see it in her eyes when she watched him leave. They both knew that would be the last time they would see each other. How could their friendship continue after she had helped him kill his best friend. It was necessary. Cloe deserved justice for what Harper had done to her, but it didn't heal the hole it left in Jace's life. If anything, it only made it bigger. *Don't consume yourself with revenge, forget you knew us, allow yourself to heal*, those were the words Harper said to him when she was trying to get Jace to drop his search for Cloe's killer, but who was she really trying to protect? Him or herself? He never would have believed Harper was the vampire who fed off Cloe. They were best friends when Harper was human, but he saw the guilt in her eyes and then she allowed him into her mind for a brief moment. Bitterness and rage were all he felt at that moment when he stuck the dagger through her heart. It was afterwards that all the pain and grief sank in. Pain and grief for the losses he felt and sorrow for Cloe who had been betrayed by her best friend the one person beside himself, human or vampire, who should have kept her safe.

Sarah had greeted him as soon as he knocked on her door. "Hi. Please come in." She lowered her gaze and stepped out of the way allowing Jace to pass through the doorway. An awkward silence followed their initial greeting as Jace followed Sarah into the kitchen. Jace took a seat at the round kitchen table while Sarah offered him a warm cup of coffee.

"So, what's this all about?" Jace finally asked as Sarah set down the coffee mugs and sat across from him at the table.

"I got a visit at the shop the other day from a girl from Noxwood."

Jace's heart dropped into his stomach at the mention of Noxwood. This could lead to nowhere good. "What does this have to do with me?" he asked.

"She came to me looking for answers to a dream she believed was repressed memories. Someone, a friend of hers I guess, told her to come here. But what she described to me was not a dream. It was visions. And it is because of who is in those visions that I called you."

"I don't think I want to know. Whoever it is, whatever it is, I don't want anything to do with it."

"Jace, it was Dac. He's entering into her mind and calling to her. I'm scared for the girl. We have to help her. We have to find out what he wants." Sarah's pleas cut through him like a knife.

Jace's skin grew cold with the mention of the vampire's name. He wrapped his hands around the warm coffee mug more as a nervous gesture than to warm them. He stared at Sarah for a moment. "I can't," he finally said. "I'm sorry, I just can't be involved with this anymore." Jace began to get up to leave but Sarah grabbed his hand.

"Please, will you just meet with her first, hear her story before you say no." She pleaded.

"Sarah, listen. I'm only here a few days for my niece's birthday party. Then I'm leaving again the day after tomorrow. I can't get involved with vampires again. I can't bring that into their lives. That part of my life is done." This time Jace did get up to leave. "I'm sorry," he said as he walked out the door.

The birthday party was the next day. Jace still had not gotten his niece a gift and he had no idea what to even get for her. On his way back to the motel, he stopped at the local grocery store, grabbed some food for dinner, picked out a birthday card for his niece and retrieved two hundred dollars from the atm machine. What teenage girl didn't like cash right? She could use it to buy herself something that she liked or go out with her friends, and he wouldn't end up feeling stupid for buying her something she hated.

Back in his room he picked at the food he bought from the store as he tried to choke down each bite. The talk of vampires earlier that day had left a bitter taste in his mouth and a sour feeling in his stomach. What would Dac want with some random girl from Noxwood and why would he be entering her mind? That didn't even sound like something Dac would do. That seemed more like Luca's or Alex's style. Jace had no idea what went down that night after he set Nikolai free. He knew Dac had some type of plan, but that was none of his business. Could they all still be feuding after all these years? He supposed they could be considering they had been feuding for centuries before that. Whatever was going on now though Jace wanted nothing to do with it. It was none of his concern. As he had said to Sarah, he left that life behind him a long time ago. If you could consider ten years a long time. Maybe it wasn't to an immortal vampire, but to him it felt like a lifetime ago.

If only he could get the thoughts of vampires out of his head. Especially these particular group of vampires. Jace put on a jacket and decided to take a walk and try to clear his head. The evening sun was sitting atop the horizon. The autumn air made him shiver a bit. The streets were quiet aside from the random passing car or two. Most businesses had closed up already for the season. Only a few stayed open year-round on this side of town.

He stopped in a bar whose neon sign said open. The scent of alcohol accosted him as soon as he stepped inside. Another thing he hadn't done in a long while was drink alcohol. Not that he stopped completely. He'd have a beer or two here and there over the years, but after leaving Aura Springs those first few years had been rough and liquor became his best friend. Then one night he found himself in the emergency room with cuts to his face and knuckles from a fight with a stranger that he didn't even remember getting into. But the story he was told was that he started that fight and since he had no memory of it, he didn't bother disputing the fact. He went home that night and decided he needed to get his life back on track. He had gathered all the liquor bottles from around his apartment and poured their contents down the sink. He discarded all the empty bottles in the recycle bins at the apartment's trash room and from that moment on he steered away from the hard stuff. Only on a few social occasions would he drink a beer or a glass of wine, but tonight he sat at the bar, and he ordered himself a whiskey.

The deep amber liquor felt smooth as it slid down his throat. The rich flavors of honey, vanilla, and oak lingered on his tongue with each sip. As the warmth settled in, he felt his body begin to relax for the first time in days. He ordered another drink taking in its sweet aroma. Someone sat on the bar stool next to him. The man's voice sounded vaguely familiar as he spoke to the bartender though Jace couldn't place who it belonged to until he saw his face. Great, just what he needed. Another person from a past life he would rather not remember.

"Hey, long time no see," The man said to him. It was Zaine's old friend Chris. They had never been friends though they had known each other for years. They were cordial when Zaine and Harper had been together, but everyone knew Jace hadn't liked Zaine very much.

"Yea, it's been a while," Jace said.

"When did you get back in town? Heard you moved away a while ago."

"Yea, I did. Just came in for my niece's birthday then I'll be gone the day after tomorrow." Jace wasn't really in the mood for small talk. Not that he harbored any sort of dislike for Chris, he would rather just not be around people who reminded him of Zaine and Harper. He turned his head and took a drink from his glass hoping Chris would get the message. He must have because he picked up his beer and turned to leave, but not before saying, "Hey, we should get together before you leave, you know just for old times' sake or whatever." Jace nodded to him, and Chris walked away to meet his friends at the other end of the bar. For old times' sake as if they had ever been friends. They were barely ever acquaintances.

Jace finished his drink, paid for his tab, and left the bar. That was enough human interaction for one day. He did, however, stop inside the liquor store next door and buy a small bottle of whiskey to drink back at the motel.

He didn't even bother pouring the whiskey into a cup. He drank it straight from the bottle. He sat on the bed in his motel room. His phone in one hand. The whiskey bottle in the other. He opened his phone to Sarah's number. His thumb lingered over the call button, then he swiped back to the home screen and put the phone on the table next to him. He connected the charger this time, turned on the tv and finished his drink. He was going to regret this in the morning but right now he didn't care. All he cared about at this moment was numbing the anxiety that took over his entire mind and body. He wanted to feel nothing, he wanted to think of nothing. He wanted the world to disappear, and he wanted to disappear with it. And eventually it did as he drifted off into a deep dreamless sleep.

# Four

When Sophia had last spoken to Sarah, Sarah told her she had to talk with someone, and she would get back to her. That was two days ago. Still no call back from Sarah. Had she forgotten about her? Did she decide not to help her after all? Maybe she just hadn't spoken to whoever this someone was she needed to talk to. But Sophia could not get that look on Sarah's face out of her head. It was a look of pure fear. And with all these things Sarah had given her, the man outside that house yesterday in Aura City, Sophia felt whatever she was getting ready to uncover was something dark.

She sat on the plush white couch with her legs curled up underneath her wondering if she should just give up and go back to Noxwood. She hadn't had the dream or vision as Sarah called it since she started using the lotion Sarah had given to her. Maybe this was for the best, but something inside her told her to stay and see this through. It nagged at her like an annoying hangnail. She looked down at her phone resting on the table next to her with all the missed calls and unread text messages from her uncle and her best friend. She had been avoiding the two of them since she left Noxwood. A part of her wished her bestie was there with her but she knew it was best that she was here alone.

Sophia turned on her laptop and searched the archives of the local newspapers looking for anyone that may have looked familiar. Sarah's scared expression had her wondering if the man from her dream had lived in Aura Springs at some point. Had he done something horrible? Is that why Sarah looked so shaken by his description? She must have known him. When Sophia's internet search turned up fruitless, she grabbed her purse from the other end of the couch and her jacket that hung by the door and got into her rental car.

She walked into the Aura Springs café, walked up to the counter at the back of the café and ordered a sandwich and a drink for lunch. She still had not managed to get many groceries other than some coffee, milk, and a box of cereal from the nearby convenience store. When the server behind the counter handed her the sandwich and drink, she sat down at one of the tables. Just as she took her first bite of the sandwich, she heard the chair across from her scrap against the hardwood floor. She looked up to see Sarah standing across from her with her hand on the chair.

"Hi, sorry to interrupt your lunch, but I have some bad news." Sarah said as she sat down.

"Oh." Sophia felt her heart sink a little bit and placed the sandwich on the plate in front of her.

"I talked to an old friend the other day. Someone I thought could help. But he's not interested."

"Oh, ok. Well, thank you for trying. I really appreciate it." Sophia tried to hide the disappointment in her voice. She knew it was a long shot coming here and expecting some stranger to help her, but still she had hoped she would.

"Oh no don't worry, I'm still going to help you, just seems we'll be on our own."

"Oh, that's fine. I expected it would be just the two of us anyway." A wave of relief washed over her.

"Yea, I was really hoping for a little help, but I'll explain more later. Finish your lunch and if you're not busy today come by my house afterwards. I'll text you the address."

Sophia took her phone out from her purse as soon she heard the message ping. She could barely finish her food after speaking to Sarah. Her stomach was tying itself in knots. She tossed the remaining half of her sandwich in the garbage, took one last sip of her drink, and immediately left the café. Putting Sarah's address into her GPS, she started up the rental car and drove directly to meet Sarah.

Sophia knocked on the door and after only a short wait Sarah answered. She ushered her inside and invited her to sit in the living room. The room was cozy with a chocolate-colored sofa and matching reclining chair. Another large armchair sat on the other side of the sofa. The square coffee table in the middle of the room held the remote for the tv which hung on the wall, a couple of old magazines, and a bowl that appeared to be full of small branches. As she looked around the room, she noticed the same bowl of branches on the windowsills and on the side tables next to both the front and back doors. The room smelled of the same mixture of frankincense and peppermint that Sarah had sprayed at the shop and had told Sophia to spray around her house.

"Make yourself comfortable, I'll be back in a minute." Sarah said before disappearing down the dark hallway on the other side of the stairs.

Sophia sat down on the sofa and flipped through one of the magazines while she waited for Sarah to return. Her stomach still twisted and turned inside of her. Her legs began to shake, and she rested her elbows on her thighs to try and steady them. Again, a sense of doubt came over her as she wondered if she had made the right decision. Maybe coming here wasn't a good idea. But she pushed that thought down deep. She needed to know what that dream was all about. She needed to know what really happened to her parents. And somehow, she knew it was all connected. She didn't know how just yet, but that's why she was here. This woman was going to help her fit the pieces of her memory together. She had to do this. She took a deep breath, swallowed her anxiety, and waited for Sarah and whatever lay beyond the dark hall.

A few minutes later Sarah returned and with her an elderly woman whom Sarah held caringly by the arm as she led her to the large armchair. The woman leaned on her cane as she sat down. Sarah put a blanket over the woman's legs before she herself sat in the other chair.

"Sophia, this is my great grandmother Brigid. A long time ago she hunted vampires and she once help a friend of mine and me to do the same."

Sophia swallowed hard. "Vampires?" She had to make sure she heard that correctly. Why was this woman talking about vampires. And vampire hunting. That was the stuff of books and horror films. She definitely should not have come here. This woman was clearly out of her mind. "I'm sorry, maybe this was a mistake," Sophia began to get up to leave when Brigid reached out and grabbed her hand. Her hand was cold and soft. Her grasp was gentle, almost comforting.

"Please," Brigid said. "Let us explain. I know how this sounds but if you can give us a chance, we can help you." Brigid let go of her hand and Sophia sat back down on the couch. She was not sure if she was ready to believe what they were saying but she was willing to listen. Really, what did she have to lose? She came all this way to find answers. But vampires? Were vampires really the answer? Were they even the answer she wanted? Probably not, but at that moment, she decided once again to see this through.

"The man you described in your dream, I think I know who he is." Sarah explained.

"You do?"

"Yes, and he is a vampire. A living, breathing, real vampire. I know it sounds insane, but it's true. That's why I wanted you to meet my friend. Years ago, he went through a similar situation where he had to face that yes, vampires really do exist. Unfortunately, he has refused to get involved. As you can imagine, it was a very traumatic time. He hasn't spoken about it in years, and he wants to keep that part of his life behind him."

"I see, but what would this vampire want with me? Why would he be in my dream and why do I feel like I've seen him before?" Sophia was still having a hard time believing any of this.

"I believe you may be like my sister once was. She was able to hear the vampires through telepathy although she could not communicate with them that way. Do you remember a music box, you had as a child." Brigid answered and she pulled the small music box out from under the blanket and placed it on the coffee table for Sophia to see.

"My music box!" Sophia reached for it, but Sarah held her back. It was the music box that she had as a child. It had mysteriously gone missing one day and she had never seen it again until now. How had she not seen them carry it into the room with them? "How did you get it? Why won't you let me touch it?"

"This music box is used to aid in capturing a vampire. When one is in earshot of it, the music will hypnotize the vampire into following its sound. It will render their powers useless and allow the owner of the box to capture and destroy the vampire. I gave this to your mother a long time ago as a gift when it was no longer any use to me. Unfortunately, it had been stolen but then we got it back and it has been here with us ever since."

All of this was a lot for Sophia to take in. This woman beside her that she had never seen in her life had known her mother. Did this mean that her mother knew about vampires too? Was she a hunter? Sophia had so many questions and yet she still wasn't sure how much of this she should believe. "You knew my mother?" Sophia asked. "How? When?"

"I did. A long time ago before you were born. She was a young woman, about your age when I met her. She came to me looking for some, should we say, spiritual advice. Over the years we became friends, I guess you could say, until she met your father and moved away. We did manage to stay in touch for a bit and I gave her the music box, like I said, as a gift when I learned of her pregnancy."

"Was she a vampire hunter too?" Sophia asked.

"No, she wasn't. As far as I know she had no knowledge of vampires."

Sophia sat there for a moment thinking about her mother. Imagining her as a young woman of nineteen. She tried to picture her mother going to a psychic or whatever seeking out spiritual guidance. That sounded nothing like the woman she had known. In the nine years of life she had before her mother died, she always saw her mother as this sophisticated, upper-class woman. A woman who stood next to her husband and hosted glamourous cocktail parties. She never spoke of the supernatural. Magic was only in fairytales she used to say. But you never know what's going on behind the face that people show you Sophia was beginning to learn. Like her uncle who had lied to her and told her the beach house was sold in order to help take care of her. Instead, it was sitting in a trust waiting for her, Sophia, to turn nineteen. Now it was hers and she wondered why he never told her about it. But all this wondering about her mother's other life wasn't getting her the answers she needed. Finally, she asked, "Ok, so how does all of this explain who this man is and what it has to do with the death of my parents? All I know is there's this intense feeling in my gut that these two things are connected and that's the reason I'm here even listening to all of this."

"For that we will need to break into your subconscious. It may take a little bit of hypnosis. If there's a memory, we will find it and figure out how to connect the dots. Are you willing to do that?"

"Yes." Sophia said.

"I want you to take tonight and really think about this. If you still want to do this, come back tomorrow afternoon and we will start then. This is a lot to unpack, I know. But if you're suppressing memories there may be a reason you do not remember them." Brigid leaned back further in her large chair resting her arms against the arm rests.

Sophia agreed. She thanked Sarah again for meeting with her and said good night to Brigid. As she drove back to her new home, she thought about everything they said. She now had more questions than when she had started. Maybe that was to be expected. Like when trying to organize a mess. Sometimes a bigger mess needs to be made before the cleaning begins.

# Five

Finally, the day of the birthday party had arrived. Jace stepped into the hotel lobby holding the birthday card he had bought for his niece tight in his hand as if it were something delicate that would shatter if it slipped from his sweaty grasp. The freshly polished tiled floor felt slippery under his feet. Every joint in his body tightened up, yet he urged himself to move forward. He was here for his niece. This was her big day. He was not going to make this about himself.

The loud music coming from the ballroom oddly calmed his nerves a bit and his mood suddenly shifted. Janice appeared at the entrance. Her good mood radiated through the smile on her face. Her daughter stood next to her glowing with excitement and pure joy. Jace smiled back at his cousin and niece. Maeve ran up to him wrapping her arms around him in a familiar hug.

"Happy birthday," he said while handing her the birthday card.

"Thank you, Uncle Jace." Maeve took the card then ran off to rejoin her friends inside the ballroom.

Janice stepped over to Jace, "So glad you could make it. She really is so happy you came. Alan's inside by the bar."

"Of course, he is." Jace smiled and went to meet his best friend.

The ballroom was swimming with mostly teenagers and a few adults there to chaperone. Pink and white balloons floated about in every corner of the room. Pink roses adorned the center pieces on every table. At one end of the room was the DJ. On the other was the buffet table. Next to that was the bar where the kids ordered their sodas and the adults ordered something a little bit stronger.

The party was going on without a hitch. No teenage drama ensued. Everyone, even the adults, seemed to be having a good time. Jace checked the time on his cell phone. 5:00 pm. The sun would just be going down. It would be dark soon if it wasn't already. That's when he saw her. The glimpse of long black hair. He blinked and she was gone, just the same as what happened at his and Cloe's engagement party. It had to be an illusion. Harper was gone. He had killed her ten years ago when he found out she was responsible for Cloe's death. But then he remembered what Sarah had said to him just a day earlier. One of the vampires was reaching out to some girl from out of town. A girl from Noxwood and there was another vampire with long black hair. Another vampire who looked a lot like Harper, Una. Could it be? Was Una at this party?

Jace ran to the entrance of the ballroom. He looked down the hall in both directions. When he didn't see anyone, he went out to the lobby and through the automatic doors to the parking lot. He was right, it was dark outside already, but there was no vampire in sight. Even if she had been there, he would never have caught her if she didn't want to be caught. Jace decided to forget about it and go back to the party. He wanted nothing to do with vampires but whether it was a gut feeling or just plain old anxiety he couldn't deny the familiar dread in the pit of his stomach.

SOPHIA SHOWED UP TO meet Sarah and Brigid at Sarah's house as agreed. She was eager to get started on working out her memories. She didn't want to seem ungrateful, so she brought coffee with her from the café. Sarah graciously took them from her when she opened the door and let Sophia into the house.

The living room had been rearranged. The coffee table had been moved to one end of the room. A yoga mat had been placed on the floor. A pillow lay on top of the mat. Candles burned around the room. It smelled of lavender, jasmine, and sandalwood. Sophia stood at the edge of the room until Sarah offered her a seat at the round kitchen table in the adjacent dining room.

Sarah placed a ceramic mug in front of Sophia, "Drink this. It's chamomile tea. It will help you relax a little bit."

"Thanks." Sophia took the mug. Its warmth was comforting. The aroma sweet and the taste infused with honey. Yet as she sipped the tea, she felt anything but relaxed.

"When you're ready I'll get my grandmother from her room, and we can begin." Sarah said as she sat in the chair next to her.

Sophia nodded and took another slow sip of the tea. She would rather have had the coffee she bought from the café but who was she to question Sarah's methods? This was all too new to her, so she did as Sarah suggested and drank the tea until the cup was empty. She turned towards Sarah, "I'm ready," she said.

Sarah instructed her to lay flat on the yoga mat in the living room. "Keep your feet and head towards the ceiling," she told her.

Sophia did as instructed. She laid down on the mat. Placed her head on the pillow. The flames from the candles reflected off the pure white ceiling above her providing an orange glow to the room. Her left foot shook with anticipation. She entwined her fingers as she rested her hands against her chest. Her thumbs pressing hard into the exposed portion of her skin. This was not the relaxed state she was supposed to be in, she presumed.

Footsteps came from the hallway behind her. Brigid came into the room, her cane clicking against the laminate floor. She sat in the same large chair she had the day before. Sarah entered the room a short moment later. She placed a small clay bowl on the floor next to Sophia. The scent of lavender and sage wafted past her nose. Sarah kneeled behind Sophia. She placed her fingertips in the bowl then used the oils inside to massage Sophia's temples as Brigid spoke in slow soft tones.

"Lie still. Close your eyes. Keep your feet and head toward the ceiling," Brigid said. "Take slow deep breaths. Relax your mind with every exhale. Soon you will feel your body begin to relax as well. Take it one piece at a time. Start at your toes and move up through your feet and legs, and then your torso and up through your arms and shoulders" She continued.

Sophia listened to Brigid's instructions. With every breath she felt the tension in her muscles loosen. The thoughts began to clear out of her mind. She felt herself unwind until her body began to melt into the floor.

"When you feel completely relaxed, allow yourself to remember the face in your dreams. Follow the memory to the first time you saw the face," Brigid said. "Where were you? How old had you been?"

Sophia began to picture the pale face, the dark hair. It was nighttime. Winter. The weather was cold. Snow covered the ground. She was a young girl. A child still. There were two of them. Tall men standing in the driveway of her home. She remembered being drawn to them. The way the moonlight reflected off their skin. They were so pretty she remembered thinking. Like porcelain dolls. One of them kneeled down to her level. He spoke to her in a calm tone. His voice almost melodic. But he was not the one in her dreams now. No. It was the other one. The silent one with the dark eyes.

"Now have you seen him again?" Brigid continued. "When was that? Where?"

Once. Outside her window. A few months later. It was summer this time. She was in her room playing with her music box. She glimpsed him. Only for a second, but she knew it was him.

"Good. Now go further. Allow yourself to remember the last time you saw him. Remember you are safe here."

It was dark. She was nine years old. Not long after her birthday. A thunderstorm had eagerly rolled in, and power was out throughout the city. There was a loud bang outside the house. Then something like stomping on the roof. Her mother pushed her into the closet. Sophia sat in the corner. She pulled a coat down from the hanger and covered herself with it. Even with her hands over her ears she could hear shuffling outside. Glass shattered somewhere in the house. Then footsteps. The door to the closet opened. She hugged the coat, pulling it up to her face but allowing her eyes to peek out. The silhouette of man stood there. A dark shadow with a pale face and nothing but a red glow in the space where the eyes should be.

Sophia gasped when the knock on the door came. Sarah put a hand on her shoulder, and she remembered where she was. She was safe in Sarah's house. She was not that nine-year-old little girl hiding in a closet. Still a tear fell from her right eye. She wiped it away as she sat up curious to see who was at the door. She looked over at Brigid whose face was unreadable. If she was worried about what Sophia had remembered she wasn't letting on.

Sarah was standing at the front door. One hand on the door, the other on her hip. She was talking to someone. A male voice was on the other side of the door. Sophia tried to listen, but her mind was still feeling overwhelmed by the memories she had just uncovered. Still so many questions. Still no real answers.

Sarah came into the living room. The man standing at her side said, "I came here to help." Brigid smiled. Sophia relaxed.

# Six

Emmaline sat in her windowless room. Footsteps traipsed across the floor above her. Una's exasperating voice vibrated through the walls. "I think he saw me." She was saying to Nikolai. "How could you let him see you! I told you to stay away from him," Nikolai shouted back at her. "If he's back in town we need to know why," Una insisted. Nikolai and Una always fought like this whenever Jace was nearby.

Emmaline turned the music up in her earphones hoping to drown out the yelling. Quentin's old townhouse was nowhere near as quiet as the huge house she once shared with Dac, Nikolai, and Quentin. Things had certainly changed over the years.

Ten years ago, Nikolai returned home with Una at his side. He had told Emmaline and Quentin, how she had rescued him from a drawer in the town morgue, but that wasn't all he said. Jace and his vampire hunting friend had been holding him there as leverage and Jace only let him out because Una had forced him to. Jace had made agreements with multiple vampires, one of them being Dac, and Una figured out that plan. But Jace wasn't the only one telling half-truths, so was Dac. Una figured out Dac was planning to meet Alex alone. He had Jace set it all up. Once Una figured out the meeting place, she forced Jace to take her to Nikolai so they could rescue Alex together. But when they arrived, Alex was already dead and so was Luca. Dac had killed them both and not only that he also consumed the demon that lived inside of Luca. After that Nikolai gave Una her own room and she moved into the house with them.

Days had passed before anyone had seen or heard from Dac. At that point, no one had heard from Harper either. Dac had banned her from the house when she had turned to his brother, but with Luca dead they all had to wonder where she had gone. Emmaline remembered calling her several times a night with no answer. Quentin didn't seem too concerned mumbling things like, "she made her bed." Then Dac showed up out of the blue. Quentin had requested they all meet in the dining room that night. When they opened the doors to the room Dac was seated in his usual spot at the head of the table. Blood stained the corners of his mouth. The right sleeve of his jacket was torn at the shoulder seam. His shirt hung loose and untucked. But it was his eyes that gave Emmaline pause. The faint red glow gleaming from the pupils sent chills down Emmaline's spine. She knew that glow. It was the same glow she had saw in Luca's eyes when he kidnapped and fed from her before turning her into a vampire. Now that glow was in the eyes of Dac. The eyes of the one who had rescued her and given her a home so long ago. The one she trusted and relied on. For the first time since she'd known him, she feared him. Or maybe she feared for him, for what he would now become.

Dac stood as the others entered the room. "Things are going to change from here on out," he had said. "It is time we embrace our true nature. It is time we become the vampires we were always meant to be."

Emmaline noticed a bit of a smile begin to form on Una's face. Oh, how she despised that woman. Quentin only agreed to let her stay for Nikolai's sake, so that Nikolai would stay, but Emmaline hated the idea. Una had tried to kill him and now she was acting as his protector. It made no sense.

"But that's..." Emmaline began to protest. Dac was at her feet before she could finish the sentence. He stood towering over her and pressed his forefinger to her lips.

"My dear Emmaline," he whispered. "You have always been my favorite. Always so innocent, so naïve." Emmaline rolled her eyes at the word naïve. "But there is more to this life than I've allowed you to experience," he continued. "Now is your time to grow."

Emmaline took a step back and that's when they all heard the whimper in the corner. As they each turned their heads in the direction of the cry Dac raced back to his spot at the table and in the chair next to him was a woman. Dac snatched the woman up by her hair. Her neck torn open dripping with blood. Her eyes clouded with tears and terror.

"Dac what have you done!" Nikolai yelled out. Quentin rushed towards Dac grabbing one of his arms. Nikolai followed, taking hold of the other. They scuffled about the dining room. Chairs were broken, glass shattered. The woman cried out in faint screams. The life slowly, painfully draining from her as she bled out from her wounds. Una snatched the woman up from the floor, placed her lips to her neck and drank the remaining life from her.

"What are you doing?" Emmaline yelled.

"Ending her misery." Una replied licking the blood from her lips as she pushed past Emmaline.

Emmaline stood frozen in the doorway as she watched the only family she had known since becoming a vampire fall apart. It was as if her brain no longer knew the words to communicate with her legs. Her hands and arms became numb. The vision of her friends a blur as her eyes focused on the dead woman. A woman she realized she knew. A woman who had for years kept their secret and watched over their house. Had been loyal to them. It was Charlotte.

That night Quentin and Nikolai managed to subdue Dac despite his strength. They locked him inside one of the rooms on the lowest level of the house, though it was not his own. Quentin told Emmaline and Una to pack their things and go to his old townhouse while he and Nikolai boarded up the house.

The next night after settling into their new home, Emmaline called Jace to ask if he heard from Harper. His answer told her all she needed to know. "She's gone." He had said. Then he hung up. He gave no details of what happened or how he knew but she heard it in his voice. The sadness and the guilt. The last time they spoke Jace was looking for a vampire he believed killed his fiancée. Looks like he found her. Emmaline shut her eyes and then laid back on the bed inside her new room. Life from that point on would be forever changed.

Things had actually been quiet for the next ten years, different but quiet. Now, Emmaline kept mostly to herself. She spent most of her time in her room listening to music and writing poetry in an attempt to avoid running into Una. Nikolai tried to convince her to give Una a chance, but Emmaline wasn't interested. She didn't like her, and she definitely didn't trust her. Besides, Emmaline had a secret of her own and it would be best if the others did not find out what she had been up to over the last few years.

QUENTIN NEVER THOUGHT he'd live in his townhouse again after the fire that had destroyed it, but he had it rebuilt anyway. Throughout the years he had a couple different caretakers to keep it inhabitable, now and then staying there himself for a day or two when he needed an escape. And now he, Emmaline, Nikolai, and Una had been living there in relative quiet for the past ten years. Una was an unexpected addition to their little family but with all of her family now dead she was all alone. Besides, she and Nikolai had been a family once, husband and wife, actually. It was for that reason alone that Quentin agreed she could stay and live with them. With

Dac now in possession of the demon and Harper gone, Quentin wanted to keep Emmaline and Nikolai close. He didn't believe the three of them should be separated. Whether or not Una could be fully trusted, well that was up for debate and according to Emmaline definitely not, but Quentin figured with her living with them he could at least keep a close eye on her. But Quentin's main objective was keeping everyone safe and Dac locked away. With the curse taken hold of him Dac was dangerous and out of control, which he showed the night he killed Charlotte.

Since confining Dac inside their old house, Quentin and Nikolai took turns bringing blood to him. Never enough to give him strength and power, only enough to keep him alive, but weak. Once a week one of the two would bring a jar of blood to Dac. They would bring it to the room they kept him locked inside of, slide in through the door and then leave as quickly as possible. Tonight, it was Quentin's turn.

In his natural form Quentin was not much more than a dark shadow. As a non-human vampire, he fed off the energies of other living beings. He didn't need blood to survive like the others but when he did drink blood, he could take on the form of whichever creature's blood he consumed. Which for him was typically human. It was his natural shadowy form he kept to this night. He swept through the city streets undetected by anyone, human or creature. It was what he mostly preferred these days, but especially on nights like tonight.

He slipped into the old boarded up vampire house. The memories of its grander still vivid in his mind despite its current decrepit condition. In the front foyer he looked around the dark interior before going to the wall that hid the staircase leading down to the lowest level of the house. The place where all of their rooms used to be when they lived here. But now it only housed an imprisoned, cursed, demon vampire. The air inside was cold and dry.

Quentin could feel the warmth of the blood through the glass jar in his hands, but it wouldn't stay warm for long in these temperatures. He fumbled around in the dark for the key to Dac's room. Each time he came Dac would ask him the same question. "Why do you keep me here? Why not just kill me?" Quentin would always answer back "Because one day we will find a way to free you from that demon."

Quentin put the key in the lock, but when he turned it, something felt different. There was no click of the latch unlocking. The door was already unlocked. He turned the knob and pushed the door open. Even with his vampire sight he didn't trust his own eyes in the darkness. He lifted the electric lantern he carried with him. As the room lit up it confirmed what Quentin had feared. The room was empty. Dac was gone.

Quentin dropped the glass jar in his other hand. The glass shattered as it crashed to the ground. The blood inside spilled out, painting the floor the color of dark crimson. He raced down the hallway and back up the stairs from which he came. He searched the first-floor rooms then ran up the next flight of stairs, checking Dac's old office, then the dining room. When he still found no trace of Dac, he hurried to the attic. He pushed open the heavy attic doors. The room had been cleared of all the weapons and oils that had been stored there, all the things that could harm them, but also the things that had assisted Dac and Nikolai back when they hunted Luca. Just like the other rooms in the house he had checked, this one was empty too. Quentin had to accept, Dac had escaped.

Quentin had no choice. He had to go home and warn the others. They had to find Dac and soon before he killed anyone. Although Quentin knew it was probably already too late for that. He sighed as he clenched his fists. How could this happen?

# Seven

Jace and Sophia arrived at Sarah's doorstep at the same time. The evening sky was beginning to turn a darker blue as the sun had only just set. Jace knocked on the door but allowed Sophia to enter first when Sarah answered and let them inside. Jace shuddered at the cool breeze that blew past as he entered through the doorway. Inside Sarah led them to a room down the hall on the first floor.

"My grandmother isn't doing too well today, but she asked to speak with all of us." Sarah said.

The curtains over the windows were pulled back. The lamp on the dresser lit up the room. Brigid sat on her bed with her back against the headboard. Pillows propped up behind her. A heavy quilt pulled up to her waist covered her legs. There were three chairs placed next to the bed. As Sarah, Jace and Sophia entered the room Brigid gestured for them each to sit. She smiled but Jace noticed her sallow complexion and hollowed cheeks. As usual she wore her white hair tied back in a bun at the nape of her neck though the sides showed thinning. The once hearty woman he knew years ago, now looked frail and wan.

Sarah sat in the chair closest to her grandmother. Sophia sat next to her and Jace took the chair furthest away. Sarah reached over and handed Brigid a small plastic bottle of water for her to drink before she started talking. Brigid took a few small sips of water then handed the bottle back to Sarah.

"I want to tell you all my history with the vampires." Brigid said.

"Are you sure?" Sarah questioned, knowing that Brigid was always very reluctant to talk about it.

"Yes. It is time. I may not have much longer and maybe it can help this poor girl to understand what is happening with her."

Sophia looked at Brigid, "thank you," she said.

Jace remained quiet as he remembered when he first met Brigid back when he was searching for vampires. She had sat with him and Sarah in her house and told them the truth about the vampires as she had known it, and how to destroy them. Now she was getting ready to tell her story to Sophia, and he was here to help this young woman, a virtual stranger, to search for possibly those same vampires. The same vampires that destroyed his life.

He had sworn off any involvement with the vampires, but after the other night at his niece's party he had no choice. If vampires were back in town, he needed to protect his family. He sat back in the chair and listened as Brigid began her story.

IT WAS A TIME OF WAR all around the world, but Brigid and her siblings were involved in a war of their own. A different type of war. A war between humans and the undead. They were hunters as were their parents before them and their grandparents before that. Their family had hunted vampires for centuries and would continue until the very last vampire was vanquished. That was the pledge that was made by their ancestors, and it had been continued ever since and would be seen through until the end. That was the reason Brigid, her sister Scarlet, and brother Edwin were standing in this cottage at the edge of Crimson Fells, just past the Crimson Fells Cemetery drinking tea with an old woman and listening to her warnings and coming into the possession of a magical music box.

"The vampires are talking," Scarlet had said just a day earlier. Scarlet had a special gift of hearing the vampires when no one else could. With this gift she could learn of their comings and goings. "They speak of a certain two that have arrived within the past few days. They fear these two. They say one of them is cursed."

It was this information they took to the old woman. She told them the story of the curse and handed them the music box. "Open the box and the melody will lead them to you. While they are hypnotized by its song that will be your chance to kill them. Vampires this old will need more than your potions and a stake to the heart to destroy them. You will need to sever the head. Be strong my hunters. The cursed one is most evil, and his companion will do anything to protect him. He may not yet have the demon inside of him, but if he is not destroyed it is only a matter of time before it finds him."

Brigid took the music box from the woman and then the three siblings made their way back home. They came up to the modest two-story home in Crimson Fells where they lived with their parents who were anxiously awaiting their return. Brigid entered the house first. Her siblings followed closely behind her. Her father set aside the newspaper he was reading.

"What did the old woman say?" He asked. The newspaper crinkled as he set it on the table.

Brigid set the music box down on the rounded kitchen table. "She gave us this," she answered and then explained to her parents how it worked. Her mother, standing at the stove stirring the stew she was cooking in a large pot glanced at the box. She walked over and picked it up admiring the whimsical pattern painted on the round wooden box.

"It looks like a child's toy," she scoffed as she placed the box back on the table and went back to her stew.

Brigid rolled her eyes. Her mother was always skeptical of magic that couldn't be cooked up in a pot over the stove. Even as much as they relied on Scarlet's ability to the hear the vampires her mother would dismiss it as folly. She would say her potions weren't magic. But to Brigid and her other family members if creatures like vampires could exist outside of fairytales and myths then so could magic.

"We'll need to come up with a strategy. Then assign roles that best suit each of us in order to properly execute our plan," her father said. "What else did the woman say?"

"She says they are some of the oldest vampires in the world. And that they kill vampires and humans alike. It is a demon's curse that plagues one of them. She says if we do not destroy him the demon will get inside him eventually."

"Then we must act quickly. Any creature that will kill his own kind is purely evil."

"I agree," said Edwin always eager to please his father.

"I will listen out for the other vampires. They seem to want them here even less than we do. We can use that to our advantage. Maybe they will mention were these two are hiding out."

Their mother placed a loaf of bread in the center of the table, then placed a bowl of stew in front of her husband and each of her children. "That's enough vampire talk for now, eat." She sat down at the table with her own bowl in front her. They all ate in silence.

The next morning Brigid awoke to the sun shining brightly through her window. Its warm rays grazed her face through the open glass. The lace curtains danced against the windowsill with the gentle breeze from outside. The smell of springtime drifted through the air. She glanced over at the magical music box that sat atop her dresser. Her family decided that she would be the one to hold on to it. Keep it safe. When the time came, she would be the one to use it. Brigid had killed her share of vampires before, but this time felt different. The butterflies fluttered about her stomach in a tizzy. She was simultaneously anxious and excited. These would be the most powerful vampires they ever come up against. If she could kill even one of them that would solidify her place amongst the other hunters.

They would finally see her as more than someone who mixed creams and potions like her mother or a seer like her sister. They would finally see her as a true hunter.

Brigid quickly dressed and met her parents and siblings in the kitchen when she heard her mother calling them all for breakfast. Everyone was seated at the table by the time she had arrived. Her mother had set a small plate of food in front of her usual seat. Brigid was picking at the scrambled eggs on her plate when a knock came at the door. She got up to answer it.

"What are you doing here?" On the other side of the door stood Patrick, another hunter. Brigid rolled her eyes and stepped out of the way to let him in.

"I came to speak with your father." Patrick brushed past Brigid as he stepped into the house. "Good morning, all," he said to the family seated around the table.

Brigid's father stood up and he shook Patrick's hand and the two of them went to talk in the den. Brigid sat back at the table. She took a few more bites of her breakfast, sipped her orange juice, and politely excused herself. Pretending to go back to her bedroom, she snuck to the den and listened through the closed door.

# Eight

Sundown was coming later and later as the spring season progressed. Brigid was growing impatient waiting for her father and brother to leave the house. They were going on a hunt tonight but told Brigid to sit this one out and stay home. She hated it when they wouldn't take her along. She could kill a vampire just as well as either of them, but it was just as well, she made other plans for herself. While everyone was sitting on their hands making plans for the newest vampires in town, she was going to be a bit more proactive. Scarlet had mentioned they were said to be mingling amongst the humans and Brigid was ready to see who they were.

Soon as she heard her father and brother leave the house, Brigid locked her bedroom door. She watched them from her window as they climbed inside of their father's car and drove down the street. Wherever they were headed tonight it wasn't nearby otherwise they would have walked. Just as well, this would mean there was less of a chance of running into them.

With her father and brother out of sight and her mother and sister in their respective rooms Brigid slipped into her covert clothing of men's slacks and button-down shirt. She twisted her hair into a tight bun on top of her head. She tip toed down the stairs where she then slipped her feet into a pair of old warn black boots and picked up one of her brother's fedoras from the hat rack next to the door. Once outside she covered her hair with the fedora and started out towards the town taverns.

She may not know what these two men looked like, but she knew vampires and she would know if she saw one. She imagined being from out of town they wouldn't be dressed as the other locals. She kept close to the buildings as she walked determined to stay out of the light of the streetlamps. Keeping her ears open to the sounds around her, she listened for any mention of strangers in town. Finally, she got her break. Coming out of the bookshop two elderly women and the shop owner were talking. One of the women speaking rather loudly. The shop owner was locking the door to the shop, most likely closing up for the day. The woman next to him was telling them about the two strangers her husband had seen recently.

"Black as the night sky, their hair was," she was saying. "And pale, pale skin. Like nothing we've ever seen before and that is saying a lot for around here."

"Mmm. That's interesting," The other woman said as she locked her arm around the elbow of her husband, the shopkeeper.

"And those accents. Certainly not from this side of the continent. They are strange, those two, I tell you. Be safe out here," She warned.

"We will. Don't worry about us. You be careful getting home,"

Brigid watched as the shopkeeper and his wife parted ways with the loudmouth elderly woman. So, the vampires have been out amongst the humans, she thought to herself. Scarlet was rarely ever wrong but now Brigid had proof, and she was sure she was in the general area of where they'd been spotted considering the woman's assumed husband had just come out of the tavern next door to meet his wife and walk home together. Men usually frequented the same places.

Brigid slipped quietly through the doors of the tavern and sat in a booth at the far corner. The room was dimly lit by orange-colored lanterns hanging from the low ceiling. It smelled of liquor, and sausage. Someone walked past her spilling beer on the floor. She picked up the paper menu on the table and pretended to read it while she scanned the room.

As her eyes surveyed the bar mostly all she saw was locals. She tried listening to the voices around her but the loud banter between patrons made it difficult to distinguish between the different conversations although she was sure she would notice an unfamiliar accent.

The sound of the glass mug hitting the table startled her. Foamy liquid spilled out and traveled across the table towards her. She quickly wiped it away with the handkerchief from her pocket. She huffed at the voice that spoke to her.

"Now it's my turn to ask you what you're doing here?" Patrick was sitting across from her sipping the straw-colored brew from the heavy glass mug.

"That's none of your business. How did you even know it was me?"

"Your disguise isn't as inconspicuous as you think. You look ridiculous."

Brigid scoffed at his insult.

"I saw you when you walked in. So, I followed you. Making sure you're not getting yourself into trouble."

"I don't need you to watch over me."

"You do if you're here doing what I think you're doing."

"And what do you think that is."

"Looking for vampires."

Brigid couldn't argue with that. It was exactly what she was there doing. "Keep your voice down," she hissed.

"Listen you'll have your role to play once we come up with a viable plan, until then keep your head down and go home."

"Fine." Brigid got up from her seat in the booth and walked out of the tavern. To her relief Patrick stayed behind to finish his drink.

She would let him believe she was obeying his order to go home but home was not where she was headed, at least not yet.

The temperature outside had become cooler and the night darker. The stars and moon were no longer visible beyond the clouds that covered the sky. A mist hung in the air. Brigid tugged on the rim of her hat, pulling it further down covering her eyes. With her hands in her pockets and her head hung low she walked on to the next pub. When she stepped inside it was set up just like the last one. Again, she chose a table in the back corner. She sat with her back to the wall, watching and listening to those around her. It was there that she saw him, sitting at the bar. He was just as that woman had described. Hair the color of obsidian and skin so translucent you could almost see right through it. When he spoke, his voice was mesmerizing. His words rang like a melody. His friend appeared in a similar fashion. They both radiated a confidence she had rarely seen in any other vampire. They were well aware of their power and influence.

Brigid sank back further into her chair. She stayed for a while watching the strange new vampires. They appeared so comfortable amongst the humans as if it were natural. They ordered drinks that they never drank, easily passing them off to someone else then ordering another and somehow no one noticed. Those that circled around them regarded them with both fascination and camaraderie. It made Brigid sick to her stomach knowing that in only a short time one of these innocent unknowing people would become the victim of these vampires.

Brigid snuck out of the tavern unnoticed. The misty weather from earlier had cleared but the ground was still wet under her feet. She headed in the direction of her house knowing her father and brother would likely be home soon. She was determined to get home before them and hopefully before anyone noticed she was gone. She needed to process what she had witnessed with these strange vampires. They were unlike any others they ever encountered. They were bold in their actions, assimilating with the towns people, instead of hiding in the background. They dressed like the upper class and spoke with elegance. They were enchanting and enigmatic. It was going to be trickier than any of them thought to get to these two. Brigid imagined they did not dwell in caves and underground tunnels, which she would later find out was true.

The area around her grew darker as the streetlamps became fewer and further apart the closer she got to her home. Behind her she heard the footsteps of someone else. She tightened her shoulders and straightened her posture. Keeping her head straight but her eyes to the ground she watched the shadow behind her rapidly approaching. She reached under her hat and snatched a hairpin from her hair and held it between her fingers. As the footsteps grew louder, she held the pin tighter.

"I thought I told you to go home," the voice behind her said.

Brigid let out a sigh of both relief and annoyance. "Patrick! You scared me to death. What are you doing here now?"

"What I should have done earlier. Making sure you get home safely."

"I don't need you to babysit me."

"Are you sure about that?"

Brigid rolled her eyes even though Patrick couldn't see the gesture. She picked up her pace as they neared her house. Patrick trailed behind her but didn't bother to keep up. When she got inside, she locked the door behind her, never saying goodbye to Patrick. As she hoped, her father and brother had not returned home yet. Her mother and sister were still in their rooms, she assumed given all the lights downstairs were turned off. She hung her brother's hat back on the hat rack she had taken it from earlier that evening. She removed the wet boots from her feet and stuffed them in the closet then quietly snuck back to her bedroom for what would turn out to be a restless sleep.

When she entered the kitchen the next morning for breakfast her family were already sitting at the table as usual. It was normal for Brigid to be the last one at the table in the morning. What wasn't normal was for Patrick to be there. For as much time as he spent at their house he typically arrived later in the morning. Brigid felt her heart drop to her stomach when she noticed the look on her father's face.

"Good morning," she said meekly as she sat in her usual seat. A plate with toast and bacon was already set out for her. She picked up a piece of bacon and took a small bite.

"Is it true?" Her father asked.

Brigid glanced up at her father before answering. The look in his eyes could cut glass. Brigid swallowed hard. "Is what true?"

"Don't play dumb. Were out in the pubs last night looking for those vampires?"

Brigid looked toward Patrick and then back at her father. Of course, Patrick would tell on her. "Listen, I just..." she started to explain.

"No, you listen! You are not to be going out there by yourself!" Her father's face reddened as he raised his voice at her. He rose from his seat and stormed out of the kitchen.

Brigid followed her father, determined to plead her case. She begged for him to listen as she explained what she observed the night before. After much argument he finally agreed to let her spy on the vampires, but only if Patrick accompanied her. Reluctantly she promised she would only go if Patrick escorted her.

Over the next few weeks Brigid and Patrick followed the vampires to the pubs and theatres. They noted their every move. They way they dazzled those around them. They looked for news of murders or mysterious deaths in the morning papers, but never found any evidence of the vampires killing. It mystified Brigid how clever these two were. The hunters would need to be more cunning than them if they wanted to succeed in destroying them. Brigid was desperate to find where they lived. She knew that would be the key to killing them.

Finally, the day came when Brigid's father called them all together to discuss their final plans. Everyone was gathered in her father's study. Brigid, as usual, was the last to arrive. Her father was seated behind his desk. Edwin and Patrick stood to the left and right of him. Scarlet was perched on the windowsill. Their mother sat in one of two leather seats in front of the large desk leaving the other seat available for Brigid. She sat down eager to hear the plan the men had laid out.

Her father spoke first, "We now know all the places the vampires frequent thanks to Brigid and Patrick. We know their patterns. I think we're ready to move forward."

"Brigid will use the music box to lead them out of the town center. There's that old, abandoned house at the edge of town. We will lead them there. Edwin and I will be there ready to take them down while they're entranced by the music." Patrick continued.

"And do you really think it's going to be that simple?" Brigid jumped in. "Patrick, we've seen them. They radiate a power none of us have encountered before, not even you, father. I think we need something more" she said.

"I agree," said Scarlet from her spot near the window. "They've been in town for weeks, maybe months and I have never heard them. They keep their minds so tightly closed not even a smidgen of thought gets through. They are smart. Even the other vampires fear them."

"Then what would you suggest?"

"I think we should wait and find out where they live. Get them in the daytime when they sleep." Brigid answered. Scarlet and her mother both nodded in agreement.

"Don't be ridiculous. We've studied them enough. It's time to take them down. That magic box of yours will trap them into a trance and Edwin and I will kill them, as is already planned."

"Patrick is right. We can't allow them to reside in our town any longer killing our friends." Her father said.

After some back and forth Brigid left the room when the men refused to listen to her plan. She went upstairs to her bedroom and took the music box out of its hiding place. She stared at it for a while as she thought of the old woman's warnings. These were very old and very powerful vampires. They would not be able to destroy them the same as they have the others. She would have to go out alone tonight and find out where they were hiding themselves. Maybe then she could convince her father and the others that she was right.

Brigid waited for night to creep in and then dressed in the slacks and shirt she wore that first night she went looking for the vampires. Tonight, however, she took a shoulder bag along with her. She tucked the music box in the bag, then snuck into her mother's pantry and stole a couple of her potions, just in case. She had no plans to actually come in contact with the vampires, but one could never be too careful.

Once Brigid was certain everyone had fallen asleep, she crept down the stairs and slid quietly out the front door. The leaves of the trees rustled in the night breeze. Clouds floated overhead occasionally blocking out the moonlight but then setting it free again. Brigid felt herself constantly feeling the side of her bag as she walked into town. She peered into the tavern windows looking for a glimpse of the vampires. When she finally found them, she waited outside the building. She stood in the dark alleyway, took a jar out from her bag, and unscrewed the top. She scooped out a handful of the cream inside it and rubbed it into the skin around her wrists, and neck.

When the vampires left the tavern, she followed. She kept a few paces behind them keeping her breath steady, praying silently that the cream worked as it was meant to, and the vampires didn't sense her nearby. She followed them to a townhouse not far from the town center. Just as she had suspected, they lived like the humans.

The next evening, she planned on making an excuse to leave the house but when her family announced an unexpected trip out of town for the night Brigid got them to agree to leave her behind. As soon as her father's car was out of sight Brigid changed back into her shirt and slacks. She grabbed the same bag from the night before, slathered on her cream and left to the vampire's house. She wanted to be there early to see them leave.

It was just before sunset when she arrived in front of the townhouse. She stood across the street looking up at the building that housed the most powerful vampires she'd ever come to know. The windows were covered with dark curtains to keep out the sunlight, but she noticed a shadow pass by. A figure in the window. Could they be up before sunset, she wondered to herself. She looked around. The streetlamps were beginning to turn on. The sun was at its lowest point in the sky before it would totally disappear. The moon was already visible. Full darkness would be upon them soon.

Brigid stood and watched a while longer. As the sky grew darker, she wondered how long it would be until they emerged from their hiding place. She thought about turning around and leaving but she couldn't take her eyes away from that window. Who had been there? Then the lights turned on inside the house. The curtain was pulled back and her suspicion had been confirmed. The vampires stood side by side staring down the window. And, they had seen her.

She ran as fast she could back to her house, heart pounding with every step she took, never looking back to see if they followed her. As she reached her front door, she rushed inside slamming the door shut behind her. Her heart still raced and her breath was heavy. What was she going to do now?

The next morning when her family returned, they informed her they were going ahead with their plans later that night. She agreed to do her part keeping quiet about the events from the last two nights. When the time came, she pinned her hair to the top of her head. She gathered the music box, a few candles, and her potions. When they arrived at the old house Brigid lit the candles. This would give them just enough light to see and also provide some cover of shadow so hopefully the vampires wouldn't see them right away. They each slathered a bit of the cream onto their skin. Brigid took her place while Patrick and Edwin checked their weapons. When given the signal, Brigid opened the music box. The serene melody sounded all through the room. The song calmed every nerve Brigid may have had while she watched the tiny ballerina twirl in circles inside of her box on top her tiny stage. The room came alive as the flames of the candles danced to the song. Then they arrived.

The two vampires stood in the entryway. Their eyes glazed over. They moved with slow intention as if following the music just as the old woman said would happen. But then one rushed towards her. A hand grabbed her and pulled her back. The lid to the box slammed shut. The vampires were gone. It all happened so fast she barely saw it happen. The vampires somehow managed to break out of the trance before Edwin or Patrick could get to them. Luckily her father had been there to yank her out the path of the vampire.

"Are you ok?" he asked, still holding Brigid close to his chest.

"Yes, I'm fine," she said through shallow breaths.

"Maybe you were right. We need to get them where they sleep," he admitted.

When they returned home Brigid confessed to knowing their hideout and told them about the townhouse. They discussed a plan for the morning to attack the vampires unaware while they slept, but then Scarlet entered the room with news.

"Tomorrow will be too late," she said. "The vampires are scheduled to be on a train out of town at midnight."

"Then we will be there." Brigid said.

"No, that's too risky," her father declared.

Brigid rested upstairs in her bed watching the minutes on the clock tick by. The thought of letting the vampires disappear into the night and move into another city didn't sit well with her. She couldn't believe the others were going to willingly let them get away. There was no way Brigid could let that happen. She peaked her head outside her door peering down the hall. The house was quiet. Just as she had done those other nights, she crept down the stairs and out the front door, only this time grabbing a knife and a harsher potion to take with her. She was going to stop those vampires tonight.

She didn't have her bag with her this time. Only two vials of potions, one in each pocket of her trousers and the knife she had strapped to her side. As she crossed the field leading to the train station, she saw no sign of the vampires yet. She only hoped she had arrived before them, that she was not too late. She glanced around the empty field. This would be her only chance. She would have to get to them here before they reached the station surrounding themselves with people.

She hid behind an old torn down shed watching and listening for any sign of movement nearby. It would only be a matter of minutes before she would see the vampires hurrying for the train. She reached into her pocket and took out the first vial. She unscrewed the top and as they passed by unaware of her presence, she tossed the vial in their direction. The liquid potion spilled onto one of the vampires. He fell to the ground. The other distracted trying to help him. Brigid rushed towards them, her knife in her hand. She lifted the knife ready to strike when she was stopped by a strong force. A cold hand grasped tightly around her wrist. His skin felt like ice against her own. She pressed forward against his strength pushing the knife forward. As it dangled inches from his chest, she maintained her stance. Her eyes watered and her arm trembled, but she was unwilling to give up. The knife then slipped from her hand. The vampire had her now by the throat. She kicked her feet as he lifted her from the ground. With one hand she tugged at his arm. With her other hand she dug through her pocket for the potion. For a mere second, she felt the glass vile between her fingers before it fell to the ground. The vampire still had her in his clutches. He bared his fangs. She continued struggling to break free when an oily liquid hit her face. She screamed as the burning liquid dripped into her eyes. The incoming train whistled. The vampire dropped her as he and the other raced for the platform.

Brigid lay on the grass alone. She wiped her face with the sleeve of her shirt. Tears ran down her face. She recoiled when she felt the touch of a hand on her shoulder.

"Brigid," she heard the voice of her brother call out. Everything was dark.

"Are you ok?" It was Patrick's voice she heard this time.

"I can't see," She whimpered softly as her brother and Patrick lifted her off the ground. She leaned into one of them. Which one she did not know, but she felt comfort in his embrace, whoever he was.

"THAT WAS LAST TIME I had ever seen the vampires, though at that point I was not ready to stop looking. I was more determined than ever to catch them after they took my eyesight." Brigid continued. "A few weeks later my sister had heard that the vampires had landed in a place called Aura City. Patrick escorted me there knowing I would go it alone if he hadn't. We spent months looking for them, but it was a big city and they had either moved on or were keeping well hidden. Not long after that I discovered I was pregnant, and Patrick convinced me to give up the hunt. We moved out of the city and agreed we'd never speak of anything vampire again. From that moment on they were creatures of myths and scary stories. I never thought I'd hear of them again until you, Sarah, came knocking on my door ten years ago." Brigid coughed and Sarah handed her the water bottle. She sipped slowly before handing it back. Her hands trembled. Her breath became shallow revealing her fragility.

Sophia looked to the left and right of her at both Sarah and Jace and then back at Brigid, this old frail woman lying on the bed knowing that each of them had been in contact with these same vampires at different points in their lives. She was still new to the knowledge of the vampire's true existence, but she felt inspired by these three people in this room with her. She had come here seeking help and guidance from them but now she was determined to help them continue their legacy. Maybe her dream wasn't to help the man in it but to help Brigid finally get her victory. One last win before she dies.

# Nine

The view from the townhouse terrace stretched out over the city. The city lights twinkled in the midnight sky. The streets down below still bustled with people. Cold wind blew in from behind whisking his hair around his face but that didn't faze him. Nikolai stared off into the distance. From this height he could almost see his old house. The news of Dac's disappearance weighed on him. Quentin, Emmaline, and Una were all inside discussing ways to find him. Arguing mostly. Nikolai stepped outside to try and get a clear head while the other three bickered. An unfettered Dac was a disaster. Failure to capture him would only end in more tragedy. The demon inside him had completely taken over his mind. Nikolai tried for years to understand what happened. Dac had spent centuries escaping that curse, running from it, denying its existence. Then one day he just decided he wanted it. All that power lived inside him now. All that evil.

Nikolai turned towards the French doors and back to the group inside. Emmaline looked exacerbated as she always did in the presence of Una. Quentin held a glass half filled with blood. He appeared in his human form. The scar on his cheek was clearly visible. The group became silent when Nikolai stepped back inside. He sat on a chair in the corner of the room. Crossed one leg over the other. He searched each of their faces for any hint of resolution but found none.

"You know him best. Where would he go?" Una finally asked, turning towards Nikolai.

"Searching for revenge." Nikolai answered. "It's all he knows. Except those who hurt him are already gone. He made sure of that ten years ago when he killed Luca and sent Jace after Harper."

"What about you and Quentin? Will he come after you two, do you think?" Emmaline's voice was shaky.

"Maybe, but I don't really think so. We may have locked him up, but we've been taking care of him. He understands why we did what we did. Deep down I know he does."

"Does he though? The Dac you knew is gone." Una said.

"I have to believe he does, that he's still in there somewhere. It's the reason we've kept him alive."

"I agree." Emmaline remarked as she allied herself with Nikolai ignoring Una's attempt at shaping Dac into the enemy.

"I'll be back. I'm going out for a while." Nikolai exited the room before anyone could protest or offer to tag along.

Before leaving the house, he took a swallow of blood from the stash they kept locked in the basement, a level up from the underground space in which they kept their rooms. The townhouse was smaller than the last place and here they needed to be much more discreet.

The crowded streets from earlier in the night finally began to clear away. Only a few people passed by as he walked. Nikolai preferred it this way.

He got on the train going towards the old house. The yellow overhead lights flickered on and off making the already poorly lit train car dark. The train was mostly empty but for one other person at the other end. A woman sat quietly with her face buried in a book. Her jeans raised above her ankles revealed a pair of yellow socks that matched the colors in the argyle sweater she wore under her green and beige checkered jacket. The long scarf wrapped once around her neck almost reached the colorful sneakers she wore on her feet. Nikolai pulled up the collar of his wool jacket and stared straight ahead while he waited for his stop.

The station smelled of stagnant water and decaying animal flesh. Nikolai made his way quickly to the main street level and then the few blocks to his old home. Although he had been coming here every other week for the past ten years the boarded windows and unkempt lawn saddened him. He unlocked the front gate and then the front door, stepping into the foyer. He took the steps to the third-floor attic. The doors had been left open by Quentin earlier that evening. Most of the things in this room had been cleared out the day they moved into Quentin's townhouse, but there was one thing hidden in here which no one knew about.

Nikolai kneeled down to the floor. With his fingertips he lifted up the loose floorboard. Underneath hid the leather-bound case he knew would be there. The leather was tattered and worn. He untied the string which held the ends together. Loose cream-colored pages and old black and white photos slipped out as he opened it.

Beneath him he could hear footsteps approaching from the stairwell. He gathered up the papers and photographs, placing them back into the case. As he began to stand a voice spoke out, giving him pause.

"I thought you'd come here." Emmaline said.

"You followed me?" he asked, still stooped in his kneeling position.

"Not exactly, just came to the spot I thought you'd be," she shrugged and sat down beside him on the cold hardwood floor. "What's that?" she asked.

Nikolai relaxed and sat back down next to Emmaline. "Some old things that belonged to Dac. I thought about what Una said about me knowing him best." Emmaline rolled her eyes at the mention of Una's name, but Nikolai pretended not to notice. "I was thinking maybe there could be some clue in here to where Dac might have gone to hide out."

"I didn't want to say anything in front of Una or Quentin, but I heard you and Una arguing earlier about Jace being back in town. Do you think he and the other hunters could have taken Dac?"

"I don't think so. Jace seems to have kept to whatever agreement he and Dac had made and left us all alone. I don't see why he would do something like that now."

"You know, I often wonder why you didn't kill him after he killed Harper."

"I won't say I didn't want to, but at the end of the day I can't say I wouldn't have done the same. I could ask you the same question."

"I guess for the same reason. Besides I've never killed anyone before."

"You know we may never know why Harper did what she did, but my guess is Jace is suffering much worse having to live with his choices. It's best to just let him be."

"You're probably right."

Nikolai tapped Emmaline's shoulder, "Let's get out of here."

"Can we stop by Harper's old room before we go. Just thinking maybe she's got something secret hidden under the floorboards."

"The floors down there are cement," Nikolai chuckled. "But sure."

Harper's room looked exactly as she had left it only now covered in years of dust and cobwebs. While Emmaline rummaged through Harper's drawers and armoire, Nikolai looked about the room. He pulled away the coverings of the canvases leaning against the wall. Each one painted in her blood. He stared at the images, abstract shapes, and swirls of black and red. He tried so hard to understand what she must have been feeling in those moments. Nikolai missed so much of the last year of Harper's life. He had spent months in a coma healing from the stab wounds Una had inflicted on him. In the short time after he woke up, he could sense all the tensions around the household. Then Jace took him and imprisoned him in that freezer. He had been too weak still to resist the sounds of the music box. He shook away those memories. What was done was done. Can't change the past, only try to understand it, and understand they would try. That was the reason he and Emmaline were here now, to see if maybe Harper left behind some clues to the past. Why she had done the things she done.

"I should have noticed something was off about her back then." Emmaline said, breaking the silence between them.

"She was good at hiding her intentions. If she didn't want you to know, you wouldn't have." Nikolai tried to ease Emmaline's pain. He knew she felt the losses of Harper and Dac deeply.

"It's just you know, maybe I could have stopped her."

"We both know there was no stopping Harper once she had her mind set on something."

"But feeding on people. Her best friend. It just makes no sense. And before you start, I already know what you're going to say." Emmaline had been saying for years how it didn't make sense to her and everyone always said the same thing to her. It was Luca who was to blame. He gave her that first taste of human blood and she craved it afterward just like any vampire would.

Nikolai blamed himself also, although silently. He was the one who had made her a vampire in the first place. But it wasn't only that. The fact was Harper's fate was sealed long before she was even born. Centuries long in fact. The night Nikolai left his wife alone to be taken by vampires. It was that moment that set all the others in motion. It was that moment in the long ago past that made all the other moments possible.

"Here, maybe this will help ease your mind a bit. Give you some of those answers your searching for." Nikolai tossed a book towards Emmaline's direction. It landed on the edge of the bed.

Emmaline picked it up, "where did you find this?" It was a journal. The smooth soft cover held closed with an elastic strap that wrapped around its edges. When Emmaline opened it, the pages came alive with Harper's bubbly handwriting.

"It was under the mattress."

"Ah. Such a simple hiding place." Emmaline smiled at Nikolai and closed the book.

They locked up the old house and rode the train across the city together. They quietly reminisced about the old days. They stopped at an all-night diner and ordered coffee they pretended to drink while they laughed and joked and watched the people come in and out. Most of them drunk after spending the earlier hours of the night at the bars and clubs. There was a group of clearly underage teens, but drunk, nonetheless. A girl with long pink hair. Another with short blue hair. Both in leather miniskirts and fishnets. Just humans doing human things. Nikolai tried to imagine what it would be like to be human in this day and age. The closest he could get were the stories that Emmaline told of her years as a human girl.

By the time they returned to the townhouse the sun was nearing its early morning rise. Emmaline held out the journal towards Nikolai, but he refused it. "That's for you to read. I hope it tells you the answers you're looking for. I've got this," he said as he held up the leather case he took from the old attic. "Hopefully I'll find my answers in here. But do let me know if that helps. Good luck."

"Thank you. And good luck to you too." Emmaline hugged the book close to her chest and disappeared down the stairwell to her room.

"Well, where have you been all night? I suppose not out looking for Dac." Una's voice griped from the living room where she stood next to the fireplace.

"Actually, that's exactly what I was doing. You said it yourself; I know Dac better than anyone. So, I went back to the old house to get this." He held up the leather case. "I'm hoping to find something in here that could help us figure out where Dac could be hiding out. I think he'd be someplace where he'd find comfort. Someplace that would remind him of home. And this, well this is all of his memories from when he was human. Before he became a vampire."

"So then how did you end up with her?" she asked, referring to Emmaline, not even acknowledging the fact that they may now have a clue into finding Dac.

Nikolai rolled his eyes, "I'll talk to you later." He left Una standing alone in the living room and descended down the stairs to his room locking the door behind him.

# Ten

Two days had passed since Sophia learned of Brigid's encounter with the vampires. She knew now that her dream couldn't be trusted. It was a trick. An illusion the vampire created to deceive her. Wherever he was, whatever he wanted she would have nothing to do with it. Not after he had blinded Brigid and almost killed her. Not after he had killed her own parents. It was true that it took her a couple of days to digest everything she learned since coming to Aura Springs, but it was crystal clear to her now. She knew what she needed to do.

She should have been meeting up with Sarah and Jace, but instead she found herself on a train heading into Aura City. They had told her to take her time and message them when she was ready. They understood it was a lot to take in, all of this information about mythical creatures and magical music boxes. One more day wouldn't hurt.

By the time the train arrived in Aura City the late afternoon had turned into early evening. It was not a long trip, yet somehow time seemed to escape her on the ride. Sophia stepped out of the station into the bustling city streets. The city was full of people despite the impending darkness of night. If they only knew what lurked in these streets alongside them. Maybe they wouldn't be so eager to be outside after dark. But then, here she was. Purposely coming into the city knowing the dangers that surrounded her. There was something to be said about her carelessness, but she wanted one last night to pretend as though the evils she so recently learned about did not exist. One last night to be a regular human, ignorant of what hides behind the shadows of the night. Besides she wasn't actually going to be alone.

Her uncle had been consistently reaching out to her since she left his house in Noxwood. She finally answered the phone and explained that she needed some time away and was spending that time at her beach house. Coincidentally, he was going to be in Aura City for the weekend, so Sophia agreed to meet him for dinner.

She took her time walking to the restaurant. What would she say when she actually saw her uncle? She knew he would have questions. It was easy to dodge his inquiries over the phone, but face to face would be a bit more difficult. He had known her for her entire life. He raised her for half of it. He knew when she was lying and to be honest, she wasn't that good at it. There was a reason she left in the middle of the night.

When she reached the restaurant, her uncle was already waiting for her. She noticed him immediately in his dark green overcoat and tan dress pants. He had one hand stuffed in his pocket while the other held his cell phone up to his ear. Sophia waited until she saw him put his phone away before she approached him.

"Hi." Sophia bowed her head slightly looking down at her feet avoiding eye contact.

"Nice to see you." He reached out to hug her but stopped short sensing her discomfort. Instead, he tapped her elbow. "Let's get inside out of this cold," he said.

She could tell he was attempting to be nice, but she knew it was only a matter of time before the questions started rolling in and her answers would only be met with contempt. Her uncle spoke with the hostess and they both followed her to a table on the second floor of the restaurant. Sophia lifted up her menu as soon as the hostess handed it to her and started to flip through the pages. The server couldn't get there fast enough. They sat in awkward silence until finally ordering their food. With no menus in between them, the conversation Sophia was avoiding was now unavoidable.

"So," her uncle started. "I guess what I really want to know is why you felt like you needed to sneak off in the middle of the night."

Sophia stuck a fork full of food in her mouth. She chewed slowly, buying herself as much time as possible before having to come up with an answer. She reached for a piece of bread, but her uncle, knowing what she was doing, gently grabbed her wrist, stopping her.

"Please talk to me," he pleaded with her. The pained look in his eyes almost let Sophia believe he was being genuine.

She swallowed the food her in mouth, then took a sip of her water. "I knew you wouldn't have wanted me to come so I just didn't tell you," she said rather honestly.

"Why would you think that?"

"Why did you lie to me about it?" It was the question she had been dying to ask him. If he was going to interrogate her, she could to the same.

"What are you talking about?"

"The beach house, you told me it was sold. My inheritance, you never even mentioned it."

"I thought the beach house had sold. I found out about all of it at the same time you did."

Sophia thought about all the times as a little girl she overheard her parents discussing that her uncle couldn't be trusted. Maybe he didn't know, maybe he did. She would never know the truth. She decided to let it go.

"After meeting with that layer and learning about everything, it brought up a whole lot of feelings of losing my parents. I just wanted to come out here to the beach house and feel close to them again."

"We could have come with you."

"Exactly. I wanted to be alone. That's why I didn't tell anyone." Sophia shoveled more food into her mouth. Her uncle's cell phone rang. He excused himself and walked off to find a quiet corner while answering the phone. Sophia gulped down the rest of the water in her glass. She tossed some cash on the table and slipped out of the restaurant before her uncle came back to the table.

The temperature outside had fallen a few degrees. The sky had grown darker though all the lights of the city would easily guide her way back to the train station. Sophia walked each block dodging the bodies of strangers that shared the same sidewalks. Each step brought her further away from her uncle still inside the restaurant. Had he even noticed she was gone yet? Would he try to follow her? Look for her? Did she even care? She pulled her phone out from the purse that hung from her shoulder. She tapped the screen to light it up. No missed call. No missed text. Guess he hadn't noticed yet. Or maybe he just didn't care. Either way she was free of his constraints.

As if her legs had a mind of their own Sophia found herself walking straight past the train station. Instead of buying her ticket home and getting on the train back to Aura Springs she was standing in the gateway entrance to a park. She leaned against the cold iron bars. Her arms crossed tightly across her chest. The winds picked up. Her curls blew across her face. The fallen leaves circled around her feet. The only people inside the park were the unhoused. They sat on the cold benches with their large plastic bags, canvas duffle bags, and shopping carts filled with all their belongings. A woman sat wrapped in a wool blanket. A man sipped something from a thermos. The crowds of people that passed by ignored them as if this was normal. Her heart ached for these strangers. People she had never met and knew nothing about and yet she wondered about their stories. She worried about their safety. Here they sat cold and unaware of the true dangers amongst them. And then she spotted him.

In a sea of ordinary people, he was extraordinary. Tall, clear skin that practically glowed in the dark, black hair. The black trench he wore hung loosely over his shoulders. He appeared just the same as she had seen him before. In a dream. In another life. They say he's a vampire, but he doesn't look menacing. He looked captivating and provocative. Then his eyes flared with red. And in a flash, he was gone as if wings had sprouted from his back, and he had flown away.

How had no one else noticed? Everyone around her carried on to wherever they intended. Had she really been the only one to see him? Were her eyes playing tricks on her? They must have been. That was the only explanation. Or was it? Yes, that was it. The stress of the last few days had her imagination running wild. Except she knew he existed, and he had been calling out to her. Now he was here. In the city. She had to tell Sarah. She dug through her purse again looking for her phone. The darkened sky and lack of light surrounding the park made it difficult to see. Something grabbed onto her shoulder. Her heart skipped a beat.

"There you are," A stern voice came from behind her.

Sophia swiftly turned to face her uncle who was standing behind her. "Don't sneak up on me like that."

"Sorry," he raised his hands to his shoulders. "I was looking for you. Why'd you leave?"

Sophia walked away without answering his question. She could feel him following behind her. See his shadow next to hers.

"I had the remainder of your food wrapped up." He tried handing the bag, but she didn't take it. "At least let me walk you back to the train station."

She still made no response as she continued walking. Her uncle stayed close by her side like some overprotective guardian. Which she guessed at some point that's what he was. He had taken care of her after her parents died. But now she wished he would just leave her alone.

They approached the train station and Sophia walked up to the kiosk to buy her ticket. She looked at the overhead screens that hung from the ceiling looking for her departure track and time.

"Look, I don't know why you're mad at me but whatever it is I hope we can work through it. We're family and I'm always going to be here for you. I hope you know that." Her uncle said in one last attempt to get her to talk to him.

"I told you at the restaurant."

"And I told you, I had no idea about the beach house or your inheritance."

"Well, I know my parents didn't trust you and I don't know what to believe right now. I need some time. Can you please just give me that?"

"Understood." Her uncle backed away leaving her standing alone in the station while she waited for her train.

The boarding call was finally announced for the train to Aura Springs. Sophia shuffled amongst the large crowd of people boarding the train. She found a seat in one of the cars next to the door. A cold breeze came through each time the door opened. As more people crowded in, she tucked her purse onto her lap. She realized she still needed to call Sarah but decided it could wait until she got home. She settled into her seat as comfortably as was possible on the cold hard benches and watched the world pass by through the tiny windows.

The trip home seemed faster than the trip into the city. Sophia tossed her coat and purse on the couch as soon as she entered her house. She wondered upstairs to her room and into the ensuite bathroom. She turned on the warm shower water and gathered her hair on top of her head. She stared at herself in the bathroom mirror as the steam from the shower began to fog the glass. Her mind played back the events of the night like a reel in an old timey home video. The restaurant with her uncle, the park, the vampire. The Vampire.

A noise downstairs. The shattering of glass. Banging on the door. Sophia scrunched down with her back leaning against the bathroom door. Her heart pounded. The water from the shower still rained down from the faucet sloshing against the porcelain tub. Her phone – it was still downstairs. Slowly Sophia cracked open the bathroom door. She crept down the stairs keeping her back against the wall. The front door was closed. The light in the living room was still lit. The rest of the house remained dark. She snuck into the living room and snatched her purse off the couch. She sunk down to the floor hiding behind the arm of the sofa. She felt around the inside of her bag for her phone. As soon as she found it, she sent Sarah a text begging her to come to the house.

Upstairs the shower continued running. The rest of the house was quiet. Sophia stayed perched in her hiding spot until her phone buzzed. Sarah messaged; she was outside. Steading herself on her shaky legs, Sophia opened the front door to see both Sarah and Jace. Sarah stood with Sophia on the front porch while Jace took a look inside the house.

"It's all clear." Jace confirmed once he returned to the porch. "Looks like a picture frame fell from the wall in the hallway. I swept up the glass and turned off the shower upstairs, but I don't see anyone... thing in the house."

"Do you want to stay at my house for the night?" Sarah asked. "We can come back tomorrow in the daylight if you'd like."

Sophia nodded. Sarah and Jace accompanied her to gather an overnight bag and then the three of them drove over to Sarah's house. After a few cups of tea and a little small talk, Jace left for his hotel. Sarah showed Sophia to the guest room. She settled into the comfortable bed. Pulled the covers up to her chin and left the light on.

# Eleven

Emmaline flipped through the pages of Harper's journal. Every word spawned more questions. Maybe it was time to accept she would never have the answers she so badly wanted. Why had she spent all these years living in the past anyway? She needed to move forward. Ten years of being stagnate was long enough. She slammed the journal shut and tossed it in the large wicker basket on the side of her bed along with all the other books and magazines that had begun to bore her. There were more important things to be concerned with, like finding Dac.

Quentin was already doing the obvious searches of looking for suspicious deaths in all the news articles. Nikolai had spent the last few days combing through the journal he retrieved from the old house and searching for places around the city that Dac might hide. Neither of those things had turned up any clues to his whereabouts. The truth was he could be anywhere by now.

Emmaline sat back thinking of the conversations she and Dac had had over the years. Was there something in any of the things he said that would give a hint to where he would be now? Nothing came to mind. Most of their talks were mindless chit chat. They weren't particularly close, but they were family. Dac had rescued her once and it was only fair that she returned the favor. It's the reason she left the door unlocked. Only, she thought he would have come to her. She thought he would have let her know where he was hiding out or where he was going. She thought he would have at least said goodbye.

Her room was beginning to feel small. The walls closing in and the air growing thick. She grabbed her jacket out of the closet. A walk outside in the chill night air would do her some good. Upstairs she passed the parlor room where Nikolai and Una were arguing again. This was becoming a daily occurrence. She would like nothing more than to avoid these two when they were together but in this house that seemed nearly impossible. Thankfully neither of them seemed to notice her tonight. She plugged her earphones into her ears, turned the music on, pushed her phone into the back pocket of her jeans and slipped out the front door unnoticed.

The crisp cool air was refreshing. The knots in her stomach loosened with every deep breath she took. She walked slowly through the city. The streets seemed unusually quiet for this time of night, but she welcomed the peace it brought. There was no need to keep to the shadows or hide herself. She walked along as if she were any other human. She didn't have to use her energy to blend in. She could just be herself. Being herself was something she hadn't been able to do in decades. Did she even know who that was anymore. For so long she had been hiding who she was. A vampire.

Is that what finally drew Dac to succumb to his curse? The thought hadn't occurred to her until this moment, but he spent centuries pretending, always looking over his shoulders, always suppressing his vampiric urges. Is that what drove Harper to Luca? Luca was unapologetically a vampire. He accepted who he was. Dac never did. And he never let any of them accept it either. Nikolai knew what it was like to kill his prey, but Emmaline never had that chance. She never thought much of it until now. She wasn't a hunter, or a killer. She had always held on to the part of her that was human, the values she had grown up with stayed with her all throughout her vampiric years. She never felt like she was missing out on anything by drinking the donations. That made her one of the good ones, right? Not by Una's standards. Una called her a puritan, a weak mouse. Said she wasn't a real vampire. What did Una know about being a good person, a good vampire? She came here with the intention of killing her own husband. She pretended to be dead for centuries. Who was she to try to make Emmaline feel bad about herself?

Emmaline walked into the nearby park. The area was devoid of all humans and creatures alike. The lights from the street did not reach into the park, making it dark and eerie. Emmaline closed her jacket tighter wrapping her arms around her chest. She began walking the darkened paths, but then a weariness came over her. Feeling drained she sat on a nearby bench. She hadn't drunk anything yet tonight she realized as the craving for blood came to the surface.

The bare trees overhead shook with the oncoming breeze. The only sound was the wind blowing and the thoughts in her head. She tried to remain calm as she pushed down the hunger and regained her composure.

"You should give into it. The craving. It's who you are." The voice she heard now wasn't her own. Emmaline turned her head to see Dac sitting next to her.

"You sound like Una," she scoffed at him.

"I see you two haven't yet settled your differences." He leaned back on the bench crossing one leg over the other. He looked different, stronger and the red glow that flickered in his eyes made him look like Luca.

"No and we never will," she answered. "Where have you been?"

"Around."

"You know Quentin and Nikolai are looking for you. Me too, but for different reasons." Emmaline fiddled with the zipper on the edge of her jacket avoiding any eye contact with Dac.

"I know." His voice was soft and tender unlike his brother's. "It's why I haven't visited you yet. Not ready for them to find me." Of course, he wasn't. Quentin and Nikolai would only lock him up again if they found him.

"I get it. I was afraid you left town without saying goodbye."

"Never."

"Where are you staying?"

"Someplace safe. You should get home before you pass out from hunger." He placed a hand against her cheek. "Meet me back here tomorrow night?"

He was gone before she could agree, but they both knew she would be there.

The house was quiet when Emmaline awoke the next night. She wandered through the house to find that both Quentin and Nikolai had gone out. Una was laid out across the chaise lounge in the parlor room, blood poured into a crystal wine glass on the table next to her. Emmaline rolled her eyes as she passed by on her way to the kitchen. The nightly donation was poured out into a carafe on the counter for all to use. She poured herself a drink before going out. Did not want a repeat of last night.

At the park Emmaline waited on the same bench. The temperature had dropped a few degrees from the night before. She wished she had worn a heavier jacket. Her teeth chattered and her body shivered as she waited for Dac to arrive.

Leaves danced along the ground as the breeze blew in. Loose twigs snapped under someone's feet. The figure passed by her a few feet in the distance. A human. Last night the park was empty. Tonight, not so much. Her stomach turned at the thought of Dac being near all these people.

"Don't worry, I've already fed for the night." Again, Dac appeared out of nowhere, sitting next to her on the bench.

"Ugh, don't say it like that. It sounds so gruesome."

"Ha, ha, how should I say it then?"

"I don't know," Emmaline shrugged. "What's it like? I've been reading this journal I found of Harper's. She describes it as this euphoric experience and yet she felt so much guilt."

"I suppose it could feel like that. But it's how we survive. It's how we've survived for centuries. It's my fault she felt that way. I loathed who I was for so long and taught you all to loathe it too."

"And you don't anymore?"

"No. Not anymore."

"Because of the demon?" It had to be the demon. Dac had always been so strict about not drinking straight from a living human. He said it would strip them of their humanity. Turn them evil. But had it? Dac didn't seem so evil now as he was sitting here chatting with her. But then again, he did kill Charolette.

Dac's eyes flashed red at the mention of the demon that lived within him. "Let's not talk about that now. That's not why I asked you here."

"What do you want?" Emmaline heard the shift in her own voice. She was sure Dac heard it too. He had turned his head away as she asked the question.

"I need a favor from you." Dac turned back to face her. "You're the only one I can trust for now and I need to find a more permanent place. Unfortunately, Nikolai and Quentin know all of my aliases and contacts. With them looking for me I can't take any chances. I'll need you to meet with someone for me. Just to help get my affairs in order. Will you help me?"

"Of course." That was simple enough.

"Thank you. I'll text you all of the information. Please don't let anyone see it."

"I won't." Emmaline watched as Dac got up to leave. Her heart ached for the man she once knew. The man that no longer lived inside that body. Everything about him was different now, from the way he talked, to the way he dressed, even the way he carried himself. "Dac, where are you going? When you leave, I mean." She shouted to him.

He smiled down at Emmaline still seated on the cold bench. Her arms once again hugged across her chest trying to warm herself against the bitter chill air. "Home," he said.

Emmaline knew exactly what he meant when he said the word home. Nikolai had said he'd be hiding some place that reminded him of home. Some place that would give him comfort, but Emmaline never thought that he might actually go back there. She wondered about the castle Luca had lived in. The place where Dac was first turned into a vampire. The place he lived his first few nights as newly undead. She knew the stories of how his brother showed up after years of being gone and took him to that castle. How Luca had kept him there as a prisoner until he turned him and how Dac had escaped. She didn't know much beyond that, however. She wondered now where he would go. Back to that old dreary castle? To the place he lived after he left from there? Was it his home he going back to? Or was it the home of the demon? That demon drove his every move, of that, she was sure. But she would help him get away. Then once Quentin and Nikolai found a way to get rid of the demon without hurting Dac, she would tell them where he was. In the meantime, it was best she kept these meetings secret.

Quentin and Nikolai had returned home by the time Emmaline arrived back at the house. She could hear their voices in the other room when she entered through the front door. Her attempt to slip in unnoticed was of course thwarted by Una who stopped her in her tracks.

"Where have you been?"

Emmaline paused at the grating sound of Una's voice. "Out. Now if you don't mind, I'd like to just go to my room."

"No, I don't mind. But Nikolai and Quentin are looking for you." Una stepped aside as in some silent demand for Emmaline to pass her.

Emmaline sighed, then checked her phone. No text from Dac yet. That was a relief. "Where are they?" she asked as if she couldn't hear them.

"Living room."

Emmaline brushed past Una as she went to meet Quentin and Nikolai. They were seated in the living room. Both sitting wide legged on either sofa across from each other. Nikolai leaned forward, his elbows rested on his knees, grasping tightly to the glass in his hand. Quentin leaned back looking a little more relaxed. Emmaline cleared her throat as she entered the room.

"I heard you two were looking for me."

Both men looked in her direction. "Yes," Nikolai confirmed. "Did you have a good night out?" he asked.

"Yea, it was fine. A little colder than expected," she stepped further into the room and sat down on the sofa next to Nikolai as he made room for her. Una walked in at that very moment and of course scoffed and sat on the ledge of the sofa leaning against Nikolai as if marking her territory. Emmaline rolled her eyes. "What's going on?" she asked, ignoring Una's presence. "Did you find Dac?"

"Not yet, not for certain," Quentin answered. "But we think he's still in the city and we think we might know where he is."

"Where do you think he is? What do you need me to do?" Emmaline shifted in her seat.

"We think he might be at Luca's old apartment." Interesting theory and very likely. The demon had made him a lot like Luca. Living in his apartment made sense. He looked enough like him no one there would question it.

"That's not very far from here. Seems kind of risky." Even though she knew he was close by she couldn't let on that she had seen him.

"Yea, that's what I thought at first too, but then I asked around and there's been sightings of someone fitting his description. If it is him, we don't want to scare him off. That's where you come in." Quentin was always the logical one.

"Me?"

"Yea, we think if you go there, he'll talk to you. With me or Quentin, he'll fight us off and try to flee, but we're hoping you can go over there and convince him to come back, to let us help him." This time Nikolai answered.

"How am I supposed to do that?"

"Remind him of the man he used to be, the one who saved you and brought you to live with us. Let him know we're all on his side. We're all just trying to save him."

"Ok. Is it ok that I go tomorrow? I really just want to rest tonight. Then I can figure out what I'll say to him."

"Yea tomorrow is fine. Thank you, Emmaline." Nikolai patted her lightly on the shoulder.

"Of course. I want to help him just as much as you." Emmaline got up leaving the others to continue their earlier conversation.

When she got to her room, she plopped down on her bed checking her phone one more time. Still nothing from Dac yet. He probably won't reach out until tomorrow, she thought to herself. In the meantime, at least Nikolai and Quentin were set on sending Emmaline to find him. Their trust in her was comforting. She didn't want to see him locked away again, but they did not need to know that. After all everyone's goals were the same. Help free Dac from the demon.

# Twelve

Nikolai shifted over on the sofa so that Una would have a place to sit. Instead, she stood up and walked over to the fireplace. She picked up a glass sitting on the mantle and sipped from it. Nikolai turned his attention back to Quentin. They were getting closer to finding Dac, he was sure of that. After days of combing through news articles and Dac's old possessions they realized one thing. Dac wasn't Dac anymore. Not the Dac that they knew. His speech and mannerisms were more like Luca's than his own. That is when they realized if Dac was still in the city he'd be hiding out at Luca's old place and if not there someplace like it.

Emmaline, they decided, was the perfect choice for approaching him. She was more docile than either of them, less combative. Dac would for sure be more receptive to her, while he would most likely run from, or fight him or Quentin. So, they asked Emmaline to go to Luca's apartment. Thankfully she agreed. Not that they thought she wouldn't. She cared for Dac just as much as anyone else. The only one here who didn't was Una. She would just as well kill him.

"I don't know why you're agreeing to tomorrow, when I could just go over there tonight." Una's glass clanked against the stone as she set it back on the mantle.

"You're not going over there. There's no way he would listen to you anymore than either of us." Nikolai turned his head in Una's direction.

"I'm not interested in talking." No, she was only interested in killing him.

"That's exactly why you're not going. We don't want him dead. We want to help him." Nikolai reminded her.

"I don't see why you would want to keep him alive. He killed our son, or have you forgotten?"

"Of course I haven't forgotten, but I also haven't forgotten how you tried to kill me and almost succeeded." Nikolai stood from his seat on the sofa and advanced towards Una stopping short a foot or two away from her.

"Fighting isn't helping things." Quentin sat up straighter in his seat. "Emmaline is going because if Dac is willing to talk to anyone it would be her. Dac has been our friend for years and we're not turning our backs on him. Like it or not." He then stood up and exited the room eliminating any chance for further argument. He had taken over the role of head of household since Dac had been gone. After all this was his house.

"I just don't see how you can be so forgiving, Dac has used you from the beginning." Una had moved away from the fireplace and was now standing in front of the window looking out into the street.

"Again, I forgave you, didn't I? Besides no matter how it all started Dac has been there with me through the centuries. We've looked out for each other. I'm not turning my back on him. If there's a way to cure of him of that demon than I'm going to find it." Nikolai moved closer to her now. He placed a hand on the small of her back forcing her to face him.

"And what if there's not? He's more evil with that thing than Luca ever was." Her voice had softened, though hatred still lingered in her words.

Nikolai didn't want to think about that. What would they do if they never found a cure? They've never discussed it. Never even considered that an option. But Una was right about one thing. Dac was evil with that thing living inside of him and they couldn't keep him locked up forever.

"And what if it were Alex? What if Alex had succeeded in his plan to take the demon for himself? What would you be doing then?" He asked her.

"I'd be trying to save him. He was my son."

"Exactly. And Dac is my friend, my brother, my family. For years he was all I had."

"I get it but…"

"But nothing, end of discussion." Nikolai cut her off before she could finish. "You're going to stay away from Dac. Let me and Quentin handle him."

"And what about Jace? You know Dac isn't our only threat." Una flipped the conversation. Jace was yet another contention between the two of them.

"Why are you still on that? Jace hasn't bothered us in ten years."

"He's still in Aura Springs. He never stays this long. You can't tell me that isn't suspicious." She stepped away from him, reaching once again for her glass on the mantle.

"Don't tell me you're still following him." He had told her to stop, but of course she did what she wanted.

"Fine I won't tell you, but don't say I didn't warn you." Una exited the living room leaving Nikolai alone with his thoughts. She was right. It was strange he was still in town, but he did have family in Aura Springs.

He sighed heavily as he plopped back down on the sofa. He swung his feet up over the arm. He retrieved his phone from his pocket, unlocked the screen and pulled up the internet. He typed Jace's name into the search bar. Maybe it wasn't such a bad idea to see what Jace had been up to over the years. The first thing that came up was a link to the business Jace owned with his friend Alan. Nikolai clicked on the site, then opened the about us page. He was met with only a brief description of Jace's qualifications and work history. There was a paragraph describing the same info for Alan and another couple paragraphs on the business. He backed out of the site and found a few links to some social media. There were a few older pictures and posts but nothing recent. Whatever Jace had been up to he was keeping a low profile while doing it. Then he saw something that looked like a news article. He clicked the link and skimmed the text reading something about a bar fight and trip to the hospital. He chuckled a little as he closed his phone.

He glanced over towards the window, the curtains slightly pulled back. The sky was becoming a lighter shade of blue. Nikolai got up and secured the drapes closed. With the threat of the oncoming daylight, he retreated to his underground windowless room and went to sleep.

Nikolai awoke with a tightness in his chest. His breath felt shallow. His head was spinning, and his limbs felt weak. He managed to sit up and plant his feet onto the floor. He lifted himself up. Holding on to the walls he made his way across the room and opened the door. Stepping out into the hallway he glanced around. The automatic lights hadn't turned on yet, meaning it was still daytime. That would explain the way he was currently feeling.

He went back into his room and laid back on the bed. A few more hours of sleep and he'd feel better. He rested his head on his pillow. The usual soft polyester filled inside felt like a silk covered pile of rocks. His mind raced with thoughts of Emmaline and Dac, Jace and Harper. He shut his eyes and took slow deep breaths trying to calm the steady stream of thoughts that filtered through his brain. Instead, he tossed and turned until he saw the hall lights glow under the door.

He lay still for a few moments longer. The heaviness in his chest was gone and the room finally stopped feeling like a merry go round, but the intrusive thoughts remained. This time when he stood up, he was able walk unassisted. He glanced at himself in the mirror. Brushed out his mussed hair and dressed for the night before meeting Emmaline upstairs.

Together he, Emmaline, and Quentin discussed what Emmaline should say if she found Dac at Luca's apartment. They wanted him to feel unthreatened but also understand the lengths they were willing to go to protect not only him but also themselves. Emmaline needed to be convincing, to entice him to agree to a safe place to be held. If not at the old house, then another place of his choice, but somewhere where he could be contained. Someplace where he wasn't a threat to himself, to others, and to their very existence.

"You need to remind him why he chose to live as he did, for the survival of our kind." Nikolai said to her.

Emmaline agreed and promised she'd do her best. They all knew she couldn't guarantee Dac would abide by their request, but they had to try. If he were to listen to anyone at this stage, it would be Emmaline.

Nikolai watched out the front window as Emmaline disappeared down the street. The knots in his stomach twisted tighter and tighter with each passing minute. Without a second thought he grabbed a jacket out of the closet and followed at what he felt was a safe distance behind her.

He should have asked Quentin to follow her, he thought as the shadows between them grew closer together. He paused in an empty doorway to get a greater distance between them. Emmaline hadn't noticed him following her yet, but if he got any closer, she would. Quentin at least could make himself more discreet.

When they arrived near Luca's old apartment, Nikolai stood back in an alleyway between two larger buildings across the street. He watched as Emmaline stepped into the grand lobby of the building and disappeared down the hall beyond the glass doors. If only he could know for sure what was being said behind those doors.

Was Dac even there? Were they completely wrong about where he was hiding?

It occurred to Nikolai that he had never been to Luca's apartment. He had no idea which one it was. He scanned the open windows from floor to floor looking for any sign of Emmaline or Dac. The more he searched the less confident he was that this was the right place. The windows were large reaching from floor to ceiling. They would let in so much sunlight during the day where would he hide? Emmaline had wandered in as if she'd been there before, so certain this was the place. If Luca had stayed here in the past, it must not have looked like this, maybe the building could have undergone renovations or maybe Luca only used the place during the nighttime hours and hid someplace else during the day. Was Dac doing the same? It seemed like quite an inconvenience to Nikolai but maybe he had his reasons.

It did not seem like Dac was there. As the minutes passed Nikolai was feeling the urge to give up. He was about to emerge from his hiding spot and go home when a loud static rang in his ears. They must be here. Emmaline must have found him. That sound could only come from Dac. But had they seen him? They couldn't have. Nikolai was careful not to be seen. It must be a precaution. Dac was never careless.

Moments later he saw Emmaline and Dac emerge from the building lobby onto the sidewalk. Nikolai crept further into the alleyway certain not be seen by either of them. He hopped over the fence at the other end and exited on the other side. The thought of following them had crossed his mind but he chose instead to go home.

Back at the house he paced as he impatiently awaited Emmaline's return. Neither Quentin nor Una were home. Una was probably chasing after Jace again. Nikolai rolled his eyes at that thought. She was wasting her time with him, but at least it would keep her attention away from Dac for the time being. Quentin most likely needed to recharge his energy. Nikolai hadn't seen him leave the house in days. Blood would only sustain him for so long. He needed more than that, especially if they were getting ready to go up against Dac who would be at his full power and strength by now.

Finally, he heard the click of the lock and the front door open. Emmaline stepped in. Her face was unreadable. Her mind closed tight. "I didn't find him," she said, "He wasn't there." She lied to him. Why?

# Thirteen

Jace had checked out of his motel room and began staying with Sophia ever since her scare the other night. The house was certainly large enough with its four bedrooms and two living rooms. He picked the room farthest away from hers to help make her feel more at ease, even though she had asked him to stay, still he was virtually a stranger. He tried his best to stay out of her way as much as possible.

When Sophia came down the stairs, she had her hair tied on top of her head. A few loose curls hung around her face. Jace was standing near the kitchen island eating a bowl of cereal. When he looked at her, he thought about his niece. Maeve was just a few years younger than Sophia. He couldn't imagine her going through this same nightmare as Sophia, that's why he was here to help, to make her feel safe, to make sure his family was safe. Whatever long ago deal he made with Dac was null and void has long as vampires threatened his loved ones and since he was more than certain he saw one at Maeve's birthday party all deals were officially off.

The silver spoon clinked against the porcelain bowl as he dropped it in the sink. "I'll take care of that later," he mentioned to Sophia regarding the cereal bowl. "I'm going to wash up. I have to go into Aura City for a bit this afternoon. You'll be ok until I get back?"

Sophia nodded as she took the orange juice from the fridge and drank from the carton. "I'll be fine." She assured him.

Jace smiled and turned to go upstairs. He grabbed a clean tshirt and jeans from his bag and set them on the bed. Sophia had suggested he put his things in the dresser or hang them in the closet, but that felt too much like moving in. He was only here temporarily to get rid of their little vampire problem. Then he'd be leaving town again. No point in getting too comfortable. His short visit was already becoming too long. He looked at his now empty bag and then the pile of clothes on the floor. He only brought a few things with him considering this was supposed to only be a weekend trip. He'd need to wash his laundry later.

He took a bath towel from the hall closet and headed into the guest bathroom directly next to his room. Another reason he chose this room was its close proximity to the bathroom. Less of a chase of any awkward encounters.

In no time the room was filled with steam from the hot shower. Jace quickly ran his toothbrush across his teeth, gargled a cap full of mouthwash, and then washed up. When he turned off the water, he could hear Sophia down the hall. He waited a few minutes until he could no longer hear her before wrapping himself in his towel and sneaking into his room to get dressed.

Minutes later he was on the road to Aura City. The drive there was shorter than he expected with no traffic. He sucked in a deep breath as he parked his car and stepped out into the brisk autumn air. It was just past noon and would be hours until sundown. Jace was hoping to speak with Charlotte, the vampire's housekeeper, before confronting any of them. Many years may have passed since they've last crossed paths, but Jace knew how the vampires could hold grudges. He determined that speaking with Charlotte first would best suit his interests, hoping she could help broker some type of truce between them. The truth was he didn't want to kill anyone else; he'd done enough of that ten years ago, but he would if he had to. What he really wanted was to find out why one of them was stalking Sophia's dreams and why the other showed up at a teenage girl's birthday party. What were their intentions and how could he convince them to leave everyone alone?

Armed with vials of essential oils in his pockets and a hawthorn stake and the dagger at his waist, Jace walked the few steps to the vampire house. The last time he was there, he had come to make a deal with Dac. This time it was to make a deal with them all, but when he arrived it was nothing short of shocking.

The lawn was overgrown, the windows all boarded. Vines wrapped themselves around the bars of the front gate. Jace pulled on the gate surprised to find it unlocked. His footsteps crunched over the dead leaves that littered the pathway to the front door. As he walked up the front steps he reached for the door. Its brass handle cold to the touch. He pushed the door open with ease, again surprised to find it unlocked just as he found the front gate. The inside was dark with no sunlight coming through. He flicked up the light switch on the wall but nothing. There was no electricity. Jace shivered from the cold. The door slammed shut behind him, pushed closed by a swift breeze. He reached into his pocket for his phone to use its flashlight. He searched the house room by room starting with the first floor. The furniture appeared covered in dust and cobwebs. He made his way back to the kitchen. The pantry was left open along with the door to the vault hidden inside. Its contents long emptied out.

Next, he moved up to the second floor, looking through Nikolai's office first. Most of the books that used to be housed on the shelves along the walls were now gone. The drawers to the desk had been cleared out. Jace looked inside Dac's office next, finding it in the same shape. When he opened the double doors to the formal dining room at the end of hall, he found broken chairs and shattered glass. He stepped further into the room flashing the light from his phone across the wreckage as his brain tried to comprehend what could have happened there.

He took the next flight of stairs leading to the attic a little more gingerly than the last. Each wooden step creaked as his footsteps landed against the planks. The arched double doors to the attic were wide open. A stream of light peered through the dust covered circular window near the ceiling. He hadn't noticed the window the last time he was in this room, but to be fair he hadn't noticed much more than the dagger Dac held to his throat that night. The dagger that now hung from his belt loop. The same dagger he used to kill his best friend, Harper. Harper, who killed Cloe, but who also saved him from Dac.

The attic was empty just like the other rooms in the house. There was no need to linger here any longer. He turned to leave when he noticed something off. A crack in the floorboard as though someone had lifted it. He stuffed his phone in his pocket since there was a semblance of sunlight allowing him a slight view of the room. He knelt down to the floor, putting the tips of his fingers to the raised floorboard and lifted it until it came completely loose.

Jace removed his phone from his pocket using the flashlight once again. This time to look under the floor. Whatever had been hiding under there someone had already removed, however it would appear they left a few things behind. Jace reached his hand into the crack of the floor pulling out a couple yellowed pieces of unlined paper. The pages were thick and torn at the edges. The cursive writing smeared in black ink. Underneath the papers was a photograph. A picture within a picture. The lines where the original portrait had been folded and creased were visible in the photo. In the portrait were a woman and young man, possibly in his late teens. Jace recognized the face. It was Dac, as a human. The woman must have been his mother, or the mother that raised him at least. Remembering bits and pieces of the story Luca had told him, he and Dac were raised by foster parents. Jace wondered how long Dac must have carried around that original portrait, folded amongst his things as he traveled, before taking this picture of it. He figured the picture must have been used to preserve the portrait clearly fading from years of wear and tear. He also wondered if Dac still had the original somewhere and if it were in this house.

With the photo and papers in hand, Jace descended the two flights of stairs back down to the main floor of the house. He wandered into the front room where he knew a wall hid the stairs to the vampires' rooms. Would he still be able to get down there with the electricity off? He could try, worst that could happen the wall wouldn't open, right?

A breeze broke through the boarded window and a slight ray of light peaked through a crack in the wood. It was orange light. The afternoon was coming to an end and sundown was creeping upon him. Jace turned his head toward the wall of hidden stairs and then back towards the window. He would need to be out of here quick before anyone found him. He didn't know where the vampires had gone or if they'd be coming back, but he didn't want to be here when they did.

Although every voice inside his head said to leave instead, he pushed his way through the open wall and down the stone stairs to the vampires' old sleeping quarters. Still using the flashlight of his phone to guide his way he peaked into each individual room he passed. Memories flooded his mind as he remembered each stay here, both as visitor and prisoner. He passed Harper's room and went inside. The drawers to her dresser had been left open. Pieces of clothing hung over the edges. Large sheets of fabric laid in piles along the floor. Jace sat on the bed for a moment. He brushed his hand along the soft cotton of the comforter.

He closed his eyes letting the vivid memories of her play in his head. The way she laughed, the way she cried. The way she fiercely protected those she cared about until she didn't. Until her vampiric impulses took over her. The heat rose in his body. His lower lip trembled, and his fist tightened around the fabric of the blanket he sat upon. With one deep breath he calmed himself. He opened his eyes, took one last look around and closed the door behind him as he left the room.

The next room he entered must have been Emmaline's. Strings of pearls and lace hung from the vanity mirror. A lace canopy covered the tall bed posts. Whatever she took with her when she left must not have been much. Jace cracked a brief smile when he thought of Emmaline. She had been the first to warm up to him when he first came looking for their help. They had become something almost like friends for a short time. He hoped wherever she was, that she was ok.

He continued down through the corridors of the basement floor, down hallways he had never known existed. There was a room with a desk and large plush chairs. A large chandelier hung from the ceiling. Against the far wall was a fireplace and Jace wondered if it ever worked or was it just there for show. Must have been a grand room at one time. Now just covered in dust and memories like all the others.

The longer he lingered the more time had passed. His phone was beginning to feel warm in the palm of his hand. He looked at the screen and noticed the time was nearing closer to evening the sun would be close to the horizon by now. It was time to go.

Jace began making his way back towards the stairs, every few seconds checking his phone once more. Only a minute had passed but his phone battery was now draining dangerously low. The white signal turned to red. He picked up his pace until the sound of someone else's footsteps stopped him. Holding his breath, he ducked into the empty room next to him. The footsteps grew louder. He took another step back. Something crunched under his feet. Realizing he never turned off the flashlight he pointed his phone towards the ground. Shards of broken glass were scattered across the ground. And was that blood that stained the floor?

The footsteps were closer still. Jace fussed with the screen of phone trying to switch off the flashlight. Why was this so difficult? Just swipe down. Press the icon. But every movement commanded something different than he intended.

Still struggling he pushed the phone into his pocket. The fabric of his jeans would at least dim the light. He leaned his back against the wall. Still holding his breath. A shadow loomed through the doorway. A light followed and then the silhouette of a person.

"What are you doing here?"

# Fourteen

Sophia peered through the blinds watching Jace's car leave the driveway. She said she would be fine for a few hours alone. She wanted to be fine, but the tightening knots in her stomach said otherwise. She wasn't sure if it was the fear of vampires or her uncle that kept her on edge these days. Maybe a little bit of both. At least for now it was daylight so the only threat to her at the moment was the possibility of her uncle showing up at her doorstep. She tugged at the raw hem of her sweatshirt as she leaned against the windowsill. The cold window pressed against her shoulder.

Few clouds lingered in the sky when she looked outside. Maybe some fresh air would do her some good. She slipped on a pair of sneakers and grabbed her coat on the way out the door. Remembering just then that she returned her rental car when Jace agreed to stay with her, she took her phone from her coat pocket and dialed up a taxi.

Sitting down on the cold steps of her front porch, Sophia waited for the taxi to arrive. She had no idea where she was headed but when the driver asked, she told him the train station. The train was arriving at the same time they pulled up to the station. Sophia tossed some cash to the driver and hurried up the platform, catching the train just before the doors closed. She sat down before she realized she hadn't bought a ticket and still had no idea where she was going.

The ding of a scanner sounded behind her. "Ticket, please." Groaned the voice next to her.

Sophia turned her head to see the conductor standing over her. His gaze peered down as he waited for her to hand over the ticket she didn't have. She smiled coyly as she replied. "I don't have one."

The conductor rolled his eyes as he pulled out a narrow booklet from his back pocket and flipped through the pages. "Where are you headed?" There was no attempt to hide the annoyance in his voice.

Quickly she replied, "Aura City." It was the first place that came to mind, and she wanted to get this guy away from her as soon as possible. He made a couple of marks in the booklet and tore off a sheet of paper while Sophia dug through her purse for some more cash. She handed him the money and he handed her the paper ticket in return, then walked on to the next person. Sophia stuffed the ticket in her bag and stared out the window until the train finally pulled into Aura City.

With no intended destination, Sophia walked for what seemed like miles. It probably was. When she glanced at the clock on her phone hours had passed by without her even realizing it. She had been moving about the city in a haze. Her mind racing from one thought to another. Was her uncle still in town? Would she accidentally run into him while she was actively trying to avoid that exact situation? What about the vampires? They were real. She saw one right here in the city park only a few nights ago. He saw her too. She was certain of that. Had he followed her to her house that night? Sara and Jace found no trace of him, and he hadn't returned but still Sophia feared it would not be the last she saw of that one. She knew both Sarah and Jace wanted to keep her out of whatever plan they were concocting, but that vampire wanted something from her, and she needed to know what it was. It was her dreams he was appearing in after all. Speaking of her dreams, she hadn't had any in the weeks since meeting Sarah. Were the potions and creams Sarah had given her working, or was it something else? She wondered if the vampire sensed them helping her. Was he mad? They all knew each other. He knew they were hunters. Is that why he came to her house, to scare her?

None of her thoughts made sense to her. Why would he want to scare her away if he wanted her to come to him? She may not have figured out what he wanted but it didn't matter anymore. She would not go to him. Not willingly. Not after what she learned from Brigid's story and not after realizing he killed her parents. He had to know that didn't he? Sophia only wished she remembered more about that night. She recognized him from that night of the party outside her house when she was a little girl. That was months before her parents were killed. He had shown up with another. They claimed car trouble. Her parents had been so nice to them. Inviting them inside. Offering them food and drinks. She realized now what a mistake that was. Had they planned on killing them then? Was their plan interrupted by the amount of people at the party? They hadn't seemed threatening at all that night. He didn't talk to her, but the other one had. Was that how they killed their prey? Be nice to them? Give a fake story about being stranded on the side of the road? Then what? They get invited inside, then they eat them. Was he coming back to finish the job? Is that why he appeared in her dreams? He was luring her to him so he could finish his meal. But why wait so long? Maybe they had rules about killing little children.

Her thoughts were all over the place. Her stomach was growling so loud now she could hear it over the roaring traffic. With no shortage of food places around, she walked into the first one she saw. It was a small eatery tucked in between a local grocer and hardware shop. There were deli meats and different choices of bread behind a counter. A salad bar in the isle, with lettuce, vegetables, fruits and a variety of pasta dishes. She approached the counter and ordered a sandwich and bottle of water which she ate quietly at a table near the window. Looking down the street she noticed a familiar car. Jace was nearby. His car parked only a few feet away.

Sophia finished the last bites of her sandwich and took one last large sip of water before tossing everything in the nearby garbage bin. She exited the eatery and headed towards Jace's car. With her stomach full, and her head a little clearer, she began to recognize the area. She had been here before. When she first arrived from Noxwood. She was here, standing by that house. Is that where Jace went today? Was he still there? *There's evil in that house.* That's what that man said to her that day. Evil. Did he mean vampires? Is that where the vampires live?

She walked down the side street where Jace's car was parked under an unassuming tree. She looked in through the closed windows. The sunrays highlighting the worn hoodie laid across the front passenger seat. An air freshener hung from the rearview mirror. Noticing her reflection in the glass, Sophia used her fingers to brush back her windswept hair, then tied it into a loose ponytail with the elastic she wore around her wrist.

At the end of the street was the house she now assumed belonged to the vampire. Set behind the iron gate, the house stood further back from the others on this same street. Sophia stepped through the open gate. Before attempting to go inside she crept around the outside looking for any cracks in the boarded-up windows and inspecting the entrances. Around the backside of the house, she tried the backdoor, but it was locked. She went back to the front and tried the front door. To her surprise it was open. She pushed the door gently, opening it only far enough for her to squeeze through, then shut it as softly and quietly as she could.

The inside was dark even though the sun shone bright outside. She stood in the foyer listening for any sound. It was dead silent. Not even a sound from the breeze outside broke through. Her footsteps echoed off the bare walls with each careful step she took. Feeling along the walls she walked straight forward until she found herself in what had been the kitchen. She began opening drawers, searching inside them using the light of her phone. Most of them were empty, except for a few kitchen utensils, forks, knives, things that you'd expect to find in any kitchen. But what she was looking for was evidence that a vampire lived here. What that evidence was, she had no idea. The last drawer she opened held a few household tools and a flashlight. She picked up the flashlight pressing the on/off button testing if it worked. When the light flashed on, she felt a sudden relief hit her stomach. Stuffing her phone into the purse that hung from her shoulder, she used the flashlight to light her way. She flashed the light around the rest of the room. On one side was the pantry that housed an open safe. She moved closer to inspect it. Whatever was kept inside it had been removed. Along the back wall was a bench and kitchen table that looked like it had not been used in years. Sophia wiped her finger across the tabletop leaving an S shaped mark in the dust that had accumulated. Next to the door which she assumed led to the outside was the stairwell that led to the second floor. She stepped carefully onto the first step. The wood creaked beneath her. She climbed the remaining steps on tip toes, keeping close to the wall to make as little noise as possible, but each sound she made seemed ten times louder than normal in the abandoned house.

When she reached the top of the steps, she flashed the light down the long hallway and into each open door she passed by until she got to the end. The last room stood behind two arched double doors. When she entered the room, it appeared to have once been a grand dining room. A long table with matching chairs occupied the middle. A large chandelier hung from the ceiling. Large heavy drapes hung from in front of the boarded windows. As she glanced around, she thought something bad must have happened in this room. A few of the chairs had been broken. Wood splintered into pieces on the floor. Shards of broken glass were scattered all over the table and on the floor. Whatever had happened still didn't confirm it was vampires. Mostly the house looked as ordinary as any other. A little old-fashioned, but that only proved whoever lived here liked that style. She backed out of the room and back down the hall. This time she took the front stairs back to the main floor. She landed back in the foyer by the front door, although now she could see better having the flashlight with her.

She stepped into the room to the right of her. At first sight it was a simple room. A few chairs and a side table and not much other furniture. There was no sign of anyone being in the house for a long time. Not even Jace. Sophia began to leave accepting that there was nothing here to be found. Then with one last look around the room she noticed the opening in the wall.

Holding the flashlight in front of her, she crept over to the wall. Behind the wall hid a stairwell. She covered her mouth to muffle her gasp. Her eyes grew wide, and a smile formed across her lips as she peered down the dark stairwell. This was her proof. She was right! Who else would hide a stairwell behind a wall except for vampires?

She stood at the top of stairs for a moment listening for any movement at the bottom. When she heard nothing, she descended down the stairs taking one careful step at a time. The stone walls and flooring reminded her of something she may have read in a fantasy story as a child. They were cold to the touch and the air down here felt damp. She wandered through the corridors, though she didn't get very far before seeing a shadow duck into one of the rooms. Her heartbeat picked up a pace, but she followed the shadowy figure. She could see a faint light in the room. She moved closer, shining her flashlight in front of her. She stepped inside.

"What are you doing here?" Jace's voice shouted out at her.

Sophia jumped back. Her heart skipped a beat but settled quickly back into rhythm.

"You scared me half to death. You shouldn't be here. Did you follow me?" Jace was still scolding her.

"Sorry. I didn't mean to," she tried to explain. "I saw your car down the road and remembered this house and just kind of put two and two together and thought you might be here."

"Well, still you shouldn't have come. We need to go now." Jace grabbed Sophia by the arm and led her back up the stairs and out of the house. He was angry, but more than that he was scared.

The sun had set by the time they got outside. Jace slammed the door shut and hurried to his car dragging Sophia behind him.

"Could you slow down?" She was struggling to keep up with his pace while he still gripped her arm.

Jace unlocked his car and shoved Sophia inside. She rubbed the top of her arm when Jace finally let her go. He walked around and got in the driver seat before saying anything.

"Sorry. I'm just trying to keep you safe, and that place is not safe." Jace started the car and pulled out into traffic heading back into Aura Springs.

They were mostly quiet on the drive back to Sophia's house. Sophia had so many questions, but Jace's reaction to running into her at that house had her hesitant to ask. The only thing she was certain of was that the vampire lived there at some point. Why else would Jace be so angry? She would ask him later, she decided, after he had a chance to calm down.

# Fifteen

What was Jace doing here and who was that girl he was dragging away? Emmaline asked herself, standing inside the old house. When she arrived, she saw the wall to the downstairs rooms open and she heard voices coming up from the stairwell. She could smell the human blood and hear their human heartbeats, so she hid in the darkened living room. Her back up against the wall. She saw Jace as he charged out of the front room and out the front door, dragging the unknown girl by the arm. She waited until she heard the door slam shut before emerging from her hiding spot. She had come here for one reason only and that was to retrieve something for Dac. The cash he kept hidden in his old room. In his haste to leave his imprisonment he had left it behind. He asked Emmaline to retrieve it for him in fear of running into Nikolai or Quentin. Nikolai, he said he could handle on his own, but Quentin could drain his energy and imprison him all over again. Neither he nor Emmaline wanted that to happen, so Emmaline agreed to the task.

She hated coming into this house. No matter how many times she had over the years, it still dredged up too many old memories. It made her sad to look at it in its current state. All the dust and cobwebs that covered the furniture. The boarded windows. The broken glass. The empty rooms. The silence. It all reminded her of what she lost. What they all lost. She should be mad at Dac. This was his fault, wasn't it? No, it was that demon's fault. That demon took over his mind, his soul and Emmaline was determined to free him from it. But first she needed to help get him out of the city.

She crept behind the wall and down the steps to their old rooms. It was damp and cold. Her cold body ached for warm blood. She had to start remembering to drink before leaving home. She could feel her fangs scrape against the inside of her bottom lip and her mouth began to salivate at the thought of it. For now, she had to push down the hunger. She had to find this money and bring it to Dac. Then she could go home to the townhouse and fill her veins.

Throughout the many years of living here and the years since, Emmaline had only been inside Dac's room a handful of times. The king-size bed remained perfectly made. The dresser tops clear of any belongings. The closets meticulously organized. Everything in its place as if never touched. Each of their rooms had always been a private sanctuary. Something they all respected while living together. It was a place where they could each feel safe and protected.

Emmaline took her phone from her pocket and lit up the screen with the touch of her fingertip. She opened the message from Dac detailing where he had hidden the money. *The tall dresser in the far corner of the room, pull out the third drawer, the message read. Remove the belongings. Feel around the inside edge of the drawer until you feel a latch. Open it.* She did as instructed. The wooden panel at the bottom of the drawer lifted in one corner. She used the tips of her fingers to lift the whole panel, then grasping it with her hand to completely remove it. She placed the panel on the floor next to her feet, leaning it upright against the dresser. She looked inside the bottom compartment of the drawer. It was empty.

Her heart skipped a beat. She felt the warmth of panic course through her. Where could the money have gone? Who would have known about it? Nikolai? Quentin? Nikolai was the one he was closest to, it made sense he would know about it and where it was hidden. But what was she going to do now? She couldn't tell Dac it was gone, and she didn't have enough of her own money to give him in its place. In fact, she didn't have any of her own money at all. Dac had always taken care of her. When she first came to live with them Dac had given her a weekly allowance to do as she pleased. As time went on, he eventually set her up with a bank account and deposited money in it for her to withdraw from whenever she needed. She always assumed he did it because he felt bad for her, for how she was changed against her will, so she never questioned him. She was never involved in their business and had no idea where their money came from. She honestly didn't want to know. She just accepted things for how they were, knowing she was being taken care of. After the fight and Dac was imprisoned, Nikolai took over their business affairs completely and continued the deposits into her account.

She thought for a moment. Maybe she could ask Nikolai for the money, like an advance, but what could she tell him it was for? She couldn't tell him the truth, obviously. Then she remembered Jace and the unknown girl she saw leaving the house. She could tell him it was her money that she was looking for and was stolen. She could say she had been saving it for years for something special. But what? It was a large amount of cash. Nikolai would be suspicious. She needed to figure this out quickly, and before she met with Dac in a few hours.

Before leaving she made a detour into her own room. She avoided this room any time she visited since that night they all moved out. She would visit Dac in his windowless prison, then leave always too afraid to linger, too afraid of getting caught. Now with Dac no longer here it didn't matter. She could have a look around. No one would care.

She moved around the dark room tracing her fingers along the stone wall and across the tabletop of her vanity. A long string of pearls and a few other necklaces still hung from the mirror. She reached out and touched one. The pendant rested against her fingers. The silver metal cold against her already cold skin. She pulled the necklace down from the mirror untangling its chain from the others and pulled it over her head. The cool chain dangled from her neck. She rubbed the pendant between her fingers for a moment before finally dropping it, letting it rest against her chest. After one last look around her old bedroom, she made her way back up the stairs and headed back home to the townhouse to speak with Nikolai.

"THERE'S NO WAY I CAN get that amount of money tonight. I'll need to make arraignments to get that kind of cash. I'm sorry," Nikolai answered when Emmaline asked him for the money. Sticking to her plan, she didn't mention it was Dac's money and kept the details vague, relieved when he didn't ask questions.

"I understand. Thanks." She shifted her eyes towards the ground. Somehow, she would need to tell Dac the money was gone. "There's something else," she said before turning to leave the room.

"What is it?" Nikolai's voice was calm, though his face expressed concern.

"While I was at the old house, I saw Jace there." What better way to deflect any suspicion than to bring up Jace. Knowing Jace was creeping around their old house, Nikolai would turn his attention towards him hopefully long enough for Emmaline to figure out what to do about Dac.

"Did you speak to him? What was he doing there?"

"I hid before he could see me. When I walked in, I saw the wall was open. I could hear someone downstairs and could smell their blood. I knew they were human but wasn't sure who it was. So, I ducked into the living room and waited for them to leave."

"You did the right thing and thanks for telling me."

"One more thing, he wasn't alone."

Nikolai raised his brow. "Who else was there?"

"I don't know who she was. Some young girl. He seemed irritated with her. He was dragging her out of the house and yelling that she shouldn't have been there." Emmaline noticed the shift in Nikolai's posture. Perfect, he was taking the bait as she knew he would. Nikolai's first instinct is to protect. He'd naturally want to know what's going on and get to the bottom of it.

"Well, he was right about that. Don't worry about it. I'll find out what he's up to. It's probably nothing."

Emmaline nodded. That should keep Nikolai distracted for a while. She turned to exit the room, rounding the corner Una almost knocked into her. She rolled her eyes and kept walking feeling Una's stare on her back.

Inside her bedroom she laid back on her bed. Holding up her phone and holding in her breath, she typed a message to Dac. *The money is gone.*

NIKOLAI DIDN'T NEED to ask Emmaline what she needed that money for, he already knew. He also knew it wasn't her money. It was the exact amount of cash he had taken out of Dac's old room the night before. After Emmaline had lied to him about not finding Dac, Nikolai suspected the two of them were working together. Tonight, only confirmed it. Whether Dac had come to her after he escaped or Emmaline had already been helping him, Nikolai was unsure, but he wanted to think it was the former. He could understand her wanting to help him, they all did, but Dac had clearly gotten in her head, convinced her she was doing the right thing, helping hide him from the rest of them. Maybe sending her to talk to him wasn't the best idea after all. He would have to talk to Quentin, then they would figure out how best to deal with this together. If there was one thing, he learned from all that happened in the past, it was that keeping secrets never led to anything good.

"Hi," Una's voice sounded across the room. Nikolai looked up to see her standing in the doorway. Her shoulder pressed against the frame. "So, I hear Jace is snooping around the old house. I told you he was up to no good. We're going to need to do something about him and his little hunter friends."

Nikolai let out an exasperated breath. Of course she heard Emmaline telling him about Jace. This was the last thing he wanted to deal with at the moment. "Leave that to me. Like I told Emmaline, I'll take care of it. We've got more important things to worry about right now."

"More important things, really? What can be more important than the person who wants to kill us?"

"We don't know that he wants to kill us. I'll go see him tomorrow."

"Whatever," Una stormed out of the room.

Nikolai shook his head. He knew Jace needed to be dealt with but right now making sure Dac didn't leave the city, or the country was top on his list of priorities. And with the amount of money, he had asked Emmaline to retrieve for him, out of the country was likely what he was planning.

Nikolai searched for Quentin, finding him on the rooftop. He almost didn't see him in his true form. The form he seemed to favor these days.

"Even after all these years, it's still hard to get used to you that way." He admitted as he approached Quentin sitting on the edge of the roof. Nikolai sat down beside him.

"It's easier. Takes less energy than my human form. I need to preserve as much energy as possible if we're going to get Dac back."

"That's what I came to talk to you about."

Quentin turned his head to face Nikolai. The shadowy form showed only vague features and no emotion. "Did you find him? What did Emmaline finally say?"

"No, she asked me for money. The exact amount we took from Dac's room. I think he plans on leaving the country."

"Good call going over there and getting it then, before they could. What did you say to Emmaline?"

"I told her I couldn't get that amount of cash in one night. I let her believe I believed the money was hers."

"Probably a good idea. If she's working against us with Dac it's best if she doesn't know we know."

"Exactly. Emmaline told me something else too. She saw Jace at the old house tonight." That got a reaction out of him, as his shadow flickered and the yellow of eyes flashed against the dark contrast.

"Well, that was stupid of him. What was he doing there?" Quentin asked though he probably already assumed the answer.

"Don't know. She didn't speak to him. He was there with someone else. A girl. Emmaline didn't know who she was though. Said he was dragging the girl out of the house and yelling at her." Nikolai kept his voice calm though inside he was shaking. All these things happening at once couldn't be a coincidence.

"Do you think it was just a random girl that Jace found there? Or do you think they already knew each other?"

"Don't know that either, but still doesn't explain why Jace would be there in the first place."

"So, we have two threats then?" Quentin said giving voice to what Nikolai was already thinking.

"I'm afraid so. And I'm afraid it's Una's fault. She keeps stalking Jace every time he comes to town. I keep telling her to leave him be, but she just won't, and I think he must have seen her this last time." Nikolai ran his hands through his hair and let out a sigh of frustration.

"Well then, we let her deal with him for now. Dac is the bigger problem at the moment."

Nikolai shrugged. He agreed Dac was the bigger issue, but he also didn't want Una anywhere near Jace. Nothing good would come from that. For now, however, he would focus on Dac and if Jace proved to be a bigger problem he would deal with it then.

# Sixteen

Quentin leaned against the brick façade of the chimney. His feet dangled from the edge of the slanted rooftop. He watched the clouds above floating across the starless sky. The night was about as murky as his thoughts. How had it all gone so wrong? He wasn't like the others. He didn't have the same human emotions and connections. Creatures like him were mostly loners. They didn't live in packs. How could they when they drained the energy of anyone they came in contact with, even their own? Yet Quentin learned long ago how to control his energetic needs and had spent the better half of the last century building this family. A family he would never have imagined would be possible. Now it was all falling apart, and he had no clue how to fix it.

Quentin was a rational creature. He wasn't controlled by emotions. He just needed to figure out how best to approach the current situation. Jace was a possible threat according to what Nikolai had told him, but possibly not an immediate one. Dac was consumed by a cursed demon and not acting like himself, but was he an actual threat to them? The answer to that was surely up for debate. If Dac was leaving the city, was it right to stop him or should they let him go? If he was far away, he would be no threat to them physically or to their existence here. Was it possible they were looking at things all wrong? Maybe Emmaline had the right idea.

If he gave it much more thought, he'd probably conclude that the whole reason they were so desperate to save him was not to save him from himself but to save him for their own selfish reasons. They wanted him to be the Dac they knew, the friend they loved. But he wasn't that Dac anymore. Sure, he was acting recklessly and that could put them all in danger, but if they allowed him to leave then what danger would they actually be in? Maybe trying to reason with him to go away to wherever he was already planning to go and stay gone would be the best for them all. Maybe, but that wouldn't be best for the humans who lived wherever Dac would eventually end up and that ultimately was the issue.

There had to be a cure for this curse that infected their friend, but he and Nikolai researched every book they owned, every note ever taken and found nothing. Was it time to give up? Was he ready to give up? Those were the questions that plagued him. It had been ten whole years, and they were no closer to finding a cure today than when they started. Except, Quentin wasn't the giving up type. He just had to think a little harder. There must be something they hadn't thought of yet. Jace!

Jace had helped them before, and he had access to the vampire hunting witch and all her knowledge. Maybe she would know something none of them knew. That could solve both of their problems at once. He had to find Nikolai.

Quentin found Nikolai in the room he used for his office. He was looking over some papers when Quentin knocked lightly on the door. When Nikolai glanced up and acknowledged him, he stepped into the room.

"I think I found a way to work out both our problems with Dac and Jace and I think Jace is key."

"What do you mean?" Nikolai was clearly intrigued.

"Well, I was just thinking Jace is poking around the old house for a reason, maybe he was looking for us? What if we go to him? We find out what he wants and while we're doing that, we ask for his help. I mean he's helped us out before."

"But how do you think Jace could help us?"

"Because he knows the hunter, Brigid. What if she knows a way to cure Dac of the curse."

Nikolai rubbed his chin and pointed his eyes towards the ceiling. "Mmm, maybe, but what are the chances the old woman is even still alive? And if she is I sincerely doubt she'd be in any way eager to help us."

"Good point, but even if she isn't I'm sure her granddaughter has access to all her knowledge. I'm sure Jace could convince her to help." It had worked in the past even if it did have dire consequences.

"It's worth a shot." Nikolai shrugged.

"You can't be serious." Una appeared in the doorway. "Are you really thinking of going to that human for help after he murdered one of your own? He shouldn't even still be alive."

"We're going to do whatever we need to do." Nikolai responded.

"Just let me kill him. Let Dac go on about his own way and move on with your lives. I don't see why everyone has to live up to your moral standards anyway. We're vampires. Humans are our food. It's no different than humans eating the meat of animals. This whole drinking donated blood from fancy glasses is getting old anyway." Una never did care for their ways of living.

"We were human once too, remember."

"Yea, once but not anymore. It's time to let go, Nikolai."

"Listen none of us drink from humans. That's the way we choose to live. You don't have to stay here, but if you choose to then you abide by that rule." Quentin was tired of Una.

Una rolled her eyes. "Quentin, you don't even need the blood. I don't see how your opinion even matters in this instance."

"Because it's my house. Now back to the business at hand. Una if you disagree you can leave."

Una turned and stormed out of the room. Quentin focused back on Nikolai. "We should go see Jace as soon as possible."

"Agreed. We should go now. We have time."

After a little persuasion Una finally gave up the last location where she had seen Jace. It was a house near the beach in Aura Springs. He was staying with a young woman, she informed them. Likely the same girl Emmaline seen him dragging out of the old house.

Nikolai and Quentin stood outside the ocean front property. The waves crashed loudly against the shore behind them. The smell of salt mixed with the cold winds was less than welcoming. Even worse than that was the smell of hawthorn, peppermint, and frankincense that seeped out of every crevice of the house in front of them.

The two vampires inched their way up the porch steps. Nikolai raised his gloved hand and knocked on the door. When no one answered he knocked louder until finally Jace opened the door. His hair was mussed. He yawned and wiped the sleep from his eyes. The color drained from his face as he recognized Nikolai and Quentin at his doorstep.

Quentin stepped forward knowing he'd be less sensitive to Jace's protections than Nikolai. He had made sure to drink a little blood before they left so he could appear in his human form hoping this would help Jace to feel a little less threatened. Judging by the look on Jace's face, however, he wasn't sure how much it helped.

"We would like to speak with you, if that's ok." Quentin spoke softly, keeping his tone as neutral as possible to put Jace at ease. They weren't there to harm him and he wanted him to know that.

"One minute." Jace closed the door in his face only to appear a few seconds later with a coat wrapped around his shoulders and shoes on his feet. Clearly, he was not interested in inviting them inside. He shut the door quietly behind him as he stepped onto the porch. With his arms folded across his chest he asked, "What do you want? Do you know what time it is?"

Quentin did indeed know the time and it was well past midnight. He chose to brush off Jace's rudeness since they had obviously awakened him. "We were hoping you could assist us with something. You see we have a certain situation concerning Dac and well basically we were thinking that maybe one of your hunter friends may have some information that could useful," he said getting straight to the point.

"And why should I help you?"

"Because we've looked past the fact that you killed Harper, without retaliation."

Jace's eyes dart back and forth between Quentin in front of him and Nikolai who was standing silently leaning against the porch railing. "Then why have you been following me?"

"That's not us," Quentin said, not giving any indication that he knew who it was or that it was Una.

"Umm." Jace pulled a face. "Fine, I'll see what I can do. What type of information are looking for?"

Quentin went on detailing what happened between Luca and Dac, and what happened when he showed up at home that night. He explained what happened to Charlotte and why they all moved out. He told Jace how they had kept Dac prisoner inside the house ever since until he escaped recently. He explained how they had been searching for years for a way to cure Dac. "Essentially, we need to know how we can remove that demon from inside Dac without killing him."

Jace sat quietly for a moment as if contemplating what to say next. "Damn that's heavy," he said. His voice held compassion and empathy until his expression once again hardened. "Well, like I said I'll see what I can do. I'll reach out when and if I find anything. Have a good night gentlemen." Then he turned on his heels, stepping back inside the house locking the door behind him.

Quentin descended down the porch steps with Nikolai trailing behind him. He waited for him to match his pace before speaking. "I suppose that went as well as expected."

"Suppose so." Nikolai seemed lost in thought. His attention directed towards the ocean. They were at the farthest section on the beach. The boardwalk threatening to end within a few feet. The only things in view were an old, abandoned building and an empty bench.

Quentin recognized the area as the spot where Harper used to come. He had hoped that Nikolai hadn't noticed but the melancholic energy that emitted from him said otherwise. Quentin knew Nikolai still harbored a lot of guilt for what happened to Harper, but he also felt a profound sadness. The two were close friends for the three years she had lived with them. If he had thought much of it, he would admit he felt a bit of grief himself.

"Do you want to stop here?" Quentin asked Nikolai, placing a comforting hand on his shoulder.

"No, let's just get out of here," Nikolai replied.

"It's ok if you want to sit for minute. I know what this spot meant to you."

"It meant nothing to me. It was Harper's spot. Not mine." Nikolai turned down the adjacent street leading to the train station. He picked up his pace and Quentin kept in step with him, but he remained silent.

They reached the station just as the train was pulling up to the platform. They hurried into one of the cars and sat quietly all the way back to Aura City.

# Seventeen

Jace tossed and turned the rest of the night. He watched the sunrise through the half open curtains. He couldn't believe Luca and Alex were dead. Two less vampires to worry about. Which explained why Luca had never come looking for him after killing Harper. That was good news for Jace. But thinking about Dac carrying around that demon inside of him sent chills down his spine. If he were to believe what Luca had told him, Dac wouldn't be able to control the evil of the demon, which meant he only had one choice. Kill Dac.

Jace looked at the clock hanging on the wall opposite his bed. The time read 7:30. It was early, but Sarah might be awake if she was the one opening her shop this morning. Jace retrieved his phone from the bedside table and sent Sarah a message.

*What are your plans today? Can we meet?*

Within seconds she typed back. *No plans. Let me know time and place.*

*Can we meet at your shop? I want to speak in private. ASAP.*

*No problem. Meet me there in an hour. I'll send my assistant to get breakfast or something.*

*Great. See you soon.* Jace placed his phone back on the table while he got showered and dressed. Within the hour he was heading out the door to meet Sarah.

He snuck quietly out the house careful not to wake Sophia. He didn't want a repeat of yesterday. He would fill her in when he was ready. First, he wanted to speak with Sarah.

When he parked his car in front of Sarah's shop, he could already see the lights on. Her assistant was walking out the door and down the corridor of the plaza, likely grabbing breakfast like Sarah had suggested.

Jace stepped inside. The familiar bells rung has he opened and closed the shop door. Sarah was standing behind the counter looking at something on her computer screen. She looked up at Jace, her face full of concern.

"Everything ok?" He asked.

"You tell me. You said it was urgent. What's going on?"

"Right. Of course." Jace shook his head. "Can we sit inside?" he asked pointing to the side room.

Sarah nodded and Jace followed behind her into the little side room. They both sat down on the small sofa against the wall.

"Had a couple of visitors last night," Jace said immediately as he sat down. He then began to fill Sarah in on the details of his visit from Nikolai and Quentin.

Sarah sat quietly while Jace spoke, listening intently. When he finished, she said, "I don't know of any cure other than death."

"Then we kill him."

"And what about the others? They will for sure come after us if we kill Dac."

"We kill them too. All of them. I don't care anymore. I just want my family safe and Sophia too. No one is safe with vampires running around."

"Then we kill them," Sarah agreed.

The shop's doorbell chimed alerting them to the assistant's return. The young woman's chirpy voice called from the front of the store. "Breakfast's here!" Sarah stood up from the sofa and exited the back room. Jace followed behind her though he stopped halfway standing in the doorway between the two rooms. Sarah's assistant raised an eyebrow when she saw him. Jace gave what he hoped was a friendly smile and a nod. The young woman blushed and turned to Sarah. "I can come back if you two need more time," she said.

"That's not necessary." Sarah chuckled. She grabbed a coffee cup from the to go tray and began drinking the hot beverage wiping her mouth between sips.

"Yea, I'm just leaving," Jace said to the assistant shooting her a soft smile. "I'll call you later." He looked at Sarah and she nodded back.

Jace stepped out of the shop into the cool morning air. Before going back to his car, he walked across the plaza to the bakery. He ordered himself a buttered roll and a coffee. He then drove back towards Sophia's but instead of going to the house he parked his car near the boardwalk.

He zipped his jacket shut to protect himself from the cold salty breeze. He walked onto the sand and sat down to watch the waves hit the shore. He held his coffee cup with both hands, its warmth comforting against his chilled skin. When he sipped from the cup the steam warmed his nose.

He looked around at the desolate beach. Not a single person in sight other than himself. Not even a seagull nearby. Just himself alone with his ghosts. The ghosts that haunted him not only in the darkest of night but in the brightest of day. The ghosts he had fought for years. The ghosts he was finally ready to extinguish.

A sharp breeze blew the loose lid off his cup. He watched it float through the air. The little plastic lid in a fight for its life, not unlike himself. The push between gravity and the pull of the wind keeping the lid in flight like the push/pull he felt deep within himself. The conflicting feelings between his desire to flee back into the secluded life he carved out for himself and the need to rid his old hometown of vampires. The need to keep his family and friends safe fighting against the wanting to forget it all. Finally, a break came in the wind and the lid fell into the sand. Jace reached over and picked up the lid stuffing it safely into his jacket pocket.

When he checked the time on his phone only a couple of hours had passed. The morning was still fresh, and he didn't want to go back to Sophia's until he had a plan. He decided to spend the afternoon at his cousin's house. Maybe some time with his family would give him some clarity and when he talked with Sarah again later that evening, he could approach things with a clearer head.

IT WAS WELL PAST MIDNIGHT when Sophia finally began to dose off into sleep. Most of the night she spent tossing and turning. Her eyes finally shut, and she felt her body slowly drifting into sweet paralysis when a loud bang jolted her back awake. The pounding on the door downstairs grew louder. She crawled out of her bed so she could answer it but couldn't make herself leave the bedroom. Even with her hand on the doorknob, her feet were frozen to the floor. Down the hall she could hear Jace stomp down the steps and then the door creak when he opened it. A moment of relief passed over her then curiosity crept in. She went over to the window and peered out the blinds. She could not see who Jace was speaking with, so she cracked her window just wide enough to hear what was being said. As she pressed her ear closer to the screen and peered out the glass, she saw a familiar face standing on the porch steps. His hands tucked in his pockets as he leaned against the railing. His sharp features and bright eyes were just as elegant as she remembered them. Even from this distance she could see the reflection of light in his eyes, but when he glanced her way, her heart dropped to her stomach. She ducked behind the curtain though kept her ear close to the open window. The voice that was speaking was unfamiliar to her. It was stern and intense and tied her stomach in knots with every syllable. The words he spoke painted a grisly picture and yet she could not step away. Sophia continued to listen. She was drawn into the story of torn out hearts and swallowed demons and somehow, she knew who they were speaking of, and she should have been scared and maybe deep down she was, but she was also intrigued and exhilarated. And as this vampire begged Jace for his help Sophia considered the possibilities. What if this was their way in? If Jace agreed to help them he could learn about their hiding places and they could destroy the vampires for what they did to Sarah's grandmother, Jace's fiancé, and Sophia's parents. They would each get their justice.

Sophia closed the window careful not to let it slam shut. She laid back on her bed. Her knees bent. Her eyes fixated on the ceiling fan spinning above her. She imagined herself, Jace, and Sarah sneaking to the vampires' lair in the middle of a sunny bright afternoon. Each of them carrying a wooden stake. They would open the coffins of the vampires while they slept. Catching them unaware they would drive the stakes into their hearts one by one and the vampires would perish. They would drag their bodies into the sun and watch them turn to dust and ash. Later they would go out to celebrate their victory. A smile formed on Sophia's face as she pictured the vampires' demise in her head. Her heart fluttered in her chest.

Before she knew it the sun had come up and she was still awake imagining the various ways she, Jace, and Sarah would kill the vampires. She heard the front door open downstairs and when she peered out the window, she saw Jace get into his car and drive off. She assumed he was going to meet with Sarah. She was a little annoyed he didn't invite her to go along with him, but she was too tired to make a fuss about it. She went back to her bed and slept the hours of daylight away. When she had awoken it was dark again and Jace's car was still gone from the driveway.

She picked up her phone thinking of calling Jace to ask where he was, but then decided against it. She couldn't be afraid to be alone in her own home, no matter the time of day or night. The protections Sarah and Jace had hung around her house were all still in place. She had to accept that for now she was safe. The vampires couldn't come into her house. They proved that last night. At least the two that had been on her doorstep, but what about the cursed one? Would the same protections that worked against the others work against him too? She had to believe that they would. Jace never would have left her alone this long if they wouldn't.

Sophia decided she would ask all her questions when Jace returned. Until then she was going to attempt a normal night in. She washed up and changed into a clean pair of yoga pants and a sweatshirt. She combed some leave-in conditioner through her freshly washed curls and tied her hair up on top her head.

Downstairs in the kitchen she searched the refrigerator for some food but nothing in there seemed to match her appetite. Instead, she moved into the living room, sat on the couch, ordered dinner from an app on her phone and turned on the TV while she waited for her delivery.

It wasn't long before the doorbell rang. Sophia checked her phone, but it didn't say her delivery had arrived. Maybe the app had not updated yet. She shrugged and got up from the sofa to answer the door. A cold wind blew in with the open door causing her to shiver. The person on the opposite side was not her delivery driver. Sophia took a step back.

"What are you doing here?"

"You need to come with me."

# Eighteen

It was just after dusk by the time Jace returned to Sophia's house. As he pulled into the driveway immediately, he felt something off. The lights from inside shone through the living room windows, which wouldn't be unusual except there were no shadows and no other lights seemed to be on in the house. Jace stepped carefully out of the car. His eyes darted back and forth between the house and the street. The sound of the ocean roared behind him. The air was still but cold.

Jace cautiously made his way towards the front door. The door was cracked open. A bag of takeout sat on the porch untouched. He stood to the side as he gently pushed on the open door. The house was silent. He stepped inside. The light from the living room lit up the foyer. Sophia's sneakers still sat by the door. Her coat still hung on the hook on the wall. Jace peaked into the living room. The TV was on, but the show was paused. He glanced up the dark stairwell. Two eyes glowed in the dark. He stood still as he watched the pale creature materialize in front of him. The dark-haired vampire stood before him now at the end of the steps. Her long hair grazed her elbows. Her face reminiscent of Harper, but she was definitely not Harper.

"Where is she?"

"I don't know. I didn't take her. But I saw who did." Una stepped closer to Jace. Jace reached his hand out to the side. He turned his head when he realized the bowl, he was reaching for was not there.

"I removed your hawthorn if that's what you're looking for. It makes me twitch." She said. Jace swallowed hard. "Don't worry. I won't hurt you. At least not yet." She assured him.

"What do you want? Where is Sophia?" He asked again.

"So that's the girl's name. Well, as I've said, I don't know where she is, but I can tell it wasn't a vampire that took her. It was a human."

Jace wasn't sure what to make of Una's answer. Why would a human take Sophia? Who would want to take her? There was no sign of a struggle. At first glance it appeared that she answered door willingly but then what happened after that?

"You sure it was human?"

"Of course, I'm sure. I know the difference between a vampire and a human."

"Then I need to call the police." Jace pulled his phone from his pocket, but Una grabbed his wrist before he could dial a number. The phone crashed to the floor landing on its face.

"I wouldn't do that if I were you."

"What the hell. Why not?"

"I said a human took her but I'm pretty sure he's working for a vampire. He had that glassy look in eyes and the scars on his neck only a vampire could have put there."

Jace sighed. He leaned over picking his phone up off the floor. The screen had a small crack but luckily not too much damage was done. "Why didn't you do something?"

"What business is it of mine to get into another vampire's affairs?" Una shrugged.

"Then why are you here?"

"To tell you to leave town. Stay out of vampire business. Every time you're around someone gets killed. Whatever is going on with Dac let us deal with it. Go back to wherever you've been hiding out these past 10 years. We don't need you here."

Before Jace could respond Una was gone. "I wish I could," he muttered to himself.

Jace flicked on the light in the kitchen and poured himself a drink from the whiskey bottle on the counter. He tried to stay away from the stuff, but this stay in Aura Springs was making that impossible. He looked at his phone for a minute then dialed Sarah's number. He placed the phone on the counter, hit the speaker button on the screen and took a sip of his drink. Sarah answered on the second ring.

"Jace, what's up?" Sarah asked. There was no hello or attempt at small talk. She must have sensed the urgency.

"Sophia's been taken. Vampire. Probably Dac if I had to guess." Jace said between sips of his drink.

"I'll be right there."

Jace watched the screen on his phone turn black as the call ended. He finished his drink and poured another one. Una's words invaded his thoughts. She wasn't wrong. Every time he got involved with the vampires someone ended up dead. If only he could walk away from this, but he couldn't. Especially not now. Not if one of them had Sophia. She didn't deserve any of this. All because of some chance encounter she had as a child. No, it wasn't fair. He was going to do whatever was necessary to save her, despite Una's warning.

It wasn't long before Sarah showed up. She stood in the kitchen doorway. Her hair pulled back and a sweater wrapped around her shoulders. She must have left her house in a hurry considering the cold Jace found it odd that she hadn't worn a coat.

"The door was open." Sarah said, explaining her sudden presence.

"Guess I forgot to close it. Thanks for coming. Would you like a drink?" Jace handed Sarah a glass filled with whiskey. She took the glass, thanking him.

"So, what happened? How do you know it was a vampire?"

Jace explained how he came home to find Sophia missing and Una inside the house. He repeated everything Una had said including her warning for him to get out of town.

"And you believe her?"

"I have no reason not to. What other explanation is there?" Jace could see from the look in Sarah's eye that she believed it too. With everything going on it was completely plausible. They knew that Dac was trying to communicate with her at some point. They knew they had a past acquaintance. But what did he want with her? Did he really think she could help him somehow? There were too many questions and not enough answers. "I don't know I feel it in my gut. He's got her."

"Then let's go find her."

SOPHIA WOKE UP IN THE back seat of her uncle's car. Her vision was still a little blurry, but she could see the back of her uncle's head over the headrest of the seat in front of her. Her head ached and felt heavy on her shoulders. She rubbed her temples as she tried to sit upright but the dizziness caused her to lay back down.

"Where are you taking me?" She groaned.

"You'll see when we get there, just be quiet for now." His voice remained monotoned like he was reading from a script. No emotion. He didn't sound forceful or angry. He talked as if this were a normal conversation under a normal circumstance, not as though he had just kidnapped her from her own house.

"I don't understand. What's happening?" He didn't answer. Sophia reached for her phone but realized it wasn't with her. The last thing she remembered was answering the door for what she thought was her food delivery. It turned out to be her uncle on the other side. He said she needed to go with him, but he had this glassy look in his eyes, and she said no. She began to shut the door, but he had grabbed her by the arm and pulled her towards him. Her head hit the door and next thing she knew she was waking up in a moving car. She couldn't recall if she had her phone with her when she answered the door. Had it fallen when he grabbed her? Was it still somewhere inside the house?

The car continued driving for a few more miles. Sophia could see the city lights through the windows. They were in Aura City now, but why? She still had no idea exactly where they were going. When the car stopped her uncle got out. A cold wind blew in through the open door. With the heat of the car no longer protecting her she realized she wasn't wearing a coat or shoes, only her yoga pants, sweatshirt, and a thin pair of white socks. She shivered from the frigid temperatures outside.

Her uncle pulled her from the car. Her feet hit the cold pavement. The loose gravel poking through her socks. Her uncle dragged her through a dirty and dark alleyway. At the end a gated stairwell awaited them. He pushed her through the iron gate and down the cold concrete steps. The red painted steel door opened just as they approached. A large man stood on the other side. He stepped aside allowing the two to enter. He looked Sophia up and down before closing and locking the door. He grunted, then left the room through a dark hallway.

The room was dim as they stepped inside. The small lamp in the corner gave off very little light. It was dank and dusty, but the floor was carpeted, which Sophia welcomed considering her shoeless feet.

"Sit here." Her uncle pushed her down onto a worn out two cushioned sofa. Dust flew up around her as she hit the couch. She sneezed and brushed the dust away as best she could. Her uncle disappeared through the same hallway as that other man had a moment ago. Sophia sat quietly while she waited for him to return. Her leg shook ferociously. Her heart pounded against her chest. Tears began to stream down her face.

"Please don't cry." The man standing in front of her now was no man at all but a vampire. The vampire that had called to her in her dreams. The same one who stood over her while she huddled in the closet at nine years old. He stood before her now. His eyes glowing with red then fading to black. He knelt down in front of her. He reached out his hand and wiped the tears from her face with his thumb. His skin was hard and cold. Sophia trembled at his touch. "I was truly hoping you would have found me on your own and we could have met under better circumstances, but all is well, you are here now."

"What do you want with me?" The words rattled out of Sophia's throat as she spoke them. She tried to sound strong, but her fear was evident.

"Insurance."

"I don't understand. Insurance for what? And why did you kill my parents?" The questions just came pouring out.

"That my dear I am truly sorry for, but it couldn't be helped. I had to be rid of anyone working for that retched vampire Alex. I do wish I could have spared them."

"My parents never worked for any vampire." Sophia insisted. And who was Alex? She remembered hearing that name before, recently. Was he the vampire's brother? No, Alex was the other one he killed before killing his brother. She remembered now from the story she heard those other vampires telling Jace the night before.

"Ah, I hear your mind putting the pieces together. Good for you. But I assure you your parents worked for Alex for many years. I have to hand it to him though; he was a lot smarter and a lot more patient than any of us gave him credit for. Unfortunately, they all had to be dealt with. Each and every one of them lustful for power. The power, so rightfully mine." The vampire grasped Sophia's chin fixating his gaze on her. "But you, you I spared. For you were only a child. No child should have to pay for the crimes of their elders."

"And yet now you had me kidnapped." She scoffed.

"Well had you come to me instead of the hunters I wouldn't have had to take such measures, but you made your bed." The vampire released his grip on Sophia.

"Come on Dac, is that anyway to treat a guest? You can see she's frightened." A young woman stood in the doorway. She looked around the same age as Sophia, but Sophia could see from her luminescent skin that she too was a vampire.

"Emmaline, you are right. Why don't you take her to her room? I have some phone calls to make."

Sophia sat still as the vampire Emmaline approached her. Her mouth was dry. Her hands shaking. She looked around for her uncle, but he hadn't returned since disappearing down the hall. Emmaline placed her hand gently on the back of Sophia's shoulder nudging her to get up. Seeing no other choice Sophia stood and followed Emmaline to a small room.

Inside the room was a small twin bed but no other furniture. The light which hung from the ceiling was a dim yellow. There was a small window, but it had been covered with a thin piece of plywood. Emmaline motioned for Sophia to sit, so she did. The mattress on the twin bed was thin and she could feel the planks of the bedframe underneath it. Her stomach growled and she wrapped her arms around her waist hoping the vampire couldn't hear it.

"I'm sorry for the uncomfortable accommodations. You must be cold and hungry. I'll grab you a blanket and something to eat." Emmaline shut the door and locked it leaving Sophia alone in the cold empty bedroom.

Emmaline was gone a few short minutes before returning with the blanket and food as promised. She handed Sophia a dark red colored square plate. On it was a couple slices of ham and cheese slapped between two pieces of stale bread. "It's not much but we vampires don't eat food, though we try to keep a few things around for the humans we employ." Emmaline's tone of voice was softer when she spoke to Sophia than when she had spoken to Dac a short while ago.

She seemed nice enough for someone who was holding her prisoner, but Sophia wasn't going to trust her. She took one look at the sandwich and placed the plate down beside her on the flimsy mattress.

"Where is my uncle?" Sophia asked.

"Don't worry, I've sent him back to his hotel already. He'll be on his way back home in the morning with no memory of tonight."

"So, he's not one of the humans you employ? He doesn't work for you?"

"No. We just needed him for tonight to get you here. Trust me it was the easiest way."

'I don't understand. What do you want from me?" It comforted her to know her uncle hadn't kidnapped her willingly, but still here she was an unwilling captive to two lethal vampires. Her body shook uncontrollably though she tried to steady herself by wrapping her hands around her knees while she sat on the uncomfortable bed waiting for the vampire's explanation.

"I don't know what Dac's original plan was." The vampire said. "All I know is that now he needs you for insurance. We need to get Dac out of the country before the others can stop him. But if they team up with Jace, they will win for sure. That's why we need you, to make sure that doesn't happen."

"I still don't get it."

"He'll never admit it, but Dac has feared Jace since the moment he met him. He senses something about him. I don't know what it is. But Jace also has his weaknesses."

"And you think that's me? Why? We barely know each other."

"Because of this." Emmaline tossed something onto the bed. A picture.

Sophia picked up the photograph. She easily recognized Jace, though not the woman standing next to him. They looked at each other with such affection. Their smiles radiated pure joy. Then Sophia noticed the diamond ring on the woman's left ring finger. This must have been Jace's fiancée. And now she understood. It wasn't that she and this woman exactly looked alike, but the similarities were enough and Jace would protect Sophia because he couldn't protect his fiancée. Emmaline and Dac were going to use Jace's grief to make sure Dac got safely out of town.

When Sophia hadn't said anything else, Emmaline silently left the room, closing the door behind her. To her relief Sophia didn't hear the click of a lock, but they likely had someone guarding the door so she couldn't escape. She looked over at the sandwich still resting on the plate on the mattress. She took a couple of reluctant bites and then moved the plate to the floor. She took one last glance at the photo of Jace and Cloe, then tucked it under the pillow. She laid down with a deep sigh and stared blankly at the ceiling. She knew there was no way out of this, but they needed her so for now at least she was safe. Uncomfortable, but safe.

# Nineteen

Emmaline stepped out into the cold night. She didn't want to leave the girl alone with Dac and his human bodyguard, but she knew she'd be safe for as long as Dac believed he needed her. In the meantime, she needed to get some nourishment. It had been a long, exhausting night, and she hadn't had a chance to drink yet. By the time she had woken earlier in the evening, Dac had already messaged for her to meet right away. Without even thinking about any sustenance, she immediately left the house to meet him. But being so close to humans without any blood already inside her was dangerous, especially with Dac's current influence.

By now, Jace had probably realized the girl was gone. No doubt he would be looking for her and the vampires would be the first place he looked. Emmaline was pretty sure Jace didn't know the location of their new home but still she approached with caution as she arrived in front of the townhouse. Everything was in such close proximity to each other, the townhouse, Dac's actual hiding place, the cellar where they were keeping Sophia. It was a dangerous game she was playing. So many ways it could all go wrong, but if all went how she hoped Dac would get safely away, and she and the others could move on with their lives.

Quentin and Nikolai were set on finding a cure for Dac, and keeping him hostage until they did, but Emmaline knew that was far from realistic. The chances of a cure being available were slim. If that were the case, then why hadn't Luca found one? Why had Luca lived with that Demon for so long if his true purpose was just protecting his brother. Of course, the possibility that Luca also enjoyed the power it gave him was pretty high. Seeing how much the demon had changed Dac made that the likeliest possibility. Even still, Quentin and Nikolai had spent the last ten years searching for a cure and had yet to find one. The likelihood of one existing was close to zero as far as Emmaline was concerned. Getting Dac out of town was the only choice no matter what the cost. He had saved her once. It was her turn to return the favor.

Attempting to act as normal as possible, Emmaline entered the townhouse and headed straight to the kitchen where she knew Quentin would have prepared the warm blood for everyone. As expected, the glass pitcher was waiting there on the countertop. She poured some into a glass. The blood was still warm as it slid down her throat, each sip quenching her thirst.

It wasn't until she set the glass down that she realized how quiet the house had been. Was she alone? In the large home it was hard to tell sometimes. There were only four of them and several floors and rooms. But with her vampiric hearing she could usually sense when the others were home, and yet tonight the house seemed eerily still. It felt more than quiet. It felt empty.

Every nerve in her body began to tingle. Her face felt flush. Her legs felt heavy as she moved throughout the empty house. "Nikolai! Una!" she called out. "Quen..."

"Don't bother." Quentin stood in front of her in his shadowy form. His dark figure looming over her. His voice grim.

"What's going on? Where are Nikolai and Una?" Emmaline asked, sensing something was very wrong.

"The hunters have them."

Emmaline gasped. She clenched her stomach with one arm and using her free hand she steadied herself against the wall. "How?"

"They came here. They had the music box. It doesn't affect me the same as all of you but by the time I realized what was happening, it was already too late. I'm just glad you are safe. Where were you tonight?"

Emmaline swallowed what little saliva remained in her throat. Where was she? How was she to answer that? She couldn't tell him she was with Dac. She knew Jace would blame the vampires for Sophia's disappearance, but she didn't think he would stoop to this again and definitely not this soon. She hadn't even had a chance for the next step of her plan. She was going to go to him right after she stopped here for her blood. Now what was she going to do? This was all going so wrong so quick.

She looked at Quentin who was waiting for her response. Quickly she said, "I was at the old house."

"The old house. Hmm." His shadow form flickered in and out.

"Yea, you know I figured with Dac gone it wouldn't matter if I spend some time there. You know to be alone."

"Alone with the past, I presume?" Quentin's question seemed more accusatory than any type of concern. "You know living in the past so much isn't healthy."

"Whatever. Shouldn't we be doing something to save the others." Something still seemed off. Why didn't Quentin seem more concerned? Where was his sense of urgency?

"Yes, and we will, but we need to be strategic. Remember Jace is a killer now. He had no problem killing his best friend he will have no problem killing any one of us."

"Exactly why we should be doing something now instead standing here talking about my nightly activities." She was hoping she was deflecting enough. So far it seemed to be working.

"First, we need to know why he took them. What is his end game? What does he intend to do?"

"He doesn't need a reason. He's a vampire hunter! That's his endgame! We should have listened to Una." Those last few words almost made her choke.

"Are you sure about that?" Quentin looked at her with his featureless face, yet his gaze was terrifying. A shadow that could speak words with no mouth. Hands that could reach her at any moment and send her to her knees. That would be all he needed to look human again. That or the blood on the counter. Why hadn't he drunk it? It was almost as though he wanted to intimidate her. But why? It's not like he could have known what she had really been up to. She had been so careful. She expected they would all find out sooner or later but not this soon. No, he was just worried. That's all it was. It was anxious energy she was sensing from him, not anger. It had to be.

"What else could there be?"

Quentin pushed past her disappearing into the kitchen. He removed a glass from the cabinet and poured himself some of the blood from the pitcher. As he drank the shadow faded and his human-like form appeared in its place. His demeanor softened and when he spoke his voice softened too. "I guess you could be right. Just why after all these years?"

"I don't know. I hate to admit it but maybe Una was right all along. Maybe he was biding his time."

"Maybe. I guess we better prepare then. They've had a lot of time, and they have a lot of protections."

"So, what do we do."

"I'll figure out where Jace has taken them and tomorrow we'll go get them. I have a feeling if he wanted to kill them tonight, he would have done so here. He must want something. Possibly he made another deal with Dac. I don't know but you go get some rest for tonight. You'll need all of your energy if Jace is working for Dac again."

Emmaline nodded. She knew what he wanted. He wanted Sophia back. She also knew Jace wasn't working for Dac. At least not yet, but she wasn't about to explain to Quentin how she knew that, so she kept her mouth shut. She just needed to get Jace alone. Talk to him. Convince him to go with her alone and she would take him to Sophia. Of course, she couldn't do that if she didn't know where he was. Quentin had resources she didn't have. He'd find them. She'd figure out the rest later.

NIKOLAI LOUNGED ACROSS the lengthy cushioned window seat. His eyes staring out the window at the clear night sky. Una paced the room. Jace stood uncomfortably at the door. Sarah perched herself on the opposite windowsill. She kicked her foot against the wall in a continuous rhythm. None of them wanting to be there locked in this tiny cabin together.

"This is stupid." Una complained. "How do we even know Dac has the girl? And what makes any of you believe Emmaline is really going to give up his hiding place? She's managed to evade you this long while going to visit him."

"Because Dac has been trying to contact her for a while now. It's the whole reason Sophia came to Aura Springs. It has to be him. Do you know of any other random vampires in the area?" Jace said.

"He's right. And as for Emmaline, even though she's helping Dac she wouldn't want us hurt in the process. She'll do the right thing." Nikolai added.

"Are you sure about that? I'd bet she's tasted that fresh human blood by now. Experienced the kill. She won't be the same naive vampire girl you know. She'll have changed. Just like Harper." Una antagonized.

Jace lunged towards Una. Sarah jumped from her perch to get in between them. Una hissed at Jace baring her fangs at him, but Nikolai held her back.

"Stop it! Both of you!" Sarah was not in the mood to play ref between Jace and the contentious vampire. She hated this whole idea just as much as the rest of them. She'd much rather have just killed all the vampires, but they had to find Sophia first. Fighting them now would do more harm than good. She pushed Jace into one corner while Nikolai held Una in the other. "You have to keep a level head, Jace. She's baiting you right now. Don't give in to it."

"Yea. You're right." Jace backed off, taking his stance back against the wall. Nikolai eyed him cautiously but there was a familiar friendliness in his gaze like an unspoken understanding.

Nikolai let go of Una's arm and she retreated to her own corner of the room. "Quentin and Emmaline will be here tomorrow evening. In the meantime, we just have to survive the night together. You think you can do that?" His eyes darted from Jace to Una.

"Yea," They both mumbled.

Nikolai pulled a flask from his jacket pocket and took a sip from it, then passed it to Una to do the same. If they were going to make it through this night they would need to be both strong and not hungry. He knew they were putting a lot of trust in the hunters. Especially with Sarah being around, although she was proving to be more reasonable than Jace at the moment. Still Nikolai knew to keep his senses sharp. Sarah was never on their team and Jace for whatever mutual respect they once shared that ended the day, he killed Harper. He left it alone because Jace left them alone, but if Jace got out of line he wouldn't hesitate to kill him this time.

Keeping the two humans awake through the night was the key. He had phrased it as a way to make sure everyone would be at their best if they were all well rested by tomorrow evening. But he knew it was safest for all of them if they all slept at the same time during the daylight hours.

Nikolai could feel the dawn creeping up. When he checked out the window the pale blue sky proved his senses to be right. He began walking around the cabin securing all the curtains to restrict the sunlight from entering. Jace began to do the same.

"You two can have that room over there." Nikolai said to Jace pointing to a door off the kitchen area. "We'll take this one." He pointed to the second bedroom closest to the front door.

Jace nodded and led Sarah to the far bedroom. He yawned and turned towards Nikolai. "See you in a few hours."

"See you in a few hours. Sleep well." Nikolai shot Jace a smile knowing, at least for the moment, they were all safe.

# Twenty

The sun had set, and the cold air had settled in with the dark sky. Nikolai and Una had already risen. Jace could hear them whispering not so quietly outside the room he shared with Sarah. Speaking of Sarah, where had she gone? Jace fumbled around the dark in search of the sweatshirt he had worn the night before. He had torn it off sometime during the day while he slept, but the room seemed to be taking on the temperature from outside and he was shivering. Finally, he located the shirt and pulled it over his head, the fleece inside warming him as he pushed his arms through the sleeves. Next, he felt around him for his phone. He found it when his foot tapped the screen. It must have fallen to the floor. He picked it up checking the time on the screen. Quentin would be arriving with Emmaline soon. They needed to get everyone into place before then.

Using the light of the screen he crossed the small room and exited to the common space where he found Una, Nikolai and Sarah huddled around the kitchen counter. They were chatting and Sarah even managed a slight chuckle at something Una had said. It was a strange sight to behold. Never in a million years would he have thought Sarah would be standing in a room chatting up a couple of vampires like they were old friends. Nikolai and Una each had a glass filled with the blood that they drank while Sarah sipped on a green shake. He remembered that green drink, the taste lingered on his tongue with the memory of it. Sarah pushed a glass across the counter in Jace's direction. "You'll need this," she said.

Jace looked at the glass and sighed deeply. "Don't we need to get ready for when Emmaline and Quentin get here?"

"Yes, but first drink that. You'll need your strength." Nikolai picked up the glass and handed it to Jace.

Jace took it and sipped the green shake reluctantly. He knew Nikolai was right but that didn't make swallowing the bitter tasting drink any easier. With the glass in hand, he walked over to the window seat and sat down away from the others. He wasn't exactly in the mood to be overly friendly with the vampires. He made that mistake once before. He didn't need nor want the clouded judgement. His mind was clear this time around. The vampires weren't going to survive this time. None of them. It was the only way to keep the ones he cared about safe. He'd learned that lesson the hard way last time. No need to learn it again. Once Sophia was safely away from Dac all deals were off.

After he took the last sip of the bitter green shake, he walked over to the kitchen and washed the glass clean. He looked at the others with their empty glasses. The wind outside was picking up. The branches from the trees whipped against the cabin walls. A darkness seemed to hover over the room. Both Nikolai and Una grew quiet. With a supernatural speed Nikolai was at the front of the house peering out the window through the closed blinds.

"What is it?" Jace asked, keeping his voice low.

"I don't know."

"It's probably nothing," Una said. "let's get this over with. They'll be here soon."

"Yea, you're right. Let's do this." Nikolai went over to the closet and pulled out a thick nylon rope and a roll of duct tape, handing it to Jace.

"Are you sure about this?" Jace took the rope and tape surprised at his shaking hands.

"It's not like were actually under the music box trance. We just need Emmaline to believe we are. Once you guys leave, we'll bust ourselves free."

Nikolai held out his wrist and Jace began wrapping the tape around them. He wrapped more tape around his ankles binding them together as he sat on the floor. Then he bound his arms and knees with the rope, while Sarah did the same to Una.

"Shouldn't we have them in a closet or room or something?" Sarah asked.

"Good idea," Nikolai agreed. "Use that closet over there." He pointed with his head to a large closet door across the room.

Jace and Sarah dragged both vampires to the closet, sitting them side by side then placing long pieces of tape over their mouths. Jace shut the door leaving them in dark confinement while they awaited Quentin and Emmaline's arrival.

Moments later came a knock on the door. Jace steadied himself before answering. Sarah remained positioned next to the closet. Her hand on the knob ready to reveal the prisoners when the time came. Jace cracked the door open. Once he confirmed it was Quentin and Emmaline on the other side he stepped aside and let them in. He watched Emmaline as she surveyed the room and let Quentin take the lead.

"Where are they?" Quentin demanded.

"Where is Sophia?" Jace played along.

"I'm not sure I know what you're talking about. Who is Sophia?" Quentin kept his tone even as he pretended to not know what this was about.

"The girl. I know you took her. Tell me where she is, and I'll give Una and Nikolai back to you. If it not well, I think you know what I'm capable of." Jace stood tall against the vampires. His and Sarah's bodies were both covered in oils that would harm both Quentin and Emmaline as was part of the plan to keep Emmaline from becoming suspicious of Quentin not attacking him. The smell alone would irritate their senses.

"We're well aware what you're capable of, but tell me why would we ask for your help then kidnap your new girlfriend?"

"Just show us they are safe. Please Jace. Can you at least do that?" Emmaline finally chimed in pleading with him.

"Fine." Jace relented. He motioned to Sarah to open the closet door. Emmaline growled at the sight of Nikolai and Una bound on the floor. She bared her fangs at Sarah, but Quentin held her back. Her reaction wasn't what they were hoping for.

"Jace, I don't know why you think we have this girl, but we don't. Let them go now." Emmaline pleaded again.

Jace studied her for a moment, then signaled Sarah to close the door. "They stay put until I get Sophia back."

"Can we talk alone please." Emmaline asked softly. Her eye shifted between Jace and the floor.

Jace looked to Quentin, then Sarah. "Fine." He opened the front door and stepped outside. Emmaline followed directly behind him. He leaned against the side of the cabin waiting for her to speak.

"Can we step a little further out? You know vampire hearing and all," she whispered.

"Ok." He motioned for her to lead the way then followed as she led him away from the house out of earshot of the others. The cold wind bit through his sweatshirt. His heart rate picked up and he was sure Emmaline could sense it. They had hoped Emmaline would come clean once she saw Nikolai tied up. She was holding on tight to her secret. Coming out here with her alone was risky, especially if she had told Dac and he was nearby, but he had to take the chance.

"You don't have to be scared." Emmaline's voice was soft, a far cry from the tone she used inside. It reminded Jace of the night in the van outside of Zaine's father's house. That seemed like a lifetime ago. It practically was. "I know where Sophia is, but the others can't know," she confessed. Jace remained silent and allowed Emmaline to talk. "I can take you to her, but it has to be alone. No one else."

"No, Quentin comes along or no deal."

"Can't. It has to be you alone. Jace please. It's that or I leave, and you never find her. Dac's more dangerous now than ever. He just wants a meeting with you, then he'll let the girl go. That's all. I promise, but I can't risk Quentin getting hurt."

Jace knew this was not a good idea, but he agreed. "Fine. Let's go." He led her over to his car and fished the keys out of his pocket. They got in the car and drove off. The others would be mad, he knew. This was not part of the plan. They were supposed to get Emmaline to confess in front of everyone. Quentin should have been with them to subdue Dac, but Jace's only concern was Sophia. Emmaline wasn't going to give up Dac's location to the others. She made that clear.

Emmaline rolled down the window as they drove into Aura City. The cold air mixed with the heat from the car and his already present anxiety made Jace queasy. He knew the smells of the oils were irritating to Emmaline, so he let her keep the window open. They would be there soon, he hoped. Emmaline directed him to turn down a small one-way street. She had him park about halfway down the block. Once they stepped out of the car, she led him down a narrow alley way, through an iron gate, and then she opened the red steel door to what could only have been described as an illegal basement apartment.

The small windows were boarded up with plywood. The carpet was damp from the humidity. The room smelled of mold and spoiled milk. It was dark and quiet. Jace followed Emmaline down the small hallway to an even smaller room.

"She's in here," Emmaline said. Except when she switched on the light the room was empty.

"Where is she?" Jace looked around the empty room. The sheet on the twin size bed had come undone at the corners revealing the thin mattress underneath. A thin blanket lay in a pile on the floor. "Where is she?" Jace asked again.

"I...I don't know." Emmaline ran from the room down the hall to another room. She called out for Dac, but he did not answer.

"What's going on, Emmaline? You said she'd be here?"

"I don't know. This is where I left her last night. I was supposed to bring you here tonight. That was the plan."

"Why? What did Dac want from me? Why did he take Sophia?"

"He said he wanted her as insurance. He wanted you to help get him out of town. Said he would let the girl go as soon as you helped him. He promised that was it." Emmaline pulled out a phone from her pocket. She dialed a number and put the phone to her ear.

"Who are you calling?"

"Dac. Who else?" She took the phone away from her ear. She looked at the screen and dialed the number again. This time she was sent straight to a voicemail. She stuffed the phone back in her pocket and slumped down on the chair beside her. "I don't understand."

"Looks to me like Dac double crossed you. I think it's time you told the others. Come on we're going back to the cabin."

Jace stormed out of the tiny basement and back up to the street. He raced to his car with Emmaline keeping at his side. His heart was pounding harder than before. His palms were sweating and all he could think of was as soon as he found Dac he was going to kill him.

The ride back to the cabin was tense. Neither Jace nor Emmaline spoke a word. Emmaline tried to call Dac a few more times, but each time she only got his voicemail. Jace kept his eyes on the road. His jaw remained clenched and his grip tight on the steering wheel. When they finally pulled up to the cabin Jace jumped out of the car slamming the car door shut. Emmaline stayed put until Jace yelled to her to come inside.

They walked in together. Una and Nikolai were untied and seated in the living room with Quentin and Sarah. They all rose up at once as soon as Jace and Emmaline entered the room.

"What happened? That wasn't the plan." Quentin widened his dark eyes. He advanced towards Jace but stopped short of touching him.

"Tell them, Emmaline."

"I'm sorry, I messed up." Emmaline paced the room as she told them everything from helping Dac escape the old house to meeting up with him in the park to helping him kidnap Sophia.

# Twenty-One

Sometime during the late afternoon, they had moved her, one of Dac's people, that is, one of his human servants. The middle-aged bald man had come into her tiny room. He had snatched her up by her arms and dragged her out to a minivan waiting by the curb. He smelled of onions and dried meat. The wounds on his neck had barely scabbed over. When he shoved her into the van there were no seats in the back, so she crawled up against the far side, hugged her knees to her chest and tried unsuccessfully to hold back her tears as the man slammed the door shut. There was no use fighting back, she concluded as he was under Dac's compulsion. Just like with her uncle, there would be no reasoning with him. The man climbed into the passenger seat of the van and whispered to the driver. Another one of Dac's minions Sophia presumed.

She didn't think they traveled very far but it was near dusk by the time they reached their destination. She stepped willingly out of the van on her own, although the two men kept a close distance to her. Still with only socks on her feet she walked up to Dac who was sitting on the steps of the grand house in front of her. The awning above the porch shielded him from the remaining rays of the setting sun. The shadow cast across his face revealed little beyond his glowing red eyes.

"A little early for you to be out, isn't it? Why did you move me?" Sophia tried to appear strong.

"A change in plans."

"A change in plans, or have you really just been lying this whole time?"

"You always were a smart one. It's one of the things I adore most about you." Dac grabbed Sophia by the back of the neck pulling her closer to him. "You and I are the same you know. Lied to our whole lives. Orphaned. Misunderstood. And yet, still destined for greatness."

Sophia struggled to break free of him, but Dac tightened his grip. With his free hand he took hold of her wrist, bringing it to his mouth. His lips pressed against her skin. The sting of his fangs made her body tense as they dug into her flesh. Sophia cried out as she continued to struggle. When he released her arm from his bite, he wrapped a white cloth tightly around her wrist. Sophia staggered slightly backwards but Dac still had her firmly in his grasp.

"It will hurt less soon enough. Eventually you will even find pleasure in it when you are ready. When you finally become as I am."

"I will not!" She remained defiant.

"Take her to her room."

The two men from the van dragged Sophia into the house. As she fought and struggled against them, they only held her tighter. At the top of the steps inside the grand house they tossed Sophia into a large room and slammed the door shut locking her inside. She landed on the floor. Her thigh was sore from the fall. Her arms were bruised from Dac and the other two men. She rubbed the side of her thigh then peeled herself off the ground. She looked around the room. It was considerably nicer than the one she was last in. There was a king size four poster bed. Normal size windows with lavish drapes. An ivory-colored dresser with a large vanity mirror. And there was an ensuite bathroom. As nice as it all was, she still would rather not have been the prisoner of a vampire. One who she just learned was planning to turn her into one. Shuttering at the thought, she sighed heavily as she sat down on the bed.

Moments later there was a knock at the door. Sophia's head shot up. She glared at the door as the sound of the lock clicked and the door pushed open. Dac entered.

"I trust you'll like your accommodations here much better. I hope you've had a moment to calm down."

Sophia stayed silent.

"There are fresh clothes for you in the closet. Linens and soaps in the bathroom. I do want you to be comfortable."

Sophia turned her head away from him instead facing towards the windows.

"I see you are still angry with me. What can I do to make you forgive me?"

"Let me go home."

"That's not possible."

"Then nothing."

"I'll give you some time to freshen up. Meet me in the dining hall in one hour. We will talk more then. As a show of good faith, I'll leave the door unlocked but don't bother with any ideas to escape. There will be guards outside your door."

Sophia glanced around the room one more time, noticing the large round clock hanging on the wall and noting the time. She slid off the bed, walked over to window to peer outside. The sky was turning a darker shade of blue. The sun was almost fully gone for the day and nighttime would soon be settling in. Her stomach ached and chills spread throughout her bones. Things could only get worse from here.

An hour later, Sophia emerged from her room. Her hair freshly washed and dried, she had thrown on a pair black cotton pants and a sky-blue sweater from the closet. Although she wasn't all that keen on accepting Dac's offerings, it did feel nice to have a shower and clean clothes. As she stepped out into the hall, she realized she had no idea where the dining room even was, but of course, as Dac had promised the two men from earlier that day stood diligently outside her door.

"Do you know where I am supposed to meet Dac?" She asked the men.

"I will take you." Another man, she hadn't yet met, was standing at the top of the stairs. His hair was neatly combed and slicked back on his head. His suit suggested he was at a higher ranking than those two currently standing next to her. He reached out to offer Sophia his hand.

"Thank you." She said as she took his hand and followed him down the steps. His skin was warm and his touch gentle. He was definitely human, not vampire, which gave Sophia slight relief.

"I'm Treye." He introduced himself.

"So, are you a prisoner too or are you another one of Dac's servants?"

"Neither. More of an old acquaintance, I suppose."

"Hmm." Sophia rolled her eyes.

"I met Dac years ago. He gave me my first job as a teenager. Of course, I didn't know he was a vampire then. I found out a couple of years later and then he disappeared. He was always good to me when I worked for him so when he recently asked for my help, I was happy to do it." Treye volunteered, although Sophia hadn't asked.

"So, you're just here out of the goodness of your heart?"

"Well, he also pays rather nicely."

"Of course, he does." Sophia said sarcastically.

As they approached what Sophia presumed was the dining hall, these vampires really liked their old-fashioned houses, Treye stopped a few feet away from the doors. He leaned in close to her ear.

"Be compliant, or at least pretend. It will make things a lot easier," he whispered.

Treye walked away in the opposite direction. Sophia took a deep breath before opening the double doors and entering the expansive dining room. The room resembled the one she had seen in the house in Aura City, or at least what she believed it would have looked like before it had been torn apart and left in shambles. This room, however, had no windows, but the low hanging chandeliers provided plenty of light. The long dark oak table was surrounded by richly upholstered dining chairs, ten of them to be exact, four on each side and one at each end of the table. Though somehow Sophia didn't think all those chairs would be seated tonight.

Dac was seated at the far end of the table, waiting for her when she stepped into the room. He stood as she entered. He was dressed in a full three-piece suit complete with a tie and pocket square. His shoulder length hair was pulled back and tied with a black ribbon at the nape of his neck.

"I hope you're feeling better now. Come, sit," he greeted her.

Sophia walked silently towards the vampire taking a seat in the chair next to him. On the table was a plate of food and a glass of what she prayed was red wine.

"It's cabernet," he assured her. "Don't worry, I've already eaten."

Sophia looked down at the plate of food in front of her. Her stomach ached with hunger but still she was hesitant to eat anything her kidnapper gave her.

"Go ahead, eat. It's safe, I promise you."

She twisted the fork between her fingers before picking up one of the roasted potatoes and putting it in her mouth. Dac finally sat down. He watched her eat for a few moments before finally speaking again.

"I would really like us to be friends. I'm sure you've been told some terrible things about me but I'm not all bad, I promise."

"Um...Not all bad? You kidnapped me."

"Technically your uncle kidnapped you. I just asked him to bring you to me. His methods were his choice."

"And yet you still hold me captive or am I free to leave now?"

"Unfortunately, I can't let you leave."

"Can't or won't? What do you want from me anyway?" Sophia slammed the fork down against the ceramic plate and turned to face the vampire.

"I want your friendship, your companionship. I want you alongside me while we create an army of vampires and finish what my ancestor and my brother once set out to do where we are once again the thing people fear and no longer hiding amongst mortals." Dac leaned in closer to her.

"That's crazy. I will never be your friend or companion. I will not be a vampire like you." Sophia stood to leave the table, but Dac grabbed her wrist, and she sat back down knowing she wouldn't have the strength to fight against him.

"You will and you will like it. It is your destiny. It was the moment you came into possession of that music box. The moment that old hunter gave that thing to your mother, and she accepted it. The moment your parents began working for Alex. This became your destiny, and you will fulfill it." Dac stood towering over her. Hel still held tightly onto her wrist. His eyes beamed with that red glow. "But for now, we are done here. Finish your food if you wish then, go back to your room. I have some things to do." He let her go and stormed out of the dining hall. The banging of doors echoed as they slammed shut behind him.

Sophia stared at her half empty plate. She was no longer hungry. Silently she cursed her mother and her father. Her whole life she spent worshiping them and then missing them after they died and now, she hated them. She hated them for bringing vampires into their lives. She hated them for setting this moment into motion with their past actions. She wanted to hate Brigid for giving that music box to her mother in the first place but for some reason she couldn't. She believed Brigid gave it to her for safety but somehow her mother and father used it for evil. If she ever made it out of here, she had to tell Sarah and Jace of Dac's plans and then she had to find out the truth about her parents. How had they gotten involved with these vampires to begin with? What was their reason? She needed to know.

# Twenty-Two

They had spent all night trying to think of any place that Dac could have taken Sophia. The early morning hours were approaching, and the vampires had retreated back to their home. Jace and Sarah drove back to Sarah's house. Sarah had suggested they both get some rest and then speak to her grandmother once she woke up, but Jace was restless. He tossed and turned while he watched the colors of the sky turn. There were brief moments where he would drift off into a light sleep, but the dreams came quick and vivid. He'd find himself jolted awake, his heart pounding and his head spinning. Eventually he gave up on sleeping all together and opted for caffeine instead.

By the time Sarah had woken up the house smelled of strong coffee and bacon grease. Jace had just set a plate of six slices of buttered toast on the counter when Sarah walked into the kitchen. She walked over the refrigerator, poured some orange juice into a small glass, placed two slices of the toast on a separate plate and took it to her grandmother's room. Jace had the coffee poured and was sitting at the kitchen table by the time she returned.

Jace was anxious to talk with Brigid but knew he couldn't rush the old woman. He picked at the toast and bacon and sipped his coffee while he impatiently waited. His leg shook under the table, and he eventually released a deep sigh.

"I know," Sarah said in her most understanding voice. "Give her a few minutes, then we'll go in there."

"Did you tell her anything yet?"

"I mentioned we had some questions for her, but I didn't tell her Sophia is missing. She isn't doing very well these days." Sarah looked down into her coffee cup.

"I know. I'm sorry. I wish we didn't need to involve her at all."

"It's fine. We just need to give her some time. Thanks for breakfast by the way."

"No problem. I needed to keep myself busy." It was all he could do. The only thing he had any control over at the moment were these small meaningless tasks.

Jace started clearing the dishes away as they finished eating. Sarah got up to check on her grandmother. Within minutes she returned to the kitchen.

"We can go talk to her now."

Jace wiped his hands on a dish towel and then followed Sarah to Brigid's room. There was a small radio playing which Brigid turned the volume down when she heard the two of them enter. Jace and Sarah sat down in the two chairs next to Brigid's bed.

"Is Sophia here too?" Brigid asked.

Sarah shot Jace a look, and he mouthed the words *I know.*

"No, she's not with us today." Jace replied opting to keep his answer simple.

"That's too bad. What can I help you two with today."

Sarah shifted in her seat. "Gram, we wanted to know more about the demon. Like, is there anything more you can tell us about it? Like what exactly happens when it possesses these vampires?"

"Ah, I see." Brigid blinked her eyes as she gave this some thought. "Possess is an interesting way to put it. You know I do remember Scarlet mentioning once the vampires said that demon took over the thoughts and action of any that consumed it. So, I guess possession would be pretty accurate."

"Were there other vampires besides Luca and the one he killed for it? I thought it had only been those two." Jace asked.

"Only those two that I know of, but you know the older vampires had their tales much like the humans did."

"Was there anything in those tales that could help us now?"

"Hmm, let me see if I remember." Brigid adjusted her position on the bed. She reached for her glass on the bedside table. Sarah aided her while she took a sip of the juice and put the glass back on the table. "I do remember a conversation I once had with Scarlet. It was right about the time Dac and Nikolai showed up in our town." Brigid paused for a moment. "Oh, and a visit with a very old vampire. One even older than Luca and Dac. She didn't tell me much, but she knew about the curse."

BRIGID WAS SITTING on the bed beside her sister. It had been a few days since the news of the new vampires coming to town. Those that knew of their existence were all on edge, human and monster alike. No one was too fond of the new arrivals. Brigid had wandered into her sister's room curious if she had heard anything about them. All anyone around her would say was how dangerous they were, but why? Weren't all vampires dangerous? How were these two any different? It had to be more than just their age.

"He's the product of a curse." Scarlet had said. "A curse from a demon. The demon resides within his brother, but that doesn't matter. That's what the vampires say. They whisper amongst themselves. The demon will find him, they say and once it does, he will be the most evil vampire to ever walk the earth."

"Yes, we know that from the old woman. What about his brother, the one who has the demon now?" Brigid asked.

"They say he's in the earth and the demon bides his time."

"What does this demon want?"

"Power." Scarlet shrugged and opened her eyes signaling she was done listening to the vampires.

Brigid walked out of Scarlet's room feeling less than satisfied. Someone must know more, and she was determined to find out. She couldn't ask a vampire they would never talk to a hunter, or could she? If one wanted these two gone bad enough maybe, they would be willing to talk to her. She returned to her room and waited until evening arrived.

Once the family had finished supper and everyone returned to their separate corners of the house, Brigid finished helping her mother with the dishes and then soon found herself alone in the kitchen. She snuck out the back door and ran through the yard until her feet reached the pavement. The streetlamps lit the way while she walked through town.

The tavern was dimly lit. A place where vampires could mix amongst humans without fear of being caught. Brigid surveyed the room. She was not looking for any random vampire. She was looking for someone very specific. Someone who had lived in this town for years.

"I need to speak to Alessia." Brigid said to the man behind the bar.

"Are you sure about that." The man asked.

"Very."

"As you wish." The man led Brigid through the tavern, then up a narrow set of stairs. He knocked on the door and entered the room leaving Brigid standing alone in the dark hallway. When he returned the man nodded to Brigid, left the door open and walked away.

Brigid stepped into the room. It was cool despite the growing warmth outside. Only a small number of candles and the light of the moon lit up the corner where Alessia sat in her wingback chair. Her black cat perched on the windowsill behind her.

"I have an agreement with your family, so I know you aren't here to kill me so, tell me why are you here?" The vampire's voice was soft yet powerful.

"I am hoping you can give me some information." Brigid did her best to sound confident, but her words came out shaky.

"I am not sure what kind of information a vampire could or would be willing give to a hunter, but you are brave for coming here alone. Please have a seat. Tell me, what type of information are you looking for?" Alessia gestured towards the seat across from her.

Brigid sat down. "I need to know about these new vampires. I need to know about this curse and the demon. If anyone would know I figured it would be you." And if she could get this information then her father and everyone else would finally have to take her seriously.

"Let me guess, your father doesn't know you are here."

"No, he doesn't." Brigid confessed.

"You are braver than I thought, but what makes you think I would know anything of use to you or that I would be willing to share what I do know?"

"Because you are the oldest vampire in this town and as you have already mentioned, you have an agreement with my family. Aside from that from what little I do already know it would be beneficial to all of us to be rid of these two and to my understanding you cannot kill your own kind, but I can."

Alessia laughed, "You think you can kill these two vampires? This is beyond anything you or anyone in your family have ever dealt with before."

"I have killed plenty of vampires." Brigid said defensively, crossing her arms across her chest.

"Fledglings, young ones that didn't deserve the life that was gifted them. These two are a different breed. Trust me, I was made of the same blood. From the one's ancestor."

"So, you do know about the curse. About the demon. You have to tell me. It's the best chance we have." She hated how her voice suddenly sounded. How the words came out desperate and begging.

"I understand you are a young woman trying to prove herself in a man's world, but this is not the way to do so. You'd be best to go home and forget about this."

"I have a feeling you were once the same." She couldn't give up. Not yet.

"Perhaps."

"Then how did you end up here?"

"Your sneaky tactics aren't going to work." Alessia could see right through her questioning but still she had to try.

"Please," Brigid begged. "Tell me anything, only what you feel is appropriate. That's all I ask."

"Fine, I will tell you this much, anyone made of the demon's blood possesses a piece of the demon inside of them, but they will never be as strong as the one who carries it inside himself. There are many who wish for that kind of power and many who rightfully fear it. Then there are those of us who know the truth behind the curse."

"What is the truth?"

"It is the seventh son who will become entwined with the demon, and eventually become the demon. Once that happens the demon gets what it wants."

"What's that?"

"Control, power, and an army of unkillable vampires."

JACE AND SARAH BOTH looked at each other. Was Dac already that far gone? Had the demon already taken complete control over him? Had he already started making new vampires? Is that what he wanted with Sophia?

Brigid coughed and Sarah handed her a bottle of water. She took a few sips before handing it back. "I'm sorry," she said." "I should have told you that part sooner. The vampire Alessia made me promise I would never let Dac get that demon. Patrick and I kept watching out for him for years and we truly believed we were safe when Luca never resurfaced. We eventually decided to give up that life of vampire hunting. We didn't want that for our family anymore, and I guess eventually I put it out of my mind. Now I see that was a mistake."

"Is Alessia still alive?" Jace asked.

"I don't know and don't go looking for her." For a moment Brigid sounded exactly like she had the first time Jace had met her.

"She may be the only one with the answers we need." Jace replied.

"You two have all the knowledge you need and enough vampires in your circle. You don't need anymore."

"Is there a cure for the curse? Is there some way to rid Dac of that demon inside of him?"

"Death is the only cure. You have to kill Dac."

Brigid started to cough again but this time when Sarah handed her the water bottle, she brushed it away. She slumped down in her bed and rested her head against the pillow closing her eyes. Jace and Sarah got up and left her to rest.

Once they were back in the kitchen and out of ear shot of Brigid Jace turned to Sarah and said, "I think Brigid is holding back. I think we should try to find this Alessia."

"I think you're right. Do you have ideas how to find her."

"Only one."

"Nikolai," they said in unison.

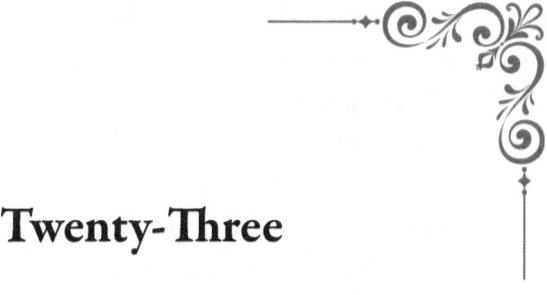

# Twenty-Three

I f only there were a way, he could travel back in time. Back to the moment they buried Luca's undead body. Back to the time they hunted all of Luca's friends and allies. Back when he and Dac hunted down any vampire or human that would have exhumed Luca's body. They did whatever they had to do in those days. It was the only way to keep the demon inside of Luca's body and keep Dac safe. They kept him alive, but immobile. They made sure there was no one left to resurrect him, and they believed they had succeeded. For centuries they lived in contentment. They felt a sense of peace and freedom from what they both knew was inevitable had they not done what they did. But it was a false sense of peace. A lie they told to the world. A lie they told for so long that they themselves began to believe it. Then one day Luca showed up and the inevitable did happen. Now, Luca was dead. The demon had possession of Dac, and the curse was coming to fruition.

Nikolai sat back in his chair. The blood in his glass swirled around coating the edges in deep crimson. He stared at the clock on the wall. Every hour that passed became more crucial than the last. He should have listened to Alessia all those years ago. Deep down he knew it back then. He just didn't want to accept it. He wanted to believe he could save Dac. That he could protect Dac. They were friends and had been for so long. No, they were more than friends. They were family. That's what he had told Alessia, and she understood, and she helped them to get out of Crimson Fells. He promised her before they left that he would look after Dac. That he would make certain that demon never got to him. He failed.

"We both failed him. It wasn't just you." Quentin said as he entered the room knowing just what was on Nikolai's mind. "We both made that same promise. All of us knew what was at stake and yet we all became a little too complacent."

"Yea, well if I had just done what Alessia asked."

"You weren't going to kill your best friend. No one should have expected you to."

"Well, if the old woman doesn't have a cure for us then we'll have no choice now."

Nikolai and Quentin sat quietly for a moment contemplating that last thought. They both knew it was true. Killing Dac was the only way. They had held onto hope for far too long. Nikolai took a sip from his glass trying to stifle the anxiety that was steadily growing inside of him. With every human life that Dac took, his power and strength would be growing, and with his so would the demon's until it finally took complete control. It had already been weeks since Dac's escape from his prison in the old house. There was no way of knowing how many lives he had already taken. How much live blood he had already consumed.

"I've been thinking lately," Quentin broke the silence. "About the girl, Sophia. If Dac wanted her dead, he would've just killed her right? He wants something from her. He chose her specifically for some reason and I don't think that reason was Jace."

"I agree. It's possible he only told Emmaline that, so she would help him. But I also think telling her to bring Jace to him was more than just a distraction. I think it was a call for help. Underneath that demon, Dac is still in there." Maybe it was wishful thinking, but Nikolai had to believe it. The alternative was too unthinkable.

"So, you don't think it's too late?" Emmaline asked from the doorway.

"No, I don't think it's too late." Nikolai extended his arm inviting Emmaline to sit next to him.

"I'm so sorry, for everything." She leaned into him as he wrapped his arm around her and squeezed her shoulder in a forgiving embrace.

"We'll get through this. We'll figure it out and save him." Nikolai assured Emmaline.

"Will we though?" Una questioned Nikolai's assertion.

Nikolai stood up. "Yes, we will."

Una scoffed. "I suggest we kill him and get it over with. He's a threat to us now. He's no longer a friend."

"You're not being helpful here."

"How am I not being helpful? I am the only one being realistic." Una picked up a crystal glass poured some blood from the carafe on the tray that sat on the far table in the room.

Even if Una had a point, Nikolai wasn't about to admit that. Especially not to her and especially not in front of Emmaline. Emmaline was struggling enough; he could see that, and Una's comments only made it worse.

"We need suggestions that are constructive to our plan right now."

"And what exactly is your plan right now? Because from what I can see you have nothing but questions and no answers. You have no idea where Dac is or what he is planning to do."

Again, Una was correct, but again Nikolai was not ready to accept it nor was he going to acknowledge it. If there was a chance to save his friend and stop what was coming, he was going to find it.

"I do know what he's planning." Nikolai blurted out. Everyone turned to him. The room filled with silence. Nikolai felt his face flush and his palms sweat in a warm contrast to his usual cold skin. The words escaped in a bout of frustration. If he could have stopped himself, in this moment he had no desire to do so. He knew the truth and it was time everyone else did too. So, he let words fall knowing that once he did there would be no turning back. "He's going to make an army of vampires. An empire of unkillable creatures unlike any of us."

QUENTIN STOOD IN STUNNED silence knowing exactly what Nikolai was about to reveal to the group. A secret knowledge they had kept between them to keep Dac safe. Nikolai, in his frustration, just gave Una all the ammunition she ever needed to find and destroy Dac. There was no time to stop Nikolai as the words spilled out of his mouth. The room fell silent except for Nikolai's voice. The energy around them grew tense and thick. Quentin soaked it up knowing he'd leave the others drained and tired. It was all he could do for now. Emmaline quietly rested her head against the back of the sofa she was seated on. Una yawned and stretched her arm out reaching for the nearest chair. Quentin grabbed Nikolai by the arm and dragged him out of the room.

"What are you doing? Are you crazy?"

"I'm sorry it just slipped out in the heat of the moment."

"I get it, but I feel it's only made things worse with Una."

"I know, it was stupid. I'll handle her."

"No, you won't. I'll handle her." Quentin walked back it the other room where Una and Emmaline sat waiting to regain their energy. Quentin stood next to Una and gently took her hand into his and she slowly slumped further into her chair.

"What are you doing?"

"What needs to be done." Quentin picked up the now comatose Una and carried her away to her room. Nikolai followed behind him watching as he placed Una onto the bed. Quentin stepped out of the room quietly closing the door. He pulled a skeleton key out of the side pocket of his pants and locked Una safely inside her room. Thank God, he thought, for these old doors.

"How long are you going keep her locked up in there? She's not going to be happy when she wakes up."

"As long as we need to. Her happiness is the least of our concerns right now."

"What about Emmaline?"

"She's fine. She'll help us." Quentin walked back up the stairs to find Emmaline who was still resting on the sofa. Nikolai again followed behind him. Everyone's emotions were running high, and it was up to Quentin to keep a cool head and take control. It seemed it was always up to Quentin to be the cool headed one. In every crisis, in every life, it was always Quentin who kept things in order while those around him wavered in the chaos. "Maybe you should rest a while," he said to Nikolai. "I'll talk to Emmaline." Nikolai agreed but Quentin heard him walk towards his office instead of downstairs to his room and knew he wouldn't rest at all. He turned to Emmaline who was now eyeing him in pure curiosity.

"How long have you both known?" She asked him. "About Dac? About his plan?"

"Since before they came to Aura City," he confessed.

"So, you've known this whole time? You've known even before he killed Luca? Why didn't you ever say anything?" Her eyes gleamed innocently but her voice held contention. She held his gaze while she waited for his answer.

"We wanted to protect you. We all decided it was best that the least amount of people that knew the truth the better."

"Better for who? For Dac or the rest of us?"

"For everyone including Dac. Do you know how many people, both hunters and vampires, would have wanted him dead? Would you have ever trusted him if you knew the truth?"

"Of course, I would have. He saved me. He took me in after Luca fed off me and then turned me and then left me to fend for myself."

"Maybe it's true that you would still feel like you owe him and maybe you'd still feel loyal to him but no, I don't believe you'd have ever trusted him knowing what he'd eventually become and to be honest none of us ever thought that Luca would ever resurface. We all thought he'd be in that grave forever."

"But he wasn't and when he did finally come around here you should have told us the whole truth. Instead, you all pretended to be shocked he was still alive when you all new the truth the entire time."

"Maybe you're right. Maybe not, but now we need to focus on what we can do now, not what we should have done in the past."

"So, what do we do now?"

"We find a way to save our friend and that girl before it's too late."

"Fine. Then I'm going to find Jace. Find out if that old woman has a cure."

"Keep this between us. Please."

"Sure. For now." Emmaline stomped out the door. Quentin could see her energy coming back though he wished she would have drunk some blood before she left. She'd need it within a few hours as her energy restored itself. Hopefully not sooner and hopefully not before she returned home.

In the meantime, Quentin needed to decide what to do next while he waited for Emmaline to return with whatever information she received from Jace, good or bad, though he wasn't optimistic. If Jace had learned anything useful, he would have reached out to them by now. He was desperate to save Sophia. There was no way he would wait too long if he had been told anything that could help her. Unless of course he decided to go out on his own. God, Quentin hoped that wasn't the case.

# Twenty-Four

Emmaline sat in the café in Aura Springs where she agreed to meet with Jace. She fidgeted with the keys in her hand while she watched the people come in and out of the café. The energy that Quentin drained from her earlier that evening had been fully restored but she hadn't expected the hunger that followed.

The scent of blood was thick. The sharpness of her fangs pierced the inside of her bottom lip. She clenched her jaw tight trying to control the urge to sink them into the neck of the nearest human. Visions swirled around in her head of the inevitable struggle, her fangs piercing the vein, and the blood flowing down her throat. She swallowed hard and pushed the thought out of her mind, doing her best to set aside her thirst. It did not occur to her to drink before she left the house. She was so worked up over her conversation with Quentin the only thing on her mind at the time was finding Jace.

She was surprised when Jace answered her text right away. She was already on the train into Aura Springs when she realized she had no idea where Jace was staying at the moment. When he responded to her text and asked to meet at the café, she was almost relieved for the neutral spot. She didn't realize how nervous she would be about meeting up with in some unknown place. They used to be friends. She used to trust him. Now everything had changed. Even if she had already been alone with him recently, she still wasn't ready to let her guard down completely.

Emmaline stared down at her phone. Her leg shook under the table. What was taking him so long? She thought he would have been here by now. The server at the café had come over to her table for the second time asking if she needed anything. What she needed the café couldn't provide her, at least not in any moral way, so she ordered an herbal tea and pretended to sip it in an attempt to blend in.

The warmth of the ceramic teacup was satisfying against the coolness of her vampiric skin. The scent of the tea helped mask the scent of blood, so she held the cup close to her face. Memories of the days she was human curled up on her mother's couch next to her sister came to mind. Their mother would bring them hot chocolate. They would watch cartoons and laugh until their sides hurt.

When the door to the café chimed, she looked up hopeful to see Jace. Instead, a woman walked in with her two young daughters by her side. Emmaline smiled at the sight of them and the memories that were still fresh in her mind although a slight pang of sadness settled in her stomach. She set her teacup down on the table and picked up her phone. She was getting ready to send Jace a message asking where he was when he finally walked into the café and sat down across from her.

"It's about time," she blurted out not bothering to mask her impatience.

"Sorry, there was a situation at Sarah's house."

"A situation?" Emmaline raised her brow. What could be more important than the situation they had with Dac?

"Her grandmother died." Jace averted his eyes away from her blinking away the tears threatening to escape.

Emmaline's heart sank to the bottom of her stomach. "What? When? Just now? Did you even get a chance to ask her about a cure for Dac?" She knew she was being insensitive, but Sarah's grandmother was their only chance.

"Just after you texted me. Sarah went to go check on her and she was already gone. I didn't want to leave Sarah alone to deal with everything, but she insisted I still come. I waited until the EMTs arrived then I drove over here. I'm sorry I should have told you."

"So, what now?" Her leg was shaking even faster now under the table. Her hands were trembling though she did her best to steady them. She held tightly to the warm teacup in front of her.

"Well, we did get a chance to talk to her this morning, but I don't think we should talk about this here. Can we go someplace else?"

Emmaline felt a small sense of relief and agreed the café probably wasn't the best place to be talking vampire business. Plus, she'd be happy to get out of there. The temptation was far too great, and the smell of blood was feeding her vampiric urges. She knew Jace would have himself protected in creams and oils and as soon as they walked outside into the fresh air her suspicions were confirmed. The smell of the essential oils wafted past her with the blowing breeze. Her nose itched as she breathed in the strongest scents of frankincense and peppermint.

She followed Jace to his car and slid into the passenger seat. Immediately she rolled down the window. "I hope you don't mind," she said.

"It's fine. I get it." He answered and she knew he did. They would both do whatever they had to do to survive this time together as limited as it may be.

As they drove across town Emmaline glanced out the window thinking about all they'd been through. She had cared for Jace at one time. Maybe deep down she still did. But it was hard to reconcile what he did to Harper. Whether or not Jace felt any regret didn't make him any less dangerous.

Jace parked the car in a space next to the boardwalk. As Emmaline stepped out the cool salty night breeze assaulted her face, but the sound of the nearby waves was surprisingly soothing. She pulled her jacket tight, followed Jace over to a bench and sat down next to him.

"I'm sorry," he said. "I know it's cold. I just thought coming someplace private to talk would be best. No one ever comes over here."

"This is where Harper used to come." Emmaline looked out at the ocean remembering her friend. Jace nodded knowingly and somehow this place suddenly felt like the perfect place to discuss everything going on.

"As I said at the café we talked to Brigid this morning. She told us a story about this vampire named Alessia."

"So, you know then?" Emmaline asked surprised. "You know what happens after that demon takes full control of Dac?"

"Yes, I know." Jace admitted.

"Nikolai told us tonight. He's known this the whole time. They all did, him, Quentin, and Dac." Emmaline found herself confessing this information so easily. "Quentin said not to saying anything to anyone else just yet, but I guess that doesn't matter now."

"And by anyone else he meant me and Sarah."

"Yea. He just doesn't want to give anyone any reason to go after Dac before we find a cure."

"That's the thing. According to Brigid there is no cure."

Emmaline lowered her eyes as she felt all hope drain from her body. This was not the answer she was hoping for.

"But..." Jace continued. "I don't think she was telling the whole truth. I think she was holding back; I think we need to find Alessia and so does Sarah."

Emmaline shifted her gaze towards Jace. The hope rising back inside of her and with that also her thirst. "I need to get back, but I'll talk to Nikolai and Quentin. If anyone can find her it would be them."

"We thought the same thing. Come on, I'll drive you to the train."

"It's fine. I can make it on my own. It isn't far from here. Thank you for everything." Emmaline gently squeezed Jace's arm, then left for the station.

EMMALINE WAS GONE BEFORE Jace could insist on taking her to the train. He climbed into his car and immediately locked his doors. A sudden uneasiness settled in his stomach. He looked out the windows and checked his rearview mirror. Total darkness surrounded him. The starless sky was covered in clouds. The one light had flickered out in the only lamppost on this end of the boardwalk. The wind had picked up howling around him. A light rain hit his windshield. Then he turned the key in the ignition of his old car, but the car's engine didn't start. He turned the key again. Still nothing. Then it dawned on him that it had been much brighter just moments before while he was sitting there talking to Emmaline. He had left the lights on. Of course, the battery died.

He got out of the car pulling the hood of his jacket over his head. He walked out towards the road to flag down any passing car for help. The heavy raindrops were cold against his exposed skin. He shoved his hands in his pockets as he continued walking.

The lights were on in the corner store. He walked inside, pushed down his hood and looked for the clerk. He swore he saw cars in the parking lot, yet the store seemed empty. He walked up and down the aisles. The lights flickered overhead. When he came across the small section of auto stuff he looked to see if they had a portable car battery charger. He didn't see one amongst the shelves but took a mental note to pick one up in the future.

"Can I help you?" A voice asked from behind him.

Jace spun around on his heels. "Oh yes. I was wondering if there was possibly someone around that could give me jump."

"Yea, sure no problem." The guy yelled to someone on the other end of store to watch over things while he was gone. They walked out of the store. The man looked around, then turned to Jace, "Where's your car?"

"It's parked by boardwalk."

The guy nodded and pointed towards his car as he unlocked it with the key fob. Jace followed him to the car and climbed in the passenger seat. When they reached Jace's car they both got out. The rain had lightened up to a light drizzle. Jace went to his car while the other guy grabbed his jumper cables from his trunk.

"So, what were you doing out here?"

"Just meeting a friend. She left and well I was stuck here."

"I see." The guys smiled and winked at him. When they got Jace's car running the guy patted Jace on the back and then drove away.

Jace got back inside his car and drove off back towards Sarah's house. He hadn't meant to leave her alone this long. He thought about his conversation with Emmaline and the one with Sarah earlier. What was he doing? He shouldn't be helping them find a cure, so why was he? Because he needed their help to find Sophia. That's why. There was no way he'd find where Dac was holding her on his own. He knew it and so did Sarah. That's why he was helping the vampires again because he needed their help in return, but once Sophia was safely away from Dac he was ready to put an end to all this vampire business for good. He would do just that he promised himself.

By the time he pulled up to Sarah's house all the lights appeared to be out. He let himself inside. The house was quiet, but he could hear the tv in Sarah's room upstairs. Not wanting to bother her but wanting to let her know he was there, he sent her a text message then made his way quietly to the kitchen for some coffee. He peeled off his wet coat and hung it over one of the kitchen chairs. He switched on the coffee pot then snuck over to Brigid's room.

He leaned against the door frame staring into the empty room. The bed had been made and the tables and dresser cleared and dusted. Jace hadn't known Brigid all that well, yet still a bit of sadness settled in the pit of stomach knowing she was gone. At least she was at peace now, he thought to himself.

"Hey," Sarah's voice came from behind him.

He turned to face her. "Hey." He wrapped his arms around her pulling her close to him in a warm embrace.

# Twenty-Five

Jace was up early the next morning helping Sarah with funeral arraignments and making the awkward phone calls to her surviving family members. It was in these moments that he learned Sarah's family dynamics weren't much different to his own. The closeness he had witnessed with both Harper's and Cloe's families was something he and Sarah both longed for and was the reason they bonded so early on. He felt a twinge of guilt now at the distance he had put between them over the past ten years and made a vow to himself not to do it again.

He listened to Sarah on her end of every phone call. Her voice wavered as she delivered the news of her grandmother's death, yet she still managed to hold it all together. Jace marveled at her strength to get these things done when he knew all she wanted to do was shut down. Sarah and her grandmother hadn't always been close but once they reconnected Sarah spent those years looking after her and caring for her.

When the doorbell rang, Jace got up to answer it, so that Sarah could continue what she was doing without unnecessary interruption. He was surprised to see it was his cousin Janice standing on the front porch with a pan full of food. He stepped aside, opening the door wider to allow Janice to pass through.

"Hey, thanks for coming by. You didn't need to do this." Jace took the tin pan from Janice and brought it into the kitchen.

"It's no problem, really." Janice followed Jace into the kitchen greeting Sarah with a gentle hug while she finished up her latest phone call.

Jace poured three cups of coffee and placed them on the kitchen table. They each took a seat and sipped at their coffees in awkward silence until Janice finally spoke up with an offer to help. "Let me know if there's anything I can do to help out," she said.

Sarah looked up from her coffee mug. "Thank you so much, but I think I've got it mostly covered. It's just going to be a small viewing and most of the arrangements are already made."

"Well still, if anything comes up, please don't hesitate to ask." Janice insisted. She then switched the conversation to tales of her own grandmother. Sarah began telling stories of her own. Jace even noticed a smile on Sarah's face after a while. He was grateful for the distraction. They sat around talking and laughing for a couple of hours before Janice had to leave.

"Thank you so much for coming by." Jace said as he walked her outside to her car. He hugged his cousin goodbye, then watched her drive away before returning to the house.

"That was really nice of her to stop by," Sarah said as Jace came back inside.

"Yea, it was," he agreed. "Are you hungry? We can heat up some of the food she brought over."

"No, not yet." Sarah fidgeted with her coffee cup. "What happened with Emmaline last night?" she finally asked. They hadn't had a chance to talk about it yet. Jace was holding off having the conversation while Sarah was dealing with her grief. He would handle the situation on his own if necessary. He wanted to give Sarah whatever time she needed, but since she brought it up, he was willing to talk about it.

"She said basically the same thing Brigid did about the demon's intentions. Apparently, Nikolai, Dac, and Quentin all knew about it for a long time. Emmaline seemed pretty upset, but she agreed to talk to Nikolai about finding Alessia."

"It's the best chance we've got."

"I agree. I just hope we can find her, and I hope it's soon. We need to find Sophia before Dac decides to turn her into a vampire. If he hasn't already." That last thought sent a chill down Jace's spine. This whole time he had been hopeful they would find Sophia in time, but the reality was it could already be too late.

"We can't think like that," Sarah said. "If Dac wanted to change her he would have done it when he first took her. Why else drag Emmaline into it and you for that matter. He wanted you know for a reason."

"And what reason would that be?"

"I don't know but think about it. As powerful as he is, especially with the demon inside of him now there's no reason he couldn't have taken her without you knowing. He wanted you to know and he'd know you'd come looking for her. There has to be more to his motives than we understand right now."

"You do have a point. I just hope you're right." Jace knew she was right but still the longer Sophia was with him the more danger she was in and the less hopeful he felt about finding her.

Jace looked at his phone hoping there would be a call or message from Emmaline. The blank screen informed him there wasn't. He thought about Nikolai and Quentin. When Emmaline went back and told them he had nothing, and that Brigid was dead, would they decide to cut him out of the rescue mission? They didn't care about Sophia. They only cared about saving Dac. He decided to push that thought out of his mind for now. Negative thoughts weren't helpful. He shoved the phone back into his pocket and decided to heat up the food Janice dropped off earlier. He made a plate for both himself and Sarah. Hungry or not they needed to eat.

While he sat at the table pushing the food around on his plate, taking small bites in between, he constantly checked his phone. He didn't want to miss the message when it came through. Emmaline would come through for him. He was sure about that. The others might decide they don't need him anymore but not Emmaline.

"THAT'S NOT A GOOD IDEA," Nikolai was saying when Jace suggested reaching out to Alessia. Jace, Emmaline, Nikolai and Quentin were all standing around the kitchen inside Sophia's beach house. They needed a private, neutral place to meet. Emmaline finally reached out to Jace. Quentin and Nikolai agreed to discuss what they had talked about the night before. Sarah still had some things to take care of with her great grandmother's funeral arraignments, so she stayed behind and Jace suggested they all meet at Sophia's house since the vampires insisted on coming to him. They had already known the address and Jace felt it safer than inviting them to Sarah's. There was a clear distrust between them still. Not that Jace could blame them. He didn't trust them much either, but they'd already been to the beach house, so it made sense to meet there.

"What other options do we have then?" Jace asked. His patience was wearing thin. They were no closer to finding a cure and no closer to finding Sophia. "You guys have been searching for ten years for a cure and haven't found one yet. Time is running out and you know it."

The longer they stood around arguing and debating the more frustrated Jace was becoming. He and Emmaline were on the side of finding Alessia. They were both in agreement that she was their best option. However, Nikolai and Quentin were strictly against it. Neither one would give an answer as to why and that was angering Jace even more.

"I'm just saying, both you and Brigid said Alessia had information about the demon. If anyone knows of a cure, it's her."

"She isn't the kind of vampire you want to encounter, Jace." Nikolai used a protective tone, but who he was protecting Jace was unsure. He doubted it was himself. Maybe it was Emmaline.

"Well, what about you? You already know her. Either one of you could reach out to her. I would never have to have any contact with her."

"It doesn't work like that. This just isn't a good idea. We'll find another way." Nikolai turned his back towards the group.

Jace exhaled heavily. He reached into the cabinet behind him for a glass. He poured himself a drink from the liquor bottle on the counter. His frustration mounting inside him, he drank his drink in one swallow and slammed the glass back on the countertop. The loud clank of glass on granite caused Nikolai to turn and face him. His dark green eyes glared into Jace's, but Jace didn't cower. Jace wasn't about to back down. He was ready to stand his ground no matter what. He never wanted anything to do with any of this vampire stuff. Time and again they dragged him into their affairs. Each time he went along with their plans and each time things turned out in tragedy. He was going to do things his way this time and to hell with what they wanted.

"I know what you're thinking, Jace. I'm telling you don't do it." Nikolai threatened.

Jace rolled his eyes and poured himself another drink. "Then figure out a way to find Sophia and do it quickly before it's too late. All I care about is getting that girl back home safely. Whatever you do with Dac after that is your business."

"Jace, we're doing everything we can. We'll find them both." Quentin promised in a soothing voice meant to abate Jace's growing anxiety. Jace wasn't falling for it but for now he'd pretend to give in for the sake of ending this argument.

"Fine, then what do you suggest we do next?" Jace asked a little less contentiously this time.

"I suggest you let us find them. You go and be with Sarah. Help her grieve for the loss of her grandmother. There's nothing left you can do for us." Quentin answered.

Just as Jace had predicted, they were cutting him loose. He knew this was what they had already had in mind before they even began this latest discussion. They wanted information that Jace couldn't provide for them. They didn't care a thing about Sophia. They only cared about saving Dac. Sophia wasn't a priority to them like she was to Jace. That was fine when they were working together but with Jace out of the picture there was no guarantee they would bring Sophia back safely.

"I can be there for Sarah and still help to find Sophia. I'm not leaving her in your hands alone."

"Jace, we will find her, and she will be safe with us. We have no ill will towards the girl. We don't even know her." Quentin tried assuring him.

"Well, I do." Nikolai announced. They all turned their attention to him. "I met her once in Noxwood. With Dac. When we were looking for Harper before we knew Luca was in town. She lived in one of the houses we were searching. Her parents were having a party, and she came outside. She saw us. She started talking to us. Couldn't have been more than nine years old at the time."

"Do you think that's why Dac took her?" Jace asked.

"I don't know. I'll have to ask Una."

"Why would Una know?"

"Because she was at that party that night. I assumed she wanted me to think she was Harper at the time, but maybe there was some other reason she was at that party. She was there before we arrived. She wouldn't have known that we'd show up. Maybe if we ask her what she was really doing there then we'll know what Dac wants with her. There must be a connection."

"The music box." Jace suggested. "Brigid new her mother and gifted her the music box."

"Maybe, but I think it's something more than that." Nikolai admitted.

"Well, whatever it is we need to find out soon."

"I still think you should let us handle this from now on." Quentin said to Jace. "When we find them, we'll have Emmaline bring her home."

"I agree. It's for the best, Jace." Nikolai said. "We'll be in touch when we find her. Til then stay put." Nikolai led Emmaline out the door. Quentin was already gone.

Jace looked around the empty room. He poured himself one more drink although he sipped it slower this time. He wasn't going to stop looking for Sophia, he decided. If they didn't want his help anymore that was fine, but he wasn't about to sit idly by while Sophia was still in danger.

# Twenty-Six

E ach day Sophia watched the sun rise and set from the bedroom she stayed locked inside. Dac had yet to allow her any chance to roam free throughout the house. The two guards still stood outside her room day and night. She wondered if they ever slept or ate. They would barely grunt a word to her except when Dac instructed them to tell her something. Otherwise, they stood like mindless zombies, with nothing more than a blank stare. She wondered if they'd even notice if she walked right past them, except she had no way out of this room unless one of them unlocked the door. Even the windows were nailed shut. She found that out on her first night here after that awful dinner with Dac.

Treye had returned to the dining room that night to walk her back to her room. He had sat and talked with her for a while, trying to convince her to show a little less defiance when it came to Dac. Sophia had scoffed at that, and once Treye left her alone, she ran to the window looking for an escape. When she tried to push the window open, it wouldn't budge. She found the lock at the top and switched it open, yet the window itself still didn't move. It was then that she noticed the nails drilled into the sash preventing it from opening. She was trapped in this house with no way out.

Each day since then Treye would knock on her door around mid-morning. He would escort her through the house, to the kitchen for breakfast or lunch and to the library where she could pick out a book or two to bring back to her room. There was an entertainment room with a large flat screen tv. They would sit there for hours watching movies and sitcom reruns until just before sunset when Treye would escort her back to her prison.

She would watch the colors of the sky change from blue to orange to black while she awaited her nightly fate. Like clockwork at the same exact time every night as soon as the sky turned dark Dac would show up to her room. Her two zombified bodyguards would unlock the door and he would step inside dressed in his fancy suits with the same smirk attached to his face.

"Are you ready, my dear?" He would ask.

Sophia rolled over on her bed turning her back to him. He would sit down beside her not deterred by her resistance.

"I wish you wouldn't oppose me. You do not understand what I am offering you."

"I do understand, and I don't want it." Sophia remained insistent. She refused to give in to him. Still, he would take her arm and bring it to his mouth. His sharp fangs punctured her skin as he helped himself to the blood flowing in her veins. Once he had his fill he would get up and leave.

Treye appeared moments later to tend to her wounds. He'd clean and bandage her arm. "I'm sorry," he would say to her. Then he'd hand her a glass of orange juice and an iron pill. Sophia placed the pill on her tongue and swallowed it down with a sip of the juice. When the dizziness subsided Treye would then escort her to dinner.

Tonight of course was no different, except when Treye came in to clean up her arm the look on his face was different. He always had this look of pity for her but tonight he looked genuinely sad.

"What's wrong?" Sophia asked.

"I just hate this for you, that's all," he said as he dabbed her wounds with a wet cloth and wrapped the gauze around her arm.

"So, why do you help him then?"

"I told you why."

"Right, because he pays you well and helped you when you were a kid. Do you know what he did to me as a kid."

Treye looked up to face her. His eyes were curious, hopeful even, but he sensed the disdain in her voice. This was the first time she had admitted to knowing Dac before now.

"He killed my parents." Sophia pulled her arm from Treye's grasp. She scooted herself up in her bed, so she was sitting up straighter. Her head felt light, and the room was beginning to tilt but she sat there in defiance of Treye's admiration for Dac. He needed to know the truth about his hero.

Treye's eye lowered. "I'm sorry," he said. "The Dac I know is not a killer."

"Well, the Dac that I know is." Sophia took her nightly iron pill and drank her orange juice while Treye stored away his box of supplies.

"We should go down for dinner. Are you feeling ok?" Treye was standing at the side of the bed now. He reached his arm out for Sophia to grab onto.

"Yea, I'm fine." Sophia shuffled to her feet ignoring Treye's offer of assistance.

Treye knocked on the door alerting the guards outside that they were ready to leave. The lock of the door clicked and door the swung open only, it wasn't the guards on the other side.

"I will escort her tonight." Dac was standing there with his arms at his side. He stepped slightly to the left allowing Treye to exit the room. Sophia took a step backwards. "Don't worry," he said to her. "I'm not going to hurt you. Not tonight anyway," he laughed.

Sophia stiffened her shoulders and slowly stepped out of the room. Dac closed the door and then the two of them walked silently to the dining hall. The table had been set as it had that first night. Sophia took a deep breath and then took a seat in front of the plate that had been provided for her. Dac sat next to her.

"Eat," he said. "Then we will talk."

Sophia took her time cutting the meat on her plate into small pieces. She chewed slowly and intently, taking sips of wine in between each bite. Dac tapped his nails against the table. Sophia could sense his impatience, but she didn't care. She was going to drag this dinner out as long as possible.

Was she curious as to what he wanted to talk about? Of course, she was. She also knew whatever it was couldn't be good and it was obvious Dac was waiting for her to finish her food before he was willing to speak, and so Sophia decided to take her time.

"I really do want you to feel comfortable here," Dac said as Sophia put the last bit of food in her mouth.

"You don't exactly make that easy," she said while looking down at her bandaged wrists.

"I know it's unpleasant now but trust me that is for your benefit."

"My benefit? How?"

"Each time I bite you I give you a tiny amount of my blood. It connects us and therefore will make the transformation process much easier for you."

"I told you I don't want to be a vampire."

"That's not up for debate. Now, I'm trying to be nice here and give you time to come to that decision on your own, but time is running out."

"I don't want to be a vampire," Sophia repeated.

"What can I do to change your mind? I really would prefer for you to come into this willingly."

"Why can't you just find someone else? I'm sure there is someone out there that would love to be like you."

"Because I chose you. Now I'll ask you one last time how can I help to change your mind?"

Sophia thought about it for a moment. There was no way she was going to change her mind. She did not want to become a vampire, but maybe she could buy herself a little time. She knew that Jace and Sarah had to be out there looking for her. There was no way they would let her disappear without a trace. They may not have known each other long but they seemed intent on helping her and in the short time they've spent together Sophia felt as though they had become friends. This gave her an idea. If she could convince Dac that she was willing to change her mind maybe she could afford herself a little more freedom around the house and stall long enough for Jace and Sarah to find her.

"Well for starters maybe you could treat me less like a prisoner." She kept her tone consistent with the start of their conversation. She knew that if she became too nice Dac would see right through her.

"I can't allow you to leave here."

"No, but you could allow me to leave my room without an escort, and maybe open a window for some fresh air."

Dac sat and thought about it for a moment. He sat back in his chair and rubbed his chin with the sides of his fingers. "Ok. I will remove the guards from in front of your door, but you won't be allowed to lock the door and there will still be guards stationed at the front and back of the house. I will have bars installed on your bedroom window so you may open it, but you may have to give me a few days for that."

"Fine, but I'm not agreeing just yet, but I will give it some thought. Is that enough for you for now."

"For now," Dac stood up as if ready to leave. "Oh, one more thing," he said. "You can go anywhere within the house unescorted, but you may not go outside, and you may not go into the basement."

"Is the basement where you sleep?" Sophia mused.

Dac winked at her and left the room without answering her question. She was surprised he had agreed to any of her requests but relieved she was no longer a prisoner in her room even if she was still imprisoned in this house. She wasn't sure how much extra time she managed to buy herself but hopefully it was enough for Jace and Sarah to figure out where she was. In the meantime, she would need to think of more ways to stall while she figured out how to get of here in case, she couldn't rely on Jace and Sarah like she hoped.

Sophia got up and started towards the door when Treye entered the dining room. She let out a soft sigh under her breath.

"I was told you longer needed an escort, but I was hoping you wouldn't mind one last time." Treye looked down at his feet. His tone was soft. He seemed nice enough, but he still worked for Dac, and it was clear whose side he was on even when he pretended to be looking out for her best interest. Still, Sophia agreed to let him escort her from the dining room.

"Can we go watch a movie or something? I don't want to go to my room just yet."

"Of course." Treye smiled and they walked side by side down through the long hallways.

Together they picked out a movie to watch and while they sat next to each other on the plush sofa Sophia took notice of Treye's sideways glances in her direction. He smiled when he realized he was caught. Again, an idea came to Sophia's mind. If she could convince Treye to help her, he could be her ticket out of here. It was risky and would take some convincing since he was seemingly loyal to Dac, but he might be her only way out if the other two couldn't find her in time. She had no idea how long Dac would wait for her to make up her mind. She had to try.

Sophia rested her hand on the soft cushion between herself and Treye. Treye placed his hand next to hers. She inched her fingers closer to his and he did the same until their skin was touching. She wrapped her pinky finger around his and they sat like that until the movie was over.

The tv screen went black as the credits finished rolling. Sophia turned her head to face Treye. "Thank you," she said. Then she got up and walked freely to her room with a smile on her face knowing Treye was watching her leave.

# Twenty-Seven

In the days since her agreement with Dac, Sophia made the most of the moments of her newfound freedom while she learned this so-called freedom came with a price. She naively believed that all she had to do was think about agreeing to become a vampire, but she soon realized that it was much more than that. During the day while Dac slept, Sophia roamed the halls as she pleased. But, at night when Dac came to her room, the exchange of their blood was more than it had been before. The fever settled in overnight. In the mornings she felt drained and tired. The orange juice and iron pills did little to restore her energy or stop the room from spinning. Still, she rose from her bed at the first sign of daylight. From dawn until dusk this time was hers.

She spent most of her time in the library. The shelves that lined the walls were filled from floor to ceiling with books. While there was plenty of fiction to choose from, she was more interested in the nonfiction selections. Sophia studied the titles on the books running her fingers across the leather spines. One book in particular caught her eye and she pulled it off the shelf. It was a thin book stuffed between two much larger encyclopedias. The pages were unbound and instead held between two thick pieces of cork and tied together with a dark blue ribbon.

Sophia took the book up to her room where she carefully untied the ribbon, setting the pages free. The words were handwritten in ink. She read them carefully, realizing that what she found was a diary revealing a piece of history of the very house she was currently imprisoned within, but what intrigued her the most was the mention of a secret passage. Sophia wondered if it was still there.

Sophia looked at the clock on the wall. She had two more hours before Dac would awaken and expected to meet her in her room for his nightly fill of her blood. She tied up the book and tucked it under the mattress. The hallway outside of her room was quiet. The guards had been moved to the outside as promised and she hadn't seen Treye all day. He was most likely out running errands for Dac which should give her enough time to explore this secret passage. If she could find it.

She ran her hands across the walls lightly knocking every now and then listening for the sound of a hollow wall as she had seen done so many times in the movies. She laughed a little to herself at how ridiculous she felt, until she noticed a crease in the wallpaper. Upon closer observation she realized behind the crease was an opening in the wall. She ran back to her room looking for something that could cut into the wallpaper. She pulled out the plastic box from under the bed and pulled out the scissors Treye used to cut the bandages for her wrists.

Back in the hallway she used the scissors to slice down the length of the wallpaper. She pushed on the wall until it began to slide open. On the other side it was dark and smelled of mold. Sophia reached into the back pocket of her jeans before remembering that she no longer had her phone. She would need something to light her way if she were to explore the passageway. Behind her she noticed a closet. She peeked inside. An old house like this must have a flashlight somewhere. She dug through the boxes on the closet shelves until she found one. She pushed the button on the flashlight to turn it on and it instantly lit up.

Pointing the flashlight in front of her, Sophia carefully stepped into the passageway. The landing was small before the steep steps began to spiral downward. She tugged on the open wall, closing it over though being sure to not shut herself in completely. She stepped down onto the first step. It was steeper than she imagined. With one hand holding the flashlight, she used her other hand to guide her taking each step slowly as they curved downward to the next level.

It took forever to reach the bottom, but once she did, she breathed a sigh of relief, although that anxious feeling in her stomach did not recede. She struggled with the rusty latch on the door in front of her but eventually managed to unbolt it. The sound echoed through the walls when the metal pieces of the lock slammed against each other. The wooden door popped open. Sophia pulled it farther so she could step through. She had expected to see light on the other side, but instead it was only darkness. The passageway did not lead to the outside as she had hoped but instead led to another room, or maybe it was a type of bunker. The book had said it led to a pond across the property, but she was staring into the dark not into the beauty of nature. Still her hopes had not faded. Somewhere there must be another door leading to the outside.

Her footsteps echoed as she shuffled across the room. She held the flashlight close as she shone the light. The shelved walls housed a variety of glass jars filled with dark liquids. Taxidermized birds and other small creatures stared back at her with their dead eyes. Wings expanded and claws outstretched. Mannequins dressed in long dark cloaks and cloths stood in a corner. Sophia held her breath as she continued her search for a way out.

Finally, she found the door she'd been looking for. She reached for its handle. A hand grabbed her from behind. She shrieked as it pulled her backwards. Another hand covered her mouth before the sound could travel too far. Her heels dragged across the concrete. The flashlight fell to the ground. She felt herself being dragged back through the door in which she entered. She heard the lock slide shut and then a familiar voice began to yell at her.

"What the hell are doing down here?" Treye yelled. "Are you trying to get yourself killed? Hurry up and get back upstairs. You're lucky it was me who found you and not someone else." He shoved her towards the steps and Sophia struggled to climb the stairs in the dark while she tried to regain her composure. Treye came to her side grabbing her by the arm and led her to the top though she struggled to keep up.

Her thighs felt tight, and her breaths were quick. Treye held onto her until they reached her room. He pushed her inside and closed the door behind them. He then stomped over to the window pulling the curtains open.

"You see that sky out there? It's almost dark. Dac will be up soon. Get yourself cleaned up and forget about that room down there. Never go down there again. Your life depends on it." Treye stormed out of the room slamming the door so hard that it popped right back open. Sophia shut it closed tight and with the adrenaline fading from her she slid down to the floor and the tears began to fall. She looked out the window through the open curtains. Treye was right. Dac would be up soon.

When Sophia emerged from the shower Dac was sitting on her bed. His legs stretched out and crossed at the ankles. His back leaned against the headboard. Sophia stood in the doorway of the ensuite bathroom wrapped only in her towel. Tension immediately filled the air around her. Slowly she stepped over to the closet and snatched a silk wrap dress from the closet draping it over her as the towel dropped to the floor. The dress was not something she'd typically wear and definitely not fit for the cold weather of the season, but it was the easiest thing to slip on in this situation. She finished tying the ribbons on the dress and turned back to face Dac. The faint red glow in his dark eyes told her to be careful.

"Come here." He demanded as he straightened his posture and planted his feet firmly on the ground. He grabbed hold of her wrist when she approached. His sharp talon-like nails wandered up her arm and back down through her fingertips tracing every inch of the veins under her skin. She shivered under his touch preparing herself for his inevitable bite. Instead, he dropped her arm, stood up from the bed and moved to the door. "Your freedom has been revoked. You will no longer leave this room and your meals will be brought to you. I'll be back for you when I decide I'm ready."

Sophia tugged on the doorknob although she knew the door was locked. She'd heard the click after Dac slammed the door shut. She went over the window and peered outside. It was almost completely dark. The sun was no longer visible. She could see Dac moving across the front lawn. His dark wings expanded she watched as he took to the sky.

Sometime later Treye came to her room with her dinner. By that time, she had covered the wrap dress with an oversized bulky sweatshirt. When he commented on her ensemble, she explained what happened.

"I'm sorry," he said. "I promise I didn't tell him a thing." His face looked somber, and his words sounded sincere.

"I know. It's alright." Sophia said between bites of her food. She sat on her bed cross-legged with a blanket covering her legs.

"I tried to get him to reconsider, but he won't budge."

Sophia nodded her head.

"It's just that room you know. Even when he sleeps, he's still aware of everything. I should've warned you. I just never thought you'd find that place. How did you find it anyway?"

"I read about it in a book."

"What book?"

"A book I found in the library. It's like a little diary or something. Tells a fascinating history of the house. Honestly, I thought it would lead to outside, not to some creepy dark room which by both your and Dac's reaction I'm guessing is part of the basement I was forbidden to go to. I swear I wasn't trying to go there."

"No, you were just trying to escape." Treye's eyes shifted downwards, and his mouth turned to a slight frown.

"Well, what did you expect? I'm a prisoner here. Dac isn't going to let me free until he turns me into a vampire and even then, I won't be free. And in any case, I don't want to be a vampire."

"I know, I'm sorry. Maybe..." Treye's words trailed off and he didn't finish the sentence. "Look I have to go, but I'll be back in the morning. Is there anything else that you need for the night?"

Sophia shrugged, "maybe some more books or a tv or something. If I'm going to be trapped in here it'd be nice to have some entertainment."

"I'll see what I can do."

After Treye left, Sophia put the bowl on the nightstand and laid back on the bed resting her head on the pillow. With nothing to do but stare at the ceiling she thought about her conversation with Treye. What had he meant to say earlier and why hadn't he said it? The more she thought about it the more she realized she had to go back to her original plan and convince Treye to help her. He was already on her side. She could see that. Even with his loyalty to Dac, he had feelings for her. She just needed to find a way to exploit that.

Moments later there was a knock on the door, and she heard the click of the lock. A woman she hadn't met yet walked through the door holding a handful of books. She handed them to Sophia and walked back out, relocking the door behind her. No introductions. No attempt at conversation. Just another one of Dac's faithful servants Sophia assumed. She wondered what he did to them to make them so compliant. Why were they all so obedient? Extortion? Witchcraft? Or were they like Treye? Had Dac helped them all in some previous life that all felt loyal to him, like they owed him something? Whatever the reason, it was going to be even harder to get passed any of them now. That's why she needed Treye on her side.

# Twenty-Eight

**B**rigid's funeral had been a small affair. Sarah's parents and siblings came and went with barely a word spoken to Sarah. A few other family members and friends had stopped by, but it was clear to Jace they all preferred to keep their distance from her. She had explained that none of them approved of her studies in the occult. They all knew the family secrets but unlike her they preferred to ignore them and pretend they didn't exist. They preferred the stories as simple fairytales. Sarah was the only one who had ever embraced the truth.

Jace stood by Sarah's side in the deserted graveyard. The wind had suddenly picked up with the setting sun. The sky grew dark. There was a crackling in the branches of the almost bare trees. A shadow loomed over them. When Jace looked up he saw the red glow in the eyes of the creature perched on the tree branch above them. He grabbed Sarah's arm at the wrist. Sarah glanced up as they both backed away. Dac glided downward to the ground to meet them. He retracted his wings.

"Wish I could say it was good to see you again," Dac said to Jace.

"Where is Sophia?" Jace asked. "We had a deal."

"And I have kept my end of the deal. Sophia was never a part of that. I have left your family and friends alone as agreed. That is until now." Dac advanced forward and snatched Sarah from Jace's grasp. He spun her around, so she was facing Jace. He pulled her close so that her back rested against his chest. His arms wrapped tightly around her waist. He dipped his head and bore his fangs. And before Jace could react Dac tore into the skin of Sarah's neck.

With no weapons on him, Jace bent down picking up a stick from the ground and thrusted it in Dac's direction. The stick embedded in Dac's shoulder causing him to release Sarah. Dac pulled the stick out from his shoulder while Jace ran over to Sarah, but Dac was faster and snatched her back up. He pushed her mouth against his open wound and forced his blood down Sarah's throat. He turned towards Jace with a smile on his villainous face. "Thanks for the assist," he said. Then he expanded his wings and flew off with Sarah still in his arms.

"I really hope you're better at killing vampires in the future than you were just now," A woman's voice said from behind him. Jace spun around to the sight of tall unknown woman. She had dark hair and dark, yet crystalline skin and when she smiled her fanged teeth exposed her vampire nature. She stretched her hand out in a gesture to shake hands. "My name's Alessia," she introduced herself and when Jace took her hand it was cold and hard like marble. "I came to pay respects to Brigid. Imagine my surprise when I find the seventh son still alive and in possession of the demon."

Jace swallowed. "So, you didn't know?"

"I heard rumors that the brother had survived and resurfaced. Then a murmur or two that Dac had killed him, but I thought his friends would have taken care of him by now. I warned them centuries ago what would happen if they had not."

"They've been looking for a cure."

"There is only one cure."

"Death"

"I see you've done your research. Tell Nikolai and Quentin I will be paying them a visit in a day or two."

"Why..." but Alessia was gone before Jace could ask the question.

Jace reached into his jacket pocket and pulled out his phone. He dialed the phone number he had for Nikolai. There was no time for a text message. This was too important. He only hoped Nikolai would answer. When he did Jace's only words were "We need to meet now. I'm at the Aura Springs Cemetery." He ended the call and sat inside his car until Nikolai arrived.

He didn't have to wait long. Nikolai was there within the hour. Quentin at his side just as Jace had expected. Jace got out of the car, walked around to the front and leaned against the hood.

"What's going on?"

"Dac was here," Jace said and recounted what happened with Sarah. Even as he was telling the story he couldn't believe it was happening.

"She'll be a vampire by tomorrow night." Nikolai said.

"I know and that's not all." Jace took a deep breath. "Alessia was here."

"What?" Nikolai and Quentin both exclaimed in unison.

"She said she will see you both in a day or two. She seemed rather unhappy to see Dac was still alive."

"What was she doing here? Did you seek her out?" Quentin asked.

"No. Of course, me and Sarah discussed it. I won't deny that, but we hadn't yet. We were too busy putting her grandmother's funeral together. Seems that was Alessia's reason for being here. She said to pay her respects to Brigid."

Nikolai and Quentin both seemed to reflect on that though neither of them said a word. A silence filled the air around the cemetery. Jace sensed fear in the two of them he had never noticed before tonight. They were afraid of Alessia for reasons unknown to him.

"While she was here, I mentioned you were searching for a cure for Dac. She said there isn't one."

"Only death." Nikolai finished the thought for him.

"Only death," Jace repeated. "I'm sorry guys. We have no choice. There's only one thing left to do to put an end to this."

"Kill Dac," Nikolai said solemnly.

"And any vampire he's made including Sarah," Jace added. Nikolai and Quentin both looked at him with surprise. "We have no choice. We know what will happen if we don't."

Jace hung his head and let the words sink in. He knew the moment Dac took Sarah into his arms she was gone. No matter what he had tried without any weapons there was nothing either of them could have done. Dac was too strong. Much stronger than any other vampire would have been, especially now with the demon inside of him. The only thing left to do now was to destroy all the vampires. He could mourn later.

NIKOLAI AND QUENTIN returned home and called Una and Emmaline into the dining room for an emergency meeting. They gathered around the table. A carafe of blood was placed in the center. Each had a full glass in front of them. Quentin drank his in large gulps as he tried to hold onto his fading human appearance without draining the energy of those around him. The stress of the night was quickly draining him. He refilled his glass before beginning to speak.

"There has been a development," he said before recounting their visit with Jace. "We don't know yet if Sarah is his first turn or not, but it is clear that Dac is already starting his army."

"What about the girl, Sophia?" Emmaline asked.

"We don't know yet." Quentin answered. He took another sip of blood. He could feel his form fading in and out with every word he spoke.

"Quentin, you should go restore your energy. There's nothing we can do here tonight, and we can all see you're struggling." Nikolia tapped him on the shoulder. Quentin felt the jolt of energy from his touch. He knew Nikolai was right. He needed to recharge.

"I suppose you're right." Quentin placed his glass on the table and stood to leave. He let himself fade into a shadow as he stepped back outside into the cool autumn night.

The streets of the city were quiet. The cold air and wind chased most of the people inside their homes. Quentin roamed for a few blocks taking what he could from anyone that passed by though it wasn't enough. The only people out and about were lone stragglers who were either heading home from a long night at work or those with nowhere to go, but none of them exuded much energy for him to steal. What he needed was a nightclub. A place full of people and liveliness.

Quentin looked at the time. It was just past midnight, and he knew just where to go. Keeping to his shadow form he traveled to the other end of the city where the nightlife was alive and full of vitality. The area was full of vibrant crowds. The music of live bands and DJs pumped out into the street. Already Quentin could feel the magnetism of the life force around him. He lingered for a while slowly siphoning the energy around him and then as he felt the night coming to a close, he took one last large pull of power and like the current of electricity he consumed the remaining life around him.

Slumped bodies staggered out of the clubs clinging to one another as they shuffled to their cars or to catch their trains home. Feeling fully rejuvenated Quentin hid in the side alley while he waited for the streets to clear. The wind began to pick up. The streetlamps flickered then went out. Quentin stood on high alert. Surrounded in darkness, he remained in obscurity surveying the area from his spot in the alleyway.

"I know you're there Quentin. I can feel you," the familiar voice of an old friend said. "I bet it felt good, didn't it? Taking all that power, all that life from all those people."

Quentin let his human appearance take form. He stepped out into the street to face his old friend. Red eyes glowed in the dark. Dac's pale skin flushed with the afterglow of a fresh kill. Blood tricked down the corners of his mouth. The whimpered cry in the corner alerted Quentin to Dac's nearby victim.

"Don't worry," Dac reassured him. "She's not dead yet."

Quentin tried draining the energy from Dac, but quickly realized he couldn't. Dac lunged forward. Quentin found himself pressed against the brick wall of the nightclub. Dac's arm pressed across his throat.

"That trick doesn't work on me anymore," Dac sneered and let out a sinister laugh. His voice sounded different to Quentin's ears now. Deeper. And Quentin knew the Dac he had known was gone. The demon had taken over. They were too late. "Tell your friends it has started. Soon I will have my army and the vampires will rise. You will either be with me or against me. I suggest you choose wisely." Dac backed off of Quentin and picked the crying girl off the ground. He bit into his wrist and shoved it against her mouth.

"We're not much different you and I, you know. We're both killers. Don't think of yourself better than I. How many of those people do you really think made it home alive. You drained every ounce of life from them as you do every time you take someone's energy. Just because you don't stick around to witness it doesn't mean it isn't true. Time to take your head out of the sand, Quentin. Join me and we can be an unstoppable team."

"I will never..." Quentin began to protest but Dac was gone carrying his newest vampire away with him. Quentin wondered how many he had made now since turning Sarah earlier that same night. He thought about Sophia. The possibility of her safety was growing slimmer with every ticking moment, and they had no real clue to what they were even up against with this demon that had possessed Dac. They had all dealt with Luca at one time or another when he had the demon inside of him, but Luca had always remained in control. This situation with Dac was something completely different. Alessia had warned them long ago what would happen if the demon ever got control of him. But he and Nikolai, they were too overrun by emotion. Dac was more than just another vampire. He was family. How could they have destroyed him? How could they do it even now? But their friend was gone now. That was the awful truth. He may look like himself, but he was no longer Dac. He was the demon.

# Twenty-Nine

The door downstairs closed with a bang. Sophia nearly jumped out of her skin from the sound as it woke her from her sleep. She ran over to the window to see it was still dark outside. She turned on the light in the ensuite bathroom not wanting to brighten up the room too much. She glanced at the clock on the wall. It was only 2am. Dac must have come home and from the sound of it he still wasn't happy.

Sophia turned off the light and crawled to the bedroom door, placing her ear to the floor. Downstairs she could hear Dac screaming for Treye. "Take these two to the basement. Put them in their boxes." He had commanded. Sophia sat up. One shoulder rested against the wall, the other against the dresser. Her breathing was shallow, and her heart pounded in her chest. What had Dac done? What or who was he putting in the basement?

Heavy footsteps sounded in the hallway. Then the lock on her door clicked. She cowered in the corner where she sat on the floor as the door swung open, almost hitting her in the face.

"You really should choose a better place to sit. You could get hurt down there." Dac walked into the room peering down at her behind the door. Sophia swallowed hard and clenched her fist as she pulled her knees closer to her chest. Dac reached down snatching her up by her arm. Pain ran down her from her shoulder to her hand like a current of electricity. She held in the scream, but she could feel the tear escape the corner of her right eye. She took a deep breath and rubbed her shoulder as Dac tossed her onto the bed and turned the light on. She covered her mouth when she saw the glow of his normally ashen skin. Blood stained his mouth and shirt.

"You think you can delay the inevitable. I may need your permission, but not the others. I wanted you to be first so you could help me build our army, but since you want to take your time to come around, I had to start without you. Tomorrow, you will meet us for dinner. Dress up nicely and be on time. 7 o'clock sharp. You'll be greeting our newest house guests. And don't try to escape again. Your next punishment will be much worse." Dac shut off the light and slammed the door closed as he stepped out of the room locking her inside.

Sophia released a long breath as she curled up in the bed. Dac had turned someone into a vampire. Two people. That was what he told Treye to bring to the basement. The boxes he referred to were coffins. Sophia shuttered and wrapped the blanket tight around her. The tears in her eyes began to fall faster.

In the morning when she woke, she stayed in bed. Treye came into the room to deliver her breakfast, and then again later to bring her lunch but she only pushed the plates to the floor without touching a single bite of the food. She watched the hours click by on the wall clock trying desperately to push down the dread that continued to creep up through her chest.

As it got closer to 7pm and the sun had set Sophia managed to finally crawl out of her bed. Her stomach growled at the sight of the two plates of food on the floor and her mouth began to salivate. She thought of the dinner she was about to get ready for and couldn't imagine what she was about to walk into or eating a meal with two very new vampires. She sat down on the floor next to the plates and shoveled the cold food into her mouth. When the plates were cleared, she stacked them on top of the dresser and got dressed for dinner.

With a light knock on the door, Treye entered the room dressed in a black suit and tie. Sophia felt slightly underdressed in her sweater dress and black tights. Dac said to dress nicely but she didn't know this was black tie event.

She followed Treye into the dining room thankful she decided to eat the food that was left in her room earlier that day. The dining room table was set with 5 crystal wine glasses, two plate settings, a bottle of wine on ice and another unlabeled wine shaped bottle. The spread of food consisted of steak cooked very rare, roasted potatoes, and a basket of fresh baked dinner rolls. Dac stood at the head of the table dressed in a finely tailored dark grey suit. The two women standing beside him were dressed in matching floor length evening gowns. Each with a deep V-neck and a ruffled hem. Sophia glanced back and forth between the two women and her heart dropped to the pit of her stomach when she recognized one of them.

"Sarah! Wha – what happened?" Instinctively Sophia began to run towards her, but Treye held her back.

"I'd like you to meet Grace and of course you already know Sarah."

Grace had long blonde hair with loose curls that reached her waist. Her features appeared soft and innocent with her round face, rounded eyes, and bow shaped lips. She held out her hand and Sophia stepped cautiously towards her. When she shook her hand, her skin was hard and smooth like marble and cold as ice. When Sophia turned towards Sarah, she glanced towards the floor unable to look Sophia in the eyes. A sorrowful expression painted deeply on her face.

"Please everyone, have a seat," Dac requested.

Treye placed his warm human hand on the small of Sophia's back and guided her towards the table. He pulled out the chair for her to sit and then seated himself next to her on the left. Dac was seated at the head of the table next to her on the right. Too close for comfort,

Sophia felt. Sarah was seated directly across from her, and Grace sat across from Treye.

A server approached the table and began to pour the drinks. He removed the wine bottle from the ice bucket first and poured a glass of red wine for both Sophia and Treye. Then he picked up the unlabeled bottle from the table and poured a thick dark red liquid into the wine glasses of Grace, Sarah, and Dac. Sarah felt her mouth turn dry and her stomach turn as she watched the thick, red substance slide into the glasses.

Dac raised his glass. "To the beginning of our new family," he toasted then put the glass to his lips and took a sip.

Treye drank his wine. Grace sipped the blood in her glass with ease. Sarah hesitated but eventually took a small taste before placing her glass gently on the table. She was holding back, but Sophia could see the craving in her eyes.

Dac turned his gaze on Sophia. "I created these two especially for you," he said. "Companions for when you decide to join us. I would like you to feel at ease. Maybe a few friends will help you do that."

When Sophia didn't respond Dac continued. "You will join us," he said. Then he leaned in close to her ear and whispered, "If you don't want to see any more of your friends turned to vampires then I suggest you do so sooner rather than later." He straightened up, lifted his glass once more and said, "Eat, drink, get acquainted. It is time to start the creation of our army. Enjoy your night. I shall return later." He drank down the remainder of the blood in his glass and then exited the dining room.

Sophia looked down at her empty plate and her full glass of wine. Treye poured himself another glass. He spooned some potatoes onto his plate then stabbed a slice of steak with his fork and placed it on his dish. He turned toward Sophia offering to make her plate. She shook her head. "No, thank you. I'm not hungry," she said.

Treye shrugged. "I hope you ate something today."

"I ate the food you brought to my room."

"That was hours ago. And when I brought you lunch, you hadn't even touched the breakfast plate."

"I ate it a little bit later. But I did eat. You can see my plates later if you wish. They are empty, piled on the dresser." Sophia watched him shovel bits of food into his mouth and her stomach turned in knots. How could he eat in this room with these vampires sipping blood across the table? She didn't understand how he could seem so comfortable with all of this, like it was normal.

Grace poured more blood from the unlabeled bottle into her wine glass. "I wonder when Dac will teach us to hunt, like him." Her voice was lively, and she seemed eager to navigate her new life as a vampire.

Sophia pushed her chair away from the table. "I think I'll just go back to my room."

"Me too" Sarah left the table and met Sophia by the door. She pulled her gently by the arm and walked with her out into the hall. "Jace will come for you. I just need to get to a phone so I can tell him where we are as soon as I figure that out. Until then, be strong. Dac cannot change you without your agreement."

"Why not?"

"I'm not sure. My grandmother hadn't told us before she died. I'm not even sure if she knew."

"Brigid is dead? I'm so sorry. It wasn't because..."

"No, it wasn't. She was old and sick. It was just her time."

"Still, I'm sorry for your loss."

"Thank you, but right now we have to focus on getting you out of here."

"Treye. He probably has a phone. He's loyal to Dac but not controlled like the others."

"Thanks for the tip."

They parted ways. Sarah disappeared down the hall behind the stairwell and Sophia climbed the stairs to her room. She shed a few tears for Brigid and a few for Sarah, but she also felt an ounce of hope return knowing that despite being a vampire now, Sarah was still on her side. Sarah would find a way to get her out of here.

She sat on her bed flipping through the magazines on her bedside table. Her stomach was beginning to rumble again so she was glad when Treye came to her room with a bowl in is hands.

"I brought you some cereal. I could tell you weren't into the food tonight, but I wanted to make sure you ate something." He handed her the bowl. "I've seen you eat this a few times, so I figured you like it."

"Thank you." Sophia took the bowl from Treye and stirred the cereal in the milk before putting a spoonful into her mouth. The cold milk and cereal were surprisingly comforting.

Treye made himself comfortable on the floor next to her bed. "I know this is rough for you, but you know maybe it won't be as bad as you think." Was he really advocating for her to allow Dac to turn her into a vampire?

"How are you ok with all of this?" She asked him. "Are you hoping Dac will turn you one day? Is that it? Do you want to be a vampire?"

"I've never really thought about it."

She knew he was lying but was he lying to her or lying to himself? Despite all his friendliness maybe he wasn't the ally she had hoped for.

When Treye left her room Sophia turned off the light and rolled over in her bed. With nothing to do she fell asleep and dreamt of her rescue.

# Thirty

It was midnight and Nikolai was sitting in the park. The nighttime temperature was rapidly dropping. The autumn trees were almost all bare. He pulled the edges of his coat closed and crossed his arms across his chest. He tucked his hands under his arms warming them against the wool fabric of his coat. Quentin was standing nearby in his shadow form keeping inconspicuous until after Alessia arrived. While she hadn't mentioned where and when she would meet them, Alessia was the type who would find you when she was ready, and they preferred she didn't find them inside of their home.

The black cat that circled Nikolai's feet alerted him to Alessia's presence. She walked up the path with another feline keeping pace at her heels. The black pants she wore graced the bottoms of her heeled boots. Her knee length leather jacket hung open revealing the deep V-neck sweater she wore underneath.

"He's already started his army." Alessia was straight to the point and down to business to as usual. She never was one to waste time on small talk and pleasantries.

"We know," Nikolai responded. "He created two of his new vampires last night."

"He's created three more already tonight. The more he creates the more his power grows. We will need to act fast."

"He's already too strong for Quentin to drain his power and we don't know where he's been hiding."

"I'm working on that. As you know I've got eyes and ears all over, but he's been unfortunately efficient at keeping his whereabouts unknown."

"Do you know about Sophia? Is she ok?"

"She is fine for now. Dac can't turn her without her permission. Seems she is holding strong for now, but we need to find her before Dac wears her down. Once he turns her there will be nothing we can do to stop him."

"Why is she so important him?" This was all new to Nikolai. He knew of the curse, yes, but still didn't understand Sophia's part in it. No one did except for Alessia. She seemed to know more about this than she had ever said in the past and Nikolai wondered what more she was holding back and why.

"Because she is a descendant of mine and therefore within her blood holds the other half of the demon."

"What?!" Quentin stepped forward, now in his human form.

Alessia didn't bat an eye. "Have a seat. It's a good choice to preserve your energy, Quentin."

Quentin sat on the bench next to Nikolai. Alessia sat across from them. Her two cats laid on the ground at her feet.

"His name was Saith. He was my husband, and we had a daughter. We were human once, witches some would call us. We practiced in both light and dark magic, but Saith dabbled more with the dark. He drew his power from a demon spirit. The longer he dabbled the more it consumed him and the more power he craved. He created the vampire with the intent to extend his own life."

"You mean Dac's ancestor?"

"Yes."

---

ALESSIA WHISPERED THE words of protection into the young girl's ear. She held her hands as they chanted the words in tandem.

When they were done Alessia peered out the window towards the barn behind their house. She closed the shutters tight before turning back to the girl.

"Run. Run as fast and as far as you can. Remember everything I have taught you and I will come for you when it is safe." Alessia had said to the child. She watched as her young daughter took off through the woods. Her braided hair bouncing off her back. Once she was safely out of sight Alessia moved through the two-room cottage. In the barn she could hear the two men arguing. She stirred her pot of herbs and poured them into a bowl. With her bowl in hand, she walked to the barn.

She knew Saith would be no match for the vampire's blood lust and so did Saith but that was his intention. His own yearning for power and immortality was much stronger than the vampire's. The vampire had no idea Saith had tricked him and planned to merge with him so they would become one. Alessia knew she couldn't stop Saith from merging with the vampire, but she could stop him from regaining his full strength once he did.

Alessia stood outside the barn waiting for her moment. She listened as Saith called the demon into himself. She stood at the door and watched as his eyes changed from black to red. The vampire grabbed him by the neck and dug his teeth into his throat. Alessia stepped into the barn chanting her spell. She grabbed the sword she had stashed in the hay bale and just as the vampire reached into Saith's chest and pulled out his heart she sliced it in half.

The vampire lunged for her and Alessia plunged the sword into his stomach. He fell back and crouched to the floor as she removed the sword's blade from his bleeding abdomen. She took one half of Saith's heart and shoved down the vampire's throat. The other half of the heart she put into the bowl of herbs. As the vampire lie on the ground healing from his wounds, Alessia finished her spell and drank from her bowl devouring the all the contents including the heart.

The vampire sat up and stared at Alessia. His eyes had the red glow of the demon. The wound in his stomach was completely healed. He crawled to Alessia putting his hands around her face.

"Saith?" She whispered.

"What have you done?"

"I have separated the demon. Now you will never be completely whole, and you will never have complete power. And to be sure of it every seventh son born to the Vladescu family will take over the demon and you will die again and again with each of their deaths." Alessia stared Saith in the eyes as his transformation completed.

Saith smiled with his new face and with his new voice he said, "You think you alone hold the other half of the demon? You forget about our daughter that she was born of the demon and therefore shares his blood. You think you can stop me, but I will have my immortality."

Alessia smiled back at Saith. "I haven't forgotten. Our daughter and her descendants have been protected by the spell."

Alessia turned her back on Saith. She returned to her cottage and Saith retreated to the vampire's castle.

"A FEW NIGHTS LATER I found where my daughter was hiding out. I explained everything to her and handed her the tools she would need to protect herself and her offspring. After that I never saw her again."

"The music box and the dagger?" Nikolai asked.

"Exactly." Alessia confirmed.

"So Dac...?"

"He is no longer Dac, the moment his heart merged with the demons he became Saith just like what happened with the first vampire."

"But what about Luca? How had he not become Saith?"

"Because he wasn't the seventh son. When he killed the vampire Saith should have died but when Luca consumed the heart it kept Saith alive but dormant. Saith couldn't become active within Luca because of the spell. He needed the seventh son in order to fully thrive. So, he waited patiently inside his new host until he reached Dac. Luca always believed he was in control of the demon, but the demon cannot be controlled and now Saith's half of the demon lives inside Dac. He needs to consume all of Sophia's blood to become whole, but I'm sure by now he's realized he can feed from her to gain strength."

"I thought he needed her permission?"

"He can feed off of her in droplets, but he cannot drain her unless she is willing. That's how the spell works. He wants to be whole. He needs to be whole to achieve true immortality." Alessia stood up and her two cats stood next to her. "Kill Dac before he kills Sophia."

Alessia disappeared beyond the trees. Nikolai and Quentin were left alone to reflect upon her story. As all the truths came to light so did their mistakes. The illusion of family had kept them together all these years, but it had also unknowingly kept them in danger.

They sat together on the bench in the park. Even in the silence they knew what the other was thinking. They had to do as Alessia had said. Keeping Dac alive was no longer an option.

Time was running out. This much they all new. If Dac was strong enough to resist Quentin draining his energy that meant Alessia was right, and he had been feeding from Sophia. Sophia wouldn't be able to hold out much longer, nobody would. Dac had already held her captive for days. How long would it have taken him to figure out he could drink from her without her permission? How often was he doing it? She could be sick with fever and ready for death by now. If she gave in to Dac and let him drain her there'd be nothing any of them could do. They had to stop him. But they had no idea where he was.

# Thirty-One

J ace stared at the number on the screen before answering the phone. He didn't recognize the number. It wasn't saved to his contacts. Any other day he wouldn't have answered it but, that little voice in his head said press that green button. So, he did. He tapped the green button on the screen.

"Hello."

"Jace, I don't have much time so listen carefully," Sarah's voice said through the other end of the line.

"Sarah?"

"Sophia is still safe for now. She's being strong, but Dac is getting impatient. We're in a house on what looks like an old farm or something. I don't know the address, I'm sorry. But I don't think it's too far outside of Aura City."

"Is there anything else you can tell me about it."

"The property is very large and open once you get through the front gates, but it's surrounded by trees on all perimeters. Doubt you can see it from the road."

"Anything else?"

"Like I said looks like an old farmhouse. Large, wraparound porch and pointed rooftops. Very big house. Maybe Victorian."

"Figures."

"Look I have to go. Reach out to Nikolai. Maybe he or Quentin know the place."

"I will. Thanks."

"Good luck."

The call ended and the screen on Jace's phone turned to black. He breathed out a sigh of relief. At least he knew that Sophia was still human, at least for now. How safe she was was up for debate, but she was still human and that's what mattered the most right now. Sarah was right about one thing though, as much as he didn't want anything else to do with the vampires, he still needed their help.

He unlocked his screen and looked at his recent texts. He found the last messages exchanged with Nikolai and typed a new message asking him to come by Sophia's beach house. Since Dac took Sarah, Jace was back at the beach house. Neither place really felt right, but all his stuff was here. Not that he had much stuff since this was supposed to have only been a weekend trip. He considered going back to the motel but decided against it.

While he waited for Nikolai and probably Quentin too, he poured himself a drink and then planted himself on the sofa in the living room. He opened the laptop that was sitting on the coffee table. The screen quickly came to life, but the internet was taking longer than usual to connect. He tapped his fingers against the edge of the computer while he waited for the connection. He checked his phone. No response from Nikolai yet. He peeked out the window through the curtains. Rain was falling in a quiet drizzle. He'd hardly noticed except for the raindrops staining the glass.

When he glanced back at the laptop the Wi-Fi had finally connected and he opened up the internet browser. He did not know exactly what he was looking for, so he searched for a map of Aura City. He zoomed out as far as he could so that he could see the surrounding towns. Then he searched each one looking for any hint of farmland.

Jace was so deep in concentration, he barely heard the knock at the door. Nikolai was waiting on the other side and as expected Quentin was at his side. Jace stepped to the side allowing them both to enter. They followed him into the living room. He explained the phone call from Sarah and showed them everything he was searching on the laptop.

"Does this house seem familiar to either of you?" he asked.

They both shook their heads. "No. It must be a new place he acquired." Nikolai answered.

"We've checked all his known hideaways already." Quentin added.

Jace sighed heavily. "Then this all we have to go one, what Sarah told me over the phone. Just a vague description and an assumption that the place isn't far."

"It's more than we had 24 hours ago," Nikolai reminded him.

"Let me take a look at that." Quentin sat on the couch next to Jace.

Jace slid the laptop closer to him so Quentin could more easily see the screen. Quentin moved the mouse around and zoomed in on a picture. "Look here," he said and pointed to the picture on the screen. "This looks exactly like Sarah described. Don't you think?"

Both Jace and Nikolai leaned in closer examining the photo on the computer. It did look like it could be the place. Jace felt a touch of excitement in his gut. This was the closest they'd come to finding Sophia since she'd been gone. He was beginning to feel the slightest amount of hope though he didn't want to raise his hopes too high.

"It does look like it could be it," Jace admitted out loud. "But do we have an address to check it out?"

Quentin copied the picture and pasted it in the search bar. It pulled up an address and Jace jotted it down in the notes app on his phone.

"So, let's go." Jace jumped up ready to go but Nikolai stopped him.

"Not so fast."

"Look I don't care what either of you say, I'm going."

"That's not why I'm stopping you, but we can't just go without some type of plan."

Jace backed down. Nikolai was right. They couldn't just show up and knock on the door demanding Sophia back. They didn't even know yet if this was the correct house and if it was, they would need a plan to get past Dac and anyone he might have guarding the place.

Jace sat back on the sofa. "So, what's the plan then?"

"Well first we need to find out if it's the right place. We should probably do that during the daytime when Dac would be sleeping. I suggest Jace go in the morning and check it out but be careful."

"Right. I know. Not exactly my first time." They had done this exact same thing back when they were looking for Harper and Luca.

"Exactly so you know the danger involved. Don't go getting ahead of yourself. Let us know what you find out tomorrow and we'll figure out the rest from there."

Nikolai and Quentin left and Jace locked the door behind them. He swallowed the last of the drink in his glass. Knowing there was nothing he could do tonight he decided to try to rest before morning. It was going to be a long day.

The morning rolled in quickly. Jace awoke not quite fresh faced, but he slept better than he had in the past few days. He drove over to Sarah's house and gathered the stakes and potions from her basement and placed them into a duffle bag. When he was back in the car, he entered the address into the gps and drove off.

Jace drove through the little farm town just past Aura City and could see why Dac would choose such a place. The properties were large and left plenty of space between neighbors. Jace parked his car about 1/3 of a mile away from his destination and then walked the rest of the way to the property. The entrance gate was smaller than he had expected. It wasn't grand like at Luca's house in Noxwood or even as tall as the vampire's old house in Aura City. It was just a simple wood gate painted white between two stone pillars. It only came up to about his waist. Not the type of security Jace would expect from a vampire. Although just as Sarah had described there were plenty of trees surrounding the property.

Jace peered over the gate. There were acres between him and the house. A long narrow driveway led to the main house and there appeared to be an old barn or shed nearby.

Jace knew he couldn't simply walk up to the front door and knock. He needed to find a way to get near without being detected. He looked towards the left and right of him. The trees were already bare due to the cold weather, but Jace decided if he could travel along the outside of the wooded area that would probably be his best bet. He moved carefully, taking each step as softly as possible trying not to rustle any leaves on the ground. He moved as close as he possibly could without being seen. As he got closer to the house, he could see through the thicket the two men sitting on the front porch. He crept further towards the back side and saw another pair of men seemingly guarding the back door. The barn was not far yet a good distance away from the house that maybe he could get a closer look without any the men seeing him.

"He's got like three more of them down there now." Jace heard one of the men say. He crouched down, leaning against the far wall of the barn. The two were speaking loud enough that even from where Jace hid he could still hear them.

"So how many of them are there now?"

"Five. Six including himself."

"What about the girl?"

"She's still locked in her room, so I guess she hasn't cooperated yet."

"Do you think he'll keep his promise once she does or what?"

"I hope so. The only alternative is he kills us."

"I don't think he'll kill us. We've done everything he asked."

"I sure hope you're right."

Jace's foot slipped on the wet grass underneath him. He braced himself for the short fall but hit his shoulder against the wall of the barn.

"What was that?" One of the men said. "Hey! Who's there?" he called out louder.

"Shit," Jace pushed himself off the ground and sprinted back towards the woods. He ran through the trees without looking back. No idea if the men were chasing him. He made it back to the road. His breath heavy and his heart racing.

"Hey!" He heard the voice call out again and took off running.

Instead of heading towards his car he ran in the opposite direction. He hopped the fence to the next yard and hid behind the giant wheel of a tractor. He stayed there for several minutes until he caught his breath.

He heard footsteps in the road and watched the two men walk past. They hadn't seen him run into the yard. He exhaled, removed his jacket and turned it inside out before putting it back on. He pulled the hood up over his head and jogged back towards his car.

If he wasn't sure about the place before he was definitely sure of it now. That was the place where Dac was hiding out. It was also where he was keeping Sophia and by the sound of it, he had made more vampires besides Sarah.

By the time Jace reached Aura City the sun was beginning to set. Perfect timing for him to text Nikolai. He pulled over in front of a coffee shop and went inside. The place was bustling with customers and Jace realized he still had his coat on inside out and his shoes and pants were covered in mud. He walked up to the counter and placed his order then headed to the bathroom to straighten himself out and wipe some of the dirt from his clothes. Once he picked up his coffee from the counter he sat down at a table and sent the message. *That's the place. Let's meet.*

# Thirty-Two

There had been a commotion outside the day before that had given Sophia a glimmer of hope that maybe Sarah had gotten through to Jace somehow. But then no one came for her, and that glimmer quickly faded out. Tonight, she stood in front of the mirror fully dressed for dinner waiting for Treye to come and escort her to the dining room as he did every night. She admired her reflection and stared at her toothy smile for the first time imagining herself as a vampire, wondering what it would be like. Maybe it wouldn't be so bad. She'd be immortal after all. No sickness, no growing old. Of course, she would never see daylight again, but did that really matter? Would an eternal existence of nighttime be so bad? She liked the nighttime. There was that part about drinking blood, however. But there were vampires that didn't kill people. She could just be like them. Would Dac let her live like that? Maybe she wouldn't have to stay with him. Maybe after she turned, she and Sarah could escape and live their lives away from Dac. She sat on the floor and imagined all the possibilities. Anything was better than being trapped in this room forever. If no one was going to save her then she would have to save herself and agreeing to Dac making her a vampire was beginning to look like the only option that she had left. And so, she decided she would tell him tomorrow when he came to her room for his nightly taste of her blood. She would give herself this last night as a human and tomorrow she would become a vampire.

When Treye knocked on the door Sophia stood up and brushed the lint from her dress. She flashed him a smile, locked her arm in his and they retreated to the dining room to meet the others for dinner. When they arrived, the vampires were already seated, Sarah, Grace, and three new commers, all men. Dac hadn't arrived yet.

Sophia and Treye took their seats. Dinner plates, silverware, and glasses were all set about the table, but the food had not yet been served. No wine for her and Treye, or blood for the vampires was available yet either. It wasn't like Dac to be late. Sophia locked eyes with Sarah who gave her a look of uncertainty. She then turned her attention to Treye.

She whispered softly, "Where's Dac?"

"I'm sure he'll be here any minute," he assured her, but Sophia could sense his unease.

Dac was a creature of tradition. He created a routine and expected everyone to follow without question and without hesitation. And one thing Dac never was, was late. If something was keeping him from the evening meal it must have been important.

Treye excused himself from the table saying he would check with the staff if anyone knew what was keeping Dac and when he could be expected. Sarah reached across the table tapping Sophia on the hand.

"Come talk with me a moment?" She asked.

"Of course." Sophia got up and followed Sarah to the far corner of the room.

"I spoke with Jace. I took your advice. I was able to sneak Treye's phone while he slept the other night." Sarah kept her voice low as she spoke. "I think he was here yesterday afternoon. There were rumblings last night amongst the guards. One of them told Dac they chased a neighborhood kid away, but I think it might have been Jace. It's too much of a coincidence." This changed everything.

"Do you think Dac figured it out? Do you think that's where he is now?" Sophia felt the pang in her stomach. If Dac figured out

Jace was here he'd most certainly kill him. The hope of being rescued rose and fell once more. It was a constant rollercoaster she couldn't seem to get off. She wanted to believe Jace would rescue her, and she did believe he would try. But was Jace enough to go up against Dac? Probably not.

Treye returned to the dining room. Sophia and Sarah both went back to their seats when they heard him enter the room. Treye stood in front of his seat. His hands clutched the chair back.

"No one knows where Dac is. I told the staff to serve dinner. So, please remain seated. If he has not returned by the end of the meal, feel free to go about your night as normal." Treye pulled out his chair and sat down.

"Are you sure this is ok?" Sophia turned to face Treye.

"Dac would want his guests to be taken care of in his absence. Wherever he is I'm sure this is what he would want."

Sophia nodded and watched as the servers placed the food for her and Treye in front of them. Next, they brought out two carafes, one with wine, the other with blood. Sarah rose from her seat and poured each vampire a glass of the dark red liquid. Treye poured a glass of wine for Sophia then himself.

It was quiet around the dinner table. The only sound was the clink of the silverware against the ceramic plates as Treye and Sophia ate their food. Normally Dac would head the conversation. In his absence no one seemed to know what to say. The vampires seemed to be drinking more than normal also. Each draining and refilling their glass. Sophia suddenly became extremely aware of the danger this posed to her and any other human in the house. These were brand new vampires alone with humans. What if they could not control their monstrous instincts? With Dac around, he could keep them under control but with him not here who would do that. Suddenly, Sophia yearned to be locked in her room.

"Don't worry. Everything will be fine." Sarah whispered to Sophia as she reached across the table gently squeezing her hand. She must have sensed Sophia's apprehension. But it was the loud crash that came from somewhere outside the dining room that gave them all pause.

The vampires hissed and growled. Their lips curled up showing their fangs. Sarah jumped to her feet and swiftly positioned herself at Sophia's side. "They smell blood. Fresh human blood." She turned to Treye. "Get Sophia out of here now!"

NIKOLAI AND QUENTIN left the house early in the evening insisting that Emmaline and Una stay behind. Of course, neither woman was having that. Emmaline wasn't exactly fond of Una, in fact she downright hated her, but they did agree on one thing, they were not being left out tonight. The men didn't get to go off and leave them behind this time. Their agendas were of course different but their motivations the same. Whereas Emmaline set out to ensure her old friend made it through this night alive, Una was intent on making sure he didn't. However, they were both certain their place was at the side of their family, not cowering alone in the house waiting for news.

"Soon as we get there all bets are off," Una said.

"Of course," Emmaline replied in agreement. She did her best to keep the contempt in her voice at bay. If not for Una, she wouldn't even know where Nikolai and Quentin were headed. It was Una who had overheard them talking the night before when they left to meet Jace. She figured it had something to do with Dac and the human girl he kidnapped so she followed them. After hearing they found where Dac was hiding out, she messaged Emmaline. Emmaline had just enough time before they all returned home to sneak onto Quentin's computer and figure out where that was. While Nikolai, Quentin and Jace were making a plan to get inside Dac's hiding place, Una was devising a plan of her own. Surprisingly that plan included Emmaline. What Una didn't know was that Emmaline was also making her own plan.

Nikolai and Quentin were meeting Jace first, which provided the ladies a far enough head start. As soon as the men were gone, they snuck out through the back door of the townhouse. Una arranged for a car rental which worked perfectly for Emmaline. While Una focused her attention on the road, Emmaline discreetly sent a text to Dac asking him to meet her. It was a meeting she wouldn't show up to, but it would keep him distracted and out of the way long enough for Sophia to be rescued and Dac to remain alive.

When the gps announced they had reached their destination, Emmaline felt a bit underwhelmed. The property was unassuming although she had imagined the house to be set back a good distance from the road. There was no one guarding the front entrance from what she could see and instead of a tall iron gate to block anyone from getting in, there was only a small gate, maybe waist high. Anyone could easily hop over it and by the look of it they probably wouldn't even need to.

Una stepped out of the car first. Emmaline followed. They walked up to the front gate. Una reached her hand over to the other side and unlocked it. She walked through it as confidently as if she lived there.

"So, this is your plan? You're just going to walk straight up to the house?"

"Well, you already warned Dac away. No need to sneak around."

"You..." how did she know?

"I figured you'd try something like that. Besides you weren't very discreet with your phone."

"Look Dac is still..."

"I know he's still your friend. You still think there's a cure for him. There isn't. You need to face that." Una picked up her pace as she marched towards the giant house in front of them. Emmaline trailed behind her.

As they moved closer the men guarding the front door came into view. The waft of human blood informed them these men were of no real threat. Una kept her pace. Emmaline stayed her few feet behind ready to follow Una's lead.

Una approached the front porch. Neither of the humans had a chance to get up before Una bared her fangs. Without missing a beat, she snatched one of the men up by his neck and tore into his artery. Blood spurted out in all directions. The other man backed away bumping into Emmaline who unknown to him was standing right behind him. Emmaline locked him in a tight grip. Una tossed her victim aside with such force he crashed through the window and landed inside the house. She grabbed the other man from Emmaline's arms and did what she knew Emmaline would not. When his dead body slumped to the ground Emmaline stepped over the body and followed Una through the front door.

As they stepped into the foyer more humans approached. A total of three men and one woman stood in front of them. They appeared to be mostly unarmed except for the man in the very front of the group holding a kitchen knife.

"Who the fuck are you?" The man shouted at them before his eyes landed on the bloodied body of his friend on the floor. Una glanced at Emmaline. She knew what they had to do but she didn't have to like it. That was the difference between her and Una.

Una struck out at the man. The knife in his hand fell to the ground and slid across the titled floor. Una tore her fangs into the man's flesh ripping opening the artery. Blood poured out from his neck and lips. A gurgling sound escaped from his mouth before his lifeless body fell to the floor.

The woman of the group screamed out in horror. Emmaline grabbed her by the throat. She placed her hand over the woman's mouth to silence her screams before tearing into her neck. Emmaline's fangs dug deep into the woman's skin. A steady stream of blood flowed into her mouth and down her throat. A sensation of euphoria spread throughout her body. Consumed by the intoxication of her first kill, her first true taste of fresh human blood, Emmaline didn't notice the man behind her holding the knife he picked up from the floor.

She felt the sting of the cold, smooth, steel blade as he plunged the knife into her back. Emmaline screeched. She dropped the body in her arms and swung herself around facing the man who had just stabbed her. With the knife still stuck in her back, she hit him with a closed fist. The punch landing across his lower jaw. The man flung backwards from the force of her vampiric strength. His head hit the corner of a wall, splitting open. Blood smeared the paint as he slid to the ground. His eyes rolled back, and breathing ceased. Una came up behind Emmaline and pulled the knife from her back and stuck it deep into the side of the third man. He screamed and pulled the knife out attempting to stab Una with it, but he collapsed to the floor within seconds. Una shook her head and left him to bleed out on the hallway floor.

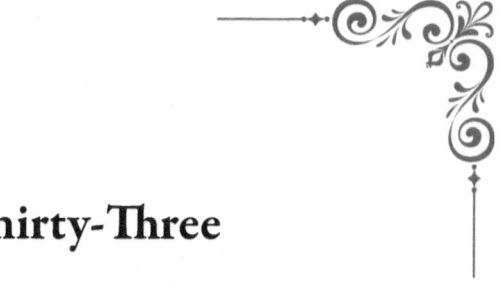

# Thirty-Three

Jace's only job was to get Sophia and get back to the car. That was the plan, but when he, Quentin, and Nikolai arrived at Dac's property what they saw changed those plans. A man lay dead on the front porch. Broken glass was scattered across the ground. Nikolai stepped onto the porch and leaned over the body.

"A vampire," he whispered as he inspected the corpse. The three men, both vampire and human, stared at each other then looked at the open door.

Quentin motioned for Nikolai and Jace to stay to the side. He switched from his human form and became a mere shadow barely noticeable. He entered through the front door nearly gasping at the carnage in front of him. Jace and Nikolai followed carefully behind him.

"What happened here?" Jace felt as if his stomach turned upside down as he took in the sight of blood and death.

"I don't know," replied Nikolai.

"We need to find Sophia."

"We need to find out what happened here. For all we know she and Dac are gone," Nikolai said. "For now, let's stick together."

Jace complied even though his mind screamed at him to search for Sophia. Remembering the dagger he had belted to his hip, he instinctively reached for it relieved to feel it still there. Footsteps stomped across the far hallway and Jace caught glimpse of Sophia running alongside some other man. He moved to chase after them, but Nikolai grabbed his arm stopping him.

"Don't. Stick together, remember?"

"But..."

"He's human. They're likely going to hide someplace safe. You'll do more for her by sticking with us."

Jace, Nikolai, and Quentin ran through the house in the direction which they saw Sophia running from, but then stopped short when they came upon the dining room. Quentin returned to his human looking form. Emmaline and Una stood before them. Both of their mouths stained with blood. This explained the scene they saw when they entered the house.

"Where is Dac?" Una was demanding from the other vampires in the room. Jace didn't recognize any of them until he saw Sarah. The others must be the new ones Dac turned over the last few days. The young fledglings hissed and snarled at Una, baring their fangs unknowing of her age and strength. They'd have no chance against her if they chose to attack. Sarah caught Jace's eye, and he turned his head when he noticed her eyes bulge and heard the voice behind him. The voice of someone from his past. The voice not from once they were allies but from when they first met, hard and commanding.

"I'm right here," Dac said from the doorway.

Una raced towards him, her fangs exposed and a steel blade in her hands. She raised the long, serrated knife above her shoulder ready to plunge it into Dac's chest. He grabbed her by the wrist and the blade fell to the floor. His eyes glowed red. Brighter than Luca's ever had. The three male fledglings let out a low growl and charged attacking the intruding vampires in defense of their creator.

Nikolai and Quetin each grabbed the two larger vampires. The smaller one managed to attach himself to Una's back and bit into her neck. Jace unsheathed the dagger at his waist and thrust it into the smaller vampire's back. He arched backed releasing himself from

Una and pounced onto Jace knocking them both to the ground. A glint of silver caught Jace's eye as he struggled under the weight of the vampire. Its teeth dripped with Una's blood. Una's serrated blade lay on the floor inches away from Jace's face. Jace pushed against the vampire's throat with one hand while reaching for the knife with the other. A sharp pain pierced Jace's neck. He wrapped his fingers around the knife's handle stabbing it into the vampire's shoulder. The vampire yelled, unlatching his jaw from Jace's throat. Jace yanked the knife free from its flesh. Blood sprayed in all directions. The vampire clutched his hands around Jace's throat, pinning his back to the floor. His head hit the tile. A thunderous clap rang in his ears. Pain engulfed his entire skull. His eyesight blurred and the air constricted in his lungs. Still clutching the knife, he stabbed at the vampire again jabbing it into his neck. He howled and released his grip. Jace retrieved his knife and jabbed it into the vampire's heart. The vampire fell back. Jace rolled away, then steadied himself to his feet.

Jace's vision cleared, and he scanned the room. The other two male vampires where dead on the floor with stakes in their hearts. The blonde one lay in the corner with blood pooled around her. Emmaline stood over her holding the blood-stained stake in her hand. Sarah stood by Emmaline's side. All four fledglings were dead. All young enough that piercing the heart was enough to kill them.

There was a momentary silence in the room. Nikolai, Quentin, Emmaline, and Sarah all stared wide eyed at Dac. Jace turned his head in Dac's direction. Blood dripped from the corners of his mouth. In his hand he held Una's severed head.

A wailing howl cried out from across the room. Nikolai rushed towards Dac. Dac dodged his advance dropping Una's head which rolled to Jace's feet. Dac positioned himself behind Sarah. He grabbed her by the waist holding her in front of him like a shield. Nikolai turned towards him, but Quentin held him back. Jace and

Sarah locked eyes. Sarah mouthed to Jace "It's ok". He looked down at the severed head next to his left foot. The dead eyes stared up at him. The same face as his old best friend. There may have been no love lost between him and Una but still an ache settled his heart. Jace shifted his gaze to the vampire he'd just killed. He bent over snatching his dagger from the dead fledging's back. He and Sarah locked eyes one more time. She nodded. Jace flicked his wrist sending the dagger straight into Sarah's heart.

Quentin let go of Nikolai's arm and Nikolai fled in Dac's direction. Emmaline moved to get between them, but Quentin stopped her. "This is between them now," he whispered.

Dac and Nikolai traded blows. Each one holding their own. The force of emotion behind every hit. Nikolai bared his fangs as they wrestled in each other's arms. He bit down into Dac's neck tearing through flesh and veins. Dac pushed Nikolai off of him with such force he flew into the dining room table. The table broke beneath his weight and crashed to the ground. Pieces of wood splintering off. Dac picked up a splintered table leg. Nikolai rolled over and snatched the dagger from Sarah's heart. He jumped to his feet. The red glow of Dac's eyes flickered. They charged each other. Weapons extended. Dac pierced the wooden staked table leg into the heart of his best friend, his family, his brother. Nikolai pushed the dagger into Dac's heart. The heart that now belonged to the demon that lived inside of him. Both men fell to the ground. Blood pooling around their undead bodies. The very force of their life draining from them.

Emmaline rushed to Dac's side. Tears filled her eyes. Dac raised his hands to her face. "This is not the end," he said. Then he took her hands and wrapped her fingers tightly around the handle of the dagger lodged in his chest. "This is yours now."

Emmaline yanked the dagger free. At the edge of the blade was the demon's heart. She took the heart in her hands and put it to her mouth.

"No!!!" Quentin and Jace screamed at that same moment. But it was too late. Emmaline had taken the demon into herself. Then the clicking of footsteps on the tiled floor averted their attention to the doorway.

"Alessia."

Alessia came into the room. In her hand she carried an axe. One much like the one Sarah had once carried with her. Methodically, she walked around the room scanning the destruction dragging the axe behind her. As she came to Dac and Nikolai a slight upturn curved in her lips. She stood over Nikolai. She raised the axe above her head and with one swift motion she brought the axe down onto his neck. Then she stepped over to Emmaline assessing the blood on her hands and mouth. She looked into her eyes. The black of Emmaline's pupils flicker with a faint red glow. Alessia placed a hand on Emmaline's cheek. "You know what you must do," she says.

Emmaline smirked and nodded. Jace caught a glimpse of her blood-stained fangs. He backed up as she advanced towards him, but she snatched him by the shoulders. He tried to pull away from her, but he was weakened in her grasp. Quentin flickered in and out between his human and shadow form. Alessia had a hold on him which he couldn't seem to shake. The leathery bat like wings extended from Emmaline's back and she wrapped them tightly around Jace obscuring him into total darkness.

Within Emmaline's tight grasp, Jace felt the sharp sting in the side of his neck. He screamed as she ripped into his skin with her fangs. As she drained his blood, she replaced it with a mix of her own and the blood of Dac's heart that lingered on her lips. A sensation ran through him as she released him, and he dropped to the floor. Every cell in his body transformed. Not into something dead. But something undead.

Alessia let go of her hold on Quentin. She walked over to Emmaline, wrapped her arm around her and whispered softly, "let's go."

SOPHIA AND TREYE SAT tucked away in the hidden staircase. Only darkness and the screams outside the walls surrounded them. Treye wrapped his arms around Sophia, and she leaned into his chest. Quietly they sat until the house grew silent. Treye shifted his weight away from Sophia. A stream of light entered their hideaway as he pushed the door open. Treye reached for Sophia's hand and helped her to her feet. Together they stepped out of the stairwell into the hallway. The house reeked of blood and death. Sophia covered her mouth and nose. Destruction greeted them at every turn. They stepped over broken glass and dead bodies as they walked the halls. Eventually they made their way back to the dining room where they had left the agitated vampires.

They were all dead. Every last one of them. Sophia surveyed the room. Splatters of blood painted the floor, walls, and ceiling. Daggers and wooden stakes strewed about the room. The dining table was destroyed. Broken plates and glasses scattered the floor. Remnants of their dinner floating in pools of blood and red wine.

She glanced around at the dead. A pang of sadness for Sarah settled in her heart, but she knew deep down this was what she would have wanted. Sarah didn't want to be a vampire. Admittedly she felt nothing for the others. They were mere strangers to her, though she did recognize one who had not been at the dinner table with them that night. She had seen him outside her beach house talking to Jace. But she knew him from a time much longer ago than that. The night in which he and Dac showed up at her parents' house pretending to be lost. The night that in hindsight was the start of this whole nightmare. She could feel no sorrow for his loss. Then a gasp escaped Sophia's lips when she noticed the expression on Treye's face fall and glanced in the direction he was staring. Dac lay on the ground. Blood pooled around his dead body. His chest cavity ripped open. His head severed almost completely from his neck. In fact, all the dead lay decapitated. And Sophia felt a wave of relief sweep over her. She was finally free.

Her solace was short lived, however, when she peeped Jace's still body on the floor and the shadowy presence hovering over him. The veiled figure turned her way. It moved closer, nothing but a sheer gloomy silhouette and yellow eyes. Sophia pulled in a deep breath. Treye tightened his hand around hers. The shadow approached, stopping directly in front of them.

"Go home, far away from here. Live in peace if you can. I will take care of him," The shadow said, and Sophia recognized the voice as the other vampire that stood with Jace on her front porch and somehow, she knew he would be ok.

Treye put his arm around Sophia's shoulder. Together they walked out of the house. Fresh air filled her lungs. The scent of pine and chimney smoke filled the atmosphere. Sophia looked up into the star filled sky. Not a single cloud lingered above them, and the late autumn night welcomed Sophia with a cold breeze.

# Thirty-Four

The brisk autumn air penetrated deep into his bones. The grinding of leaves under his feet crunched loudly in his ears. The scent of nature's death as it prepared for winter stung the insides of his nose. Every sight, sound, and touch overwhelmed his newly heightened vampiric senses. The very thing he had fought against, he had now become. That was his punishment.

"I'm sorry. I have failed you in every way possible." Jace leaned against Cloe's tombstone. "I've failed everyone." He buried his face in his hands. His elbows rested against his bent knees. The ground beneath him was hard and cold as ice. The tears that welled in his eyes refused to fall and he wiped them away with his palms.

He detested every feeling in his body, physically and emotionally. There was a hunger inside of him that he refused to satiate. This hunger ran deep, but the self-loathing ran deeper. Even on his first night as a vampire he stood in his new room inside Quentin's townhouse with a stake in his hand. Its sharp edge pressed against his chest. All he had to do was push it through his ribcage. But he hesitated and that's when Quentin came into the room. He switched out the stake for a small flask with blood from their stash. "Like Dac you never asked for this life, but unlike Dac you have control over your fate. Nikolai became a vampire to avenge his family. There was no true evil inside of him. I think you sensed that about him. You can be the same. You don't need to take human life to survive. I know this isn't what you wanted, and you can choose how you move forward, but you must move forward," Quentin had said to him, and he sat with him that entire night until the sunrise forced him into his daytime slumber.

Since that night Jace kept the flask with him at all times, taking small sips as needed, just enough to stave off the cravings. Then he closed the flask tight until the next craving returned refusing any overindulgences. He'd do enough to survive his new reality, he'd promised Quentin, but only enough, nothing more.

"Do I even want to survive?" he asked to Cloe's grave. "But how can I even die now? Who can I turn to? I have only Quentin and he refuses to end my life."

"You're damn right I do." Quentin walked over to Jace and sat on the ground next to him. "You know, I didn't like you much as a human. You're even worse as a vampire." They both laughed.

"And yet here you are." Jace patted Quentin on the shoulder.

"Well, I promised Sophia I'd take care of you." And he had kept that promise.

"At least she is safe now." Jace stared into the dark. He had set out the save Sophia and he had even though it had cost him his life.

"Yes, she is."

"And Emmaline?"

"She's been in touch. She's in Crimson Fells with Alessia. The demon lies dormant inside of her now but without Dac's bloodline it no longer holds the same power. I don't know if she will ever return. She was never truly happy here. She was always a little bit lonely, but she sounds happy now."

"That's good. She deserves happiness." Emmaline was the one who turned him into a vampire yet somehow, he could not find it in himself to hate her.

"Indeed, she does." Quentin agreed.

Quentin had lost all of his friends, his family, that night. Dac and Nikolai were both dead. Emmaline gone off with Alessia. He was alone and Jace wondered if that was the true reason Quentin kept him around. Maybe it was for his company. Whatever the reason, Jace was grateful for the support and companionship Quentin had shown him. Without Quentin, Jace probably would have shoved that stake into his own heart that first night. He hated himself for what he had become but Quentin was right about one thing, he had control over his outcome. He had control over the actions he took from this point forward as he learned to navigate his new life and Quentin was a good teacher. Maybe they weren't all monsters after all.

It amazed Jace the empathy Quentin showed towards others. He was never even human; he was born a vampire and yet he portrayed more human qualities than most humans Jace new. He hadn't noticed when they'd first met but over the course of these last few days, he saw a different side of Quentin. It made him wonder about Quentin's life. Who was he before? How was he created? Were his species born the same as humans? Did they grow from childhood into adulthood? He tried to ask him once, but Quentin brushed it off. "None of that matters. My story is boring," he had said and changed the subject. Maybe someday Quentin will tell him. He could wait. He had an eternity now.

# Acknowledgements

As always thank you to all my family, friends, and everyone who has continued to support me and cheer me on while writing this trilogy. Thanks to Elisa Pinto for your help editing and proofreading. Your work does not go unappreciated. Of course, thank you to all my readers. I hope you enjoyed reading these books as much as I've enjoyed writing them. Although this is the end for now, it may not be the end forever. I may revisit these characters some time in the future, but for now it is time for new stories and new characters. Excited for all that's to come next. Until then keep dreaming, keep creating.

# Also by Ana DiPinto

**Scorned in Blood Trilogy**
Scorned in Blood
Scorned In Darkness
Scorned Eternal

www.ingramcontent.com/pod-product-compliance
Lightning Source LLC
Chambersburg PA
CBHW020313200626
46814CB00006BA/2224